Richard Calder was born in London in 1956. He moved to Thailand in 1990, where he lived in Nongkhai, a border town overlooking Laos. He returned to London in 1996. His short stories and reviews have been published in many science fiction magazines, including *Interzone*, *Science Fiction Eye* and *Omni*, and his work has been trans-lated into several languages. *Frenzetta* is his fifth novel.

FRENZETTA

Richard Calder

ORBIT

An *Orbit* Book

First published in Great Britain by Orbit 1998

Copyright © Richard Calder 1998

The moral right of the author has been asserted.

A CIP catalogue record for this book
is available from the British Library.

ISBN 1 85723 683 1

Typeset by Solidus (Bristol) Ltd, Bristol
Printed and bound in Great Britain by
Mackays of Chatham plc, Chatham, Kent

Orbit
A Division of
Little, Brown and Company (UK)
Brettenham House
Lancaster Place
London WC2E 7EN

LOST IN CATHAY

I rose above the bed; rolled; inspected the reanimated corpse sprawled beneath me, its head pillowed in an ecstasy of flesh. The monastery had not yet been able to dissipate the heat of the day, and though the corpse – my decorticated husk – seemed appropriately at peace, the sweat beading the buxom lines of my little half-human adventuress evinced that the midnight breeze wafting through the flung-open shutters offered scant relief. Dreams stirred behind her eyes and there was a shiver of girlish movement amongst the sheets. Disturbed, my discarded body shifted, the monumental breasts which cushioned its head dimpling as they accommodated the naked steel plate that displaced the zygomatic bone. A half-putrescent, galvanic arm groped for purchase – the night table wobbled, a jar of cut flowers falling from its mother-of-pearl top – and I apprehended my corporeality's unease, its mute accusations of abandonment. I concentrated; maintained separation; even with several tours of duty behind me I was a novice still in matters of projection and could be too easily claimed by sentimental matter. Ignored, my carnal household twitched, jittered, fluttered its eyelids and then relaxed; I gazed down with satisfaction; the massive frame lay at rest, full of nostalgia for the grave. But would it remain at rest? The jar of flowers continued on its downward trajectory and there seemed little chance of anyone – undead or living – remaining insensate to its fate. The second before it impacted on the stone floor ached into an eternity; at last the jar shattered, releasing a funereal bouquet across the cell. A jungle emission, that rank perfume recalled past lives, a shadow play of mass destruction, genocide, plague and rape staged against the morbidly scented backdrop of the Nam, its skeletons of cities. Poison leaked from the torn corolla and coagulated in a sticky puddle; the puddle quivered, its surface like that of a miniature lake presaging a storm. I braced myself, waiting for my body to reclaim me, for the tug that would bring my astral form back into its confinement of dead flesh; but the explosion of glass and the gamey odour of the savage blooms had had no effect; both cadaver and guardian angel slumbered on, the couple's fidgeting indicative only of a customary sexual discontent, the living death of my material self mesmerised by the voluptuous tom-tom beating beneath that cushion of indulgent, ecstatic meat, just as the quickness of that meat was, perhaps, lulled by atavistic visions of bejewelled, underground palaces, rat-visions, goblin-visions of mines, caverns and still, black lakes that lay in the nether regions beneath blasted urban sprawls. I cast a navigational glance through the rustling, cellophane shutters; the Nam receded, its scent, like crushed petals washed away by a monsoon, coursing into a desolate chasm of confused memories; Albracca, once-proud hub of Indochina and Tartary, of Nippon and all the Oceanic Isles, imperial seat of the Empire of Cathay and refuge – in the days before its decadence – to the lost tribes of the perverse, beckoned, offering up its riches, its paltry hopes. Leaving my earthly remains in the keeping of my nursery-breasted princess, I rose higher, willed myself across the cell and floated out through the window and over the dying city, Albracca, apotheosis of the East.

East. Below me, rooftops glittered, their racks of lacquered tiles kinetic with the slitherings of house lizards. Paper-walled habitations, such as the one from which I had momentarily departed – though with few traces of the monastic austerity within which I had latterly cloistered myself, an austerity ironic considering my 'problem' – stretched to all points of the compass: ramshackle configurations of stacked, multicoloured boxes that, illuminated from within, flickered blue, green and heavenly red like rows of lanterns festooning the city's basalt-cobbled streets. Pagodas plated in platinum and steel punctured the haze of primaries, a metallic cloudscape that refracted the gaudy, histrionic light, combining and recombining to leave the horizon flushed with impossible rainbows. I passed over the Pavilion of Ch'ang-o, the Moon Goddess; looked heavenward to where the goddess held court amongst the forfeited stars. Earth's satellite was emptied of its human complement; it was a hulk, a ghost vessel, that now plied the familiar round. How did our kindred survive, harvesting its dusty shores? Rumour had it that its oceans had dried up, that there were few crops, fewer animals. Still it rained its white, legendary sap onto us, first and last divinity of the servants of the left-hand path. I flew on. Other temples, whose ferroconcrete roots entwined with the ruins of forsaken religions, shone moonily with votive candles dedicated to those usurping faiths that themselves faced imminent extinction: cults of The Shark, The She-Spider, The Wolf, The Bird of Calamity, The Snake, The Cat, and – I glanced backwards towards the monastery that sheltered my carcass, the monastery whose zoomorphic altar I had bedecked with gold in order that our planned getaway through the catacombs be unchecked ~ The Rat. But no offering, no matter how extravagant, could elevate the doomed faithful to the sanctuary of the lunar fields. That escape route, like those who would take it, was lost.

East. It was the sinuous dragons that surrounded the susurrant fountains of ice, the little stalls selling food, the people walking through the night market, laughing, drinking, sighing, the kites in the shapes of Kuan-ti, the Lord of War, and Kuan-yin, the Lady of Mercy, the mechanical men that twittered in the gilded cages hanging beside rooftop gazebos, the mechanical women performing their lickerish mimes in the gin mills along the Bund (where the princess's maid was, perhaps, even now carousing with her cronies), the great amber river with its barges laden with opium, teak and bamboo. It was all that lay beyond the continental divide: home to a confluence of tired races, scions of the self-modified who had fled persecution only to degenerate like old, senile devils whose minds were empty but for the necessity of fighting for the dubious right to exist. East, east. Near to perihelion, I watched the inhabitants of Albracca diminish into insignificance. My body had begun to tingle; it was picking up radio transmissions. Talk radio.

'And what will you be saying when you meet with the presidium on your return to Central Afric, Mr Ambassador?'

'I will be saying: Every minute of every hour, Cathay becomes more like Atlantis. No longer is it the prodigal wonder, the terror of conscience, the purulent, erotomaniacal playground of myth. Its monastic system has tempered its people's vices, effectively reining in the

*excess that formerly earned it such unwelcome notoriety.
Surely this is grounds for a conditional peace?'*

I concentrated; jammed. There was a chorus of static
and then – the crisp air knifing through the ghostly fabric of
my astral heart – a silencing of my garrulous arteries and
veins. As I broke through cumulus and sighted The Palace
of the Lady Wang, looming, apparitional, out of the bright,
almost phosphorescent mist, two other revenants –
Remarque and Stricker had known better than to be late –
streaked across the sky; I fell, and they matched my descent,
riding parabolas that would have brought them from areas
of the city obscured by K'un-lun Mountain, though never, of
course, from such a distance as might compromise their
astral umbilici. I glided across the blunt, fabulously lit summit towards the palace, and then over the palace's walls and
watchtowers, edifices built entirely of jade; dived through
the snow-freckled roof and into the audience chamber.

Beneath a cupola painted with images of the
sidereal immortals, forebears now hopelessly scattered
across the galactic arm, I hovered, enchanted by the irony
of being so near, so unbeknownst, to those that con-
gregated about the imperial dais. Peacocks, ladies in
waiting, the iron dogs whose jaws clanked menacingly at
those who drew too near, surrounded my former mistress,
she whom I had been programmed – incompetently, it had
transpired – to love, respect, worship and obey; she whose
necromancers had called back from oblivion, co-opting
the wreckage of a dead soldier's humanity so that they
might infiltrate and destroy my former comrades in their
fastness of Saigon. Tribal leaders – men and women with
gills, winged people, the chitinous, the furred, the scaled –
shuffled, waving their petitions in the faces of impassive

courtiers, or else, conceding to ennui, rehearsed amongst themselves the stale arguments of whether parthenogenesis should supersede cloning, or parasitism give way to mutation – reproduction, in these last days, being not merely the issue that divided Cathay from Atlantis, but Cathay from itself.

The ormolu clock above Lady Wang, the Empress Dowager, chimed, issuing its twelfth reminder of the hour. Drawing to the edge of her throne like a child eager to demonstrate attentiveness – a child in appearance, as well as gesture; she had had her brain transplanted into the skull of a freshly killed pubescent girl every year for nearly half a century – she spoke, and all discussion of sex-economy was stilled.

'Since the taking of Oahu, enemy forces have used long-range dirigibles to perform unheard-of bombing raids throughout Oceania, and there has been much rumour-mongering, on the streets, in the barracks and now, I am informed, at the imperial court itself, about whether Atlantis is near to discovering the secret of our city's ancient force field. *Such rumours must cease.*' The Empress's small, sharp teeth, so like the spectacular dentin of the blue-blooded, if dispossessed, creature who shared my bed, gleamed beneath the chill radiance of a chandelier. She continued with her oration, all eyes upon her, though a little to my left, two tribal elders, while dissembling attentiveness, whispered to each other, seemingly careless of whether they be arrested for *lèse majesté*.

'What of these rumours?'

'Albracca, they say, will soon be placed in peril of aerial bombardment.' Yes, I thought, the kind of bombardment I had personally experienced in the Nam.

'Always the storm, my friend, always the clash of civilisation against civilisation.'

'The storm of blood, the storm of pain.'

'And soon, it would seem, the firestorm.'

'Indeed, the storm of storms may soon be upon us.' Yes, yes. In this life and in the limbo of half-forgotten others, there had always been the storm, the fire that followed the scream of the air-raid klaxons, their wail of eternal war.

'But perhaps Cathay will fall, not to Atlantis, but to its own quarrels. Internecine conflict ~ so goes another rumour, friend ~ has already broken out in the country-side. An orgy of urban self-slaughter may follow.'

'No more talk, then, of the superiority of your own path, friend. And no more talk of the imminent breaching of our force field. Let us listen to the Empress.'

I shook my head; I had shut my ears to the Empress's *blah-blah-blah*, her pep talk to a doomed people; but other, more ethereal voices could not be so easily quelled; the air that partied with my thoughts was a-hum with multi-tracked conversations; it seemed as though a high-tension cable ~ like those of myth ~ had been threaded between my ears. I could almost hear *thought*, whispery, depraved mental murmurings that reflected the chaos of an empire fractured by what had formerly united: perversity. In that *sotto voce* of meditative despair, the assembly again rehearsed their arguments ~ *cloning, parasitism*, I heard, *cloning, parasitism, mutation* ~ each tribesperson seeking the biological high ground; The Shark affirmed the Way of the Shark; Bird, Snake, Cat their own paths, each faith hoping to subsume the others. I concentrated, shutting out the chatter; melted into the swarm, allowing myself a fleeting shrug of disgust as my naked, golden body passed, vapour-like, through the

porous wall of protoplasm, my disembodied beauty as much
at odds with the withered flock of delegates as it was with
the rotting shell that was its customary home. Tangential to
the plane of a black crêpe curtain, careful not to let myself
deliquesce into its cloying folds, I turned my attention to a
crystal vitrine, its glass cut with aboriginal calligraphy, a
display cabinet as fragile as a fairy's mortuary furniture
and one of many such to display sublime pieces of porcelain. There, tempting the fingers of the chastest of thieves,
sat Shou-hsing, the Lord of Long Life; Fu-hsing, the Lord of
Happiness; and Lu-hsing, the Lord of Salaries. Hsi Wang Mu,
consort to The August Personage of Jade, whose title the
Empress Dowager had appropriated, was also there, with
not even a bell jar to prevent the curious from caressing her
milky curves. Later pieces represented those gods and
goddesses whose devotees practised limit-experience; im-
paled, skewered, hung, roasted, flayed, dismembered, they
were transgressive deities that, if kilned in celebration of
extremes of human consciousness, were still delicate, and,
more pertinently, *invaluable* examples of the early settlers'
art. How many dynasties had passed since the exodus from
the West, when, after years of persecution, the diaspora of
the perverse had first colonised the desolate lands that lay
beyond the Urals, transplanting the old gods with their own,
the mad gods of unspeakable delight? Enough for a people
to become etiolated, to await the prospect of annihilation
with a *frisson* of expectancy, like sickly orchids eager to flower
one last time beneath the rays of a cruel dawn, the waiting
doubtless made the more easeful by a long acquaintance with
death's sweetness and with proxies such as myself to do the
dirtiest of their dying for them. I sighed; looked up from the
representations of divine torment and gazed across the hall.

Remarque and Stricker eeled their way sheepishly through the crowd; recent additions to the *wusha*, their training incomplete, a stroll through rather than around an obstacle course of living matter was still liable to induce a fit of biliousness. Sidling up to me, looking straight ahead and talking out of the corners of their mouths, they acted – dumb grunts that they were – as if they could not quite believe that they were invisible to the chattering throng.

'The deal's this,' I said, my words electromagnetic pulses that only another astral form could comprehend. I was impatient. My umbilical cord snaked behind me, wiggling like a cut worm; my projection was precarious and, I knew, could be too easily compromised. 'Tomorrow's the fifteenth day of the eighth moon. There's going to be a moon banquet, here, in the palace, and revenants who've recently been decorated–'

'And are going back to the Nam,' said Remarque, finishing my sentence, 'are invited. *Ave atque vale.* So what?'

'So what?' I laughed, hoping that neither might see through the theatricality of my incredulousness, for I was convinced that my business proposition's likelihood of making a return was, if worth an investment of time – something I had too much of, of late – of limited appeal if considered in terms of the possible expenditure of life, particularly if that life, or quasi-life, happened to be mine; *ergo*, my recruitment of Remarque and Stricker as catspaws. 'So you're invited, aren't you? This is your opportunity to pay the balance on your passage. All you have to do is – well, it's like we discussed before. You know the plan.' I gestured at the rows of glazed figurines. 'Just three or four will do. You'll be wearing capes? Good. I suggest you customise them in some way. Think concealed pockets. Think deep pockets.' There were many other treasures within easy reach. The paintings on the walls were by the Four Great Masters of the Ming, Shen Chou, Wen Chen-ming, the unconventional T'ang Yin, and Ch'iu Ying. But it was the ceramics – especially those hordes of translucent white ware, blue on white, psychedelic, that seemed ready to invade and raze an unsuspecting sensibility – that most suggested an easy portage.

'We've paid you enough already,' said Stricker. 'More than enough.' It was true; they'd been paying me ever since they'd walked into the little restaurant on the Bund that I regularly used as my office, the brightness of their eyes, the virginity of their complexion advertising their factory-fresh revivescence. But beneath the glow of unnatural health I had recognised, at once, their despair, the familiar despair of the revenant for whom reconditioning has gone awry. Like I'd done, shortly after *my* last refit, they had awoken from their brainwashed slumber, and they wanted out.

'Not enough, unfortunately, to pay the ship's captain who will take you North.'

'I said we've paid you *enough*.'

'Steady,' said Remarque. He was the older man, a former cavalry sergeant. Forgetful of his projected state, he attempted to put a hand on his friend's arm, his fingers passing through the golden energy haze and then retracting, smartly, as if they had been nipped by a small animal lurking in the oscillating patterns of astral flesh.

'Look,' I said, 'I can get you out.' I persuaded my face to assume an expression of offended hurt. 'My reputation, I think, speaks for itself.'

'Why don't you get yourself out, Duarte?' *When I have enough money,* I thought. *But not to Siberia, like you two. Siberia, where all the zombies go. I'd buy myself passage to some better land.* Smirking, I tried to convey that I enjoyed a secret that was mine to savour when and for howsoever long as I should please. *A better land. But where, where?* My smirk trembled; faltered; disappeared. I looked about at the assembled tribespeople, suddenly feeling my living death keenly, and seeing it reflected in a score of faces and fashions that had been frozen in the mid-twenty-first century and then allowed to thaw, suspended but at the same time subject to a lingering decay, for over two millennia. *Wer, wenn ich schriee, hörte mich denn aus der Engel Ordnungen?* Once, I thought, once I had been an Atlantean, with a family, perhaps, a home; but when Cathay had picked my smashed body up off the battlefield, packed it in ice and sent it to Albracca, to be rebuilt and revived, I became a non-person, an indigent, wandering soul, a fighting machine with no past, no future. 'I mean, if what you have to offer's so good, why don't you get a slice of it yourself?'

'I'll be getting out too,' I said, 'eventually. But maybe I can *afford* to prevaricate. Are you so sure you can? Deserters get a one-way ticket to the scrapyard. If you're caught, you'll be disassembled, used as spare parts. Humpty-Dumpty falls, he don't get no second chance. You know that.'

'Yeah,' said Stricker, 'well, we haven't deserted yet.'

'Oh, we're going to desert, Stricker. We can't go back to the Nam.'

'We can't go back to Atlantis, either. We're traitors, as far as they're concerned.'

'Forget Atlantis,' I said. 'Forget any notion you have

of home. For you, home doesn't exist. But with the documents I provide you can maybe *create* a home. A new start in a new country. A new name. A new life.'

'We want those documents right now, Duarte. You shouldn't be asking us to do your thieving for you. We already have too much at stake.' I turned my back on them.

'But gentlemen, we agreed. A final payment. This is the only way.'

'*We're not—*'

'Then there's no more to be said. It seems I can no longer be of help. Good luck, and *bon voyage.*' I began to rise into the air.

'Wait,' said Remarque. I rotated; spread my arms to demonstrate my willingness to accommodate their troubles, any troubles; if need be, the world's troubles, troubles mundane and marvellous, from creation until the end of time.

'The ship's captain,' I said. 'He's being really difficult. You have to appreciate that contingencies like this sometimes crop up. But with just a little extra cash ... Hell, I'm offering this to you guys on a plate.' Remarque glowered, then put his face close to his friend's; and both fell into their role-playing game of father figure and adopted son who were forming new bonds in adversity.

'The war's going real evil. We go back there – how long we going to last? How long before we get so chewed up the necromancers can't put us back together again? Siberia, I mean, it's cold, man, but we can hack that. We got to do it. We got no other options.'

'No going home, I know.'

'No staying here either, buddy.'

'It's not' – and Stricker's voice cracked, betraying the

boy who hid within the odious manhood of a *wusha* – 'it's not like we had any *choice* about becoming zombies.' Remarque stared at me, his eyes filling with a rheumy unease, the bleak, weepy shame of resignation.

'We'll go along with what you have in mind, lieutenant. But if you let us down—'

'No question of it. Shot-up, stitched-together pieces of recycled cannon fodder like us can't afford to let each other down. The princess and I will meet you at our prearranged rendezvous after you've robbed the palace blind.'

'You'll get us out through the catacombs, then?'

'It's all been arranged. You'll be taken straight to your ship. In a few days, you'll be free.'

'That orc you hang around with – you reckon you can trust her?'

'She doesn't like being called an "orc", soldier. That's what they called her in Europa. An orc, a goblin girl. And she's been trying to forget Europa for some time, understand?'

'Miss Ratty, then?' said Stricker. 'Okay if we call her Miss Ratty?'

'You call her *princess*.'

'Oh, it's princess, is it? Well, you work with the *princess* before? These ratgirls have been known to—' Remarque flashed his friend two eyeballs' worth of warning.

'Yeah, I worked with her before. In the Nam, when I was still a good, faithful servant of Cathay. She was assigned to me by the necromancers.'

'What's a Europan like her doing fighting for Cathay?' I sighed; it was time to leave; my umbilical had begun to hiss and fizz.

'Look, you don't have to worry about any of that.

She's good at what she does. She's helped get dozens of revenants across the border. Trust her.' The boy shrugged, unable to contain his doubt. Youth, I told myself, isn't always such a bad judge of character.

The boy screwed up his face; and doubt burst as from a pustule. Its contagion filled the air, infecting the older man.

'But is it true what they say about goblins? I mean rats?' said Remarque. 'That they can see us, like, even when we're projected?' I nodded, but with an extravagance that signalled that more was at stake than a simple affirmative. My head drooped, lolling onto my chest, a familiar vertigo cascading from the crown to linger in my stomach, like an indigestible brick of lard. And then the faces of my two deserters became smudged, bled paint, flitted away from me in giddy streams of kaleidoscopic light, flowing into the slipstream of the audience chamber as ground, palace, mountain rushed away from me, my umbilical snapping at my ribcage like a severed cable, whiplashing with a bittersweet tang of ion. I glimpsed the jumbled plain of paper tenements, the dark horizon, the moon-lit jagged peaks of garbage and slag that circumscribed the dream-costive tribes; and then I was smothered in an oppression of shadows, the weight of my own corporeality enough, it seemed, to have pressed me through the Earth's core to resurface in Atlantis; a sensation similar, I have read, to that experienced by primitive off-worlders who, accustomed to weightlessness, abhorred reintegrating their senses with the demands of a gravity well. My consciousness had shrunk, so that I suffered the illusion of being a homunculus trapped inside my own skull, a skull that was like a vast château curtained against the day. It seemed that that vaulted space had been my prison for a million years, that for a million years I had choked on its dark immensity. Condemned to an icy throne, blind, deaf and dumb, I struggled with my body's unseen controls, my hands brushing against gears, wheels, to at last find the joystick with which I struggled to bring my executive will to bear. At last, I opened my eyes. The princess was rubbing herself against me in her sleep with characteristic sexual irritability; it had been her unconscious frotteurism that had provided my autonomics with sufficient grounds to reel in my lifeline, summoning me back to the casket of my reanimated flesh. I disentangled myself from her arms. Stroking her hair, I heard her moan, the complaint terminating in a serene exhalation that indicated that she had returned to a deep sleep.

The projection had exhausted me. I scratched, trying to rid myself of the conceit that cockroaches roistered beneath my skin. With circumspection, I swung my legs over the side of the bed; I had no wish to rouse my bedfellow. (Little danger; a porcupine beneath her mattress was unlikely to stir *that* princess.) Then I lifted the mosquito net; rose; tiptoed across the cell; lifted the lid of the icebox. Inside, half buried in a crisp opulence of pink cubes and antiseptically bathed in a column of moonlight was the decapitated head of the young buck-about-town who only last night had drunk from the princess's slipper one drink too many and taken the unwise decision of accompanying her to her door. I put a stained cube to my ulcerated lips. The latest stress to my nervous system had resulted, I noticed, in a similar though more extensive breakout of ulcers across my chest, a patchwork of ischemia that was a reminder of the terminal putrefaction to which I was subject between meals. I dropped the cube; closed the box. Each rejuvenation lasted less than a week; I could afford, I decided, to wait until morning.

The smashed jar lay where it had fallen as I had exited through the window some fifteen minutes ago. Running a stubby, lazar's hand across the slivers of amber glass that lay scattered across the stones, I picked up the black flower, gazed into its heart, twirling the stem between my fingers. It was a mutagenic flower that I held, a war flower, and its perfume fed my imagination like some delicious poison gas. For a moment, I was again in Saigon, walking from the Eden Centre, along Le Loi Boulevard and crossing Ho Chi Minh Square. Secreted within a replica of my old uniform was the bomb I had been ordered to plant atop the Rex Hotel. Arriving, I had shown the fake pass that had allowed me through the sandbags; allowed me to ascend to the officer's bar that sprawled across the roof; allowed me to sit down amongst the assembled lieutenants, majors, colonels and hostesses. Then I had reached inside my jacket and blown the bar and myself to shreds. The princess had been quick to respond; nonchalantly following on a trishaw, sauntering through a landscape of dismembered limbs with perfect, aristocratic *sang-froid*, she had retrieved my head – a task that has, perhaps, become, for her, obsessional; she has told me that my trunk-less head permeates her dreams – and vanished into the howling panic of the streets. I pulverised the evil flower within my fist; opened my hand and lifted its ruins to my nostrils, breathing deep. Was there anything else lurking in that forbidding bouquet? The insinuation of another life? A life in Atlantis? No; I tipped the mangled remains onto the floor; attempted to straighten myself to my full, overgenerous seven feet, my height being one of the many wonders of engineering that marked me as *wusha* and made it difficult for me to walk the streets by day. My pate grazed the ceiling. Slouched, like a bipedal bug in a box, I returned to bed, a prodigy that had fallen out of love with itself.

Grimly horizontal, as if I were in another, more final box (nostalgia for the grave is endemic amongst revenants), I reflected on what Remarque had said, about why I stayed in Albracca. Was I really waiting until I could afford passage to some happier, more salubrious latitude than that which was to be his destiny? Or was it because, in this beat-up, entropic world, there was no longer a land, any land, for people such as myself? Ever since my behavioural conditioning had failed and I had disappeared into the city's papier-mâché outgrowth to try to regain some control over my life, even though that life was a life-in-death, I had had a feeling that, with the war going the way it was, the answers to these questions might, as they say, 'soon be decided for me'.

I had a dream: again I walked across the skybridges of my former home, miles-high in inviolable azure above the crashing waters of the Atlantic. Organic towers – a biomass duotone, ascetic, cankerous – rose on either side, a hybrid array of vegetation and steel meshed together by pressurised corridors such as the one I traversed, my wife and two small children accompanying me. We reached the observation deck. A wolfman and a catgirl, in the uniforms of a butler and a parlourmaid, served us chilled flutes of champagne. Looking down through the gullies to where the walls of the dying towers met, at ground level, in a wedge of darkness, I tried to escry the fabled beings who inhabited that lower world, the ones who, centuries before, had confabulated themselves, engineering strange flesh to accommodate their alien souls. Shipped from Afric and Europa – where, beyond the protection of Cathay, the confabulated fell victim to slavers – they had escaped their chains and now hid in that umbrageous perspective where Atlanteans, so long accustomed to a life above the clouds, never dared to trespass. My daughter squeezed my hand; a tremor had passed through the floor and the observation deck shook on its tendril-like supports. My wife opened her mouth to scream; then she, and the deck itself, tipped forty-five degrees. Another tremor, rising from the ungovernable shadows, had thrown all four of us to the floor. My nails dug into the nylon carpet; but inexorably, I slipped; and the eyes of all those I loved best gazed at me with terror. There was an explosion, a great *crack!* like the breaking of a gigantic twig, and I was falling backwards, as if something intangible had grasped me by the ankles and was pulling me down into its vertiginous empyrean. I felt glass shatter against my back and then I was alone, alone in the cold, empty, stark blueness of the middle air, hurtling towards the abandoned streets where the laws of Atlantis were mocked and the tribes of the perverse held sway. I knew then that I was to lose everything, that the most important things in my life were to be proved insubstantial, less than dreams, and that I was to be made into one of the perverse's servants, the enslaver to be enslaved.

My hand shaking, I drew the razor across my chin, nicking the suture that joined cheek with steel plate. Tearing a wad of tissue from the dispenser next to the commode, I dabbed at the welling bead of thick, oily ichor. The princess stood in the doorway, watching. Naked, with her hair piled into a high, rickety thatch and her make-up smeared, slatternly, she seemed at once the antithesis of the persona she presented to the world and its fulfilment, as if her daytime affectations were a rehearsal for the role she had been born to play, and would always play, the morning after. 'You're looking bad, Duane,' she said, apathetically drawing on a Javanese cigarette, 'and you're smelling putrid.'

'Thanks. So why don't you get me some breakfast?'

'Mmm,' she said, sucking in a lungful of smoke and focusing on my loins, 'I have an appetite myself.' She expelled a dense, clove-tinctured cloud that obscured my reflection in the shaving mirror; and then, tossing her cigarette aside, she stepped into the bathroom, her tail snarling about my thigh. Whatever incubus had toyed with her the previous night had stoked a fire that would not easily be extinguished. I waved the smoke away and brought my face close to its image, studying, with concern and distaste, the lurid signs of advancing decomposition. 'Breakfast can wait, Duane. Come back to bed. Little Frenzy is going to make everything right.' Our eyes met in the cracked glass. Her black irises had dilated with desire, displacing the sclerotic coat. Unfeeling, they seemed, those subterranean eyes, burning shards of jet that, like the beauty spot high on the left cheek that was like a teardrop of obsidian, failed to warm the small-boned, albescent face. I continued shaving. '*Please*, Duane.' The tail, with its deadly, purple-barbed tip, ritually pierced to accommodate a single amethyst, rose from beneath my perineum to probe and tease my poor, redundant genitalia.

'You know it's impossible.'

'They used to say that it was impossible for a revenant to break free of his indoctrination.'

'But this is different, Frenzy. We've been together for two years. And, and—' Picking up a towel I wiped the remnants of foam from my big, spatulate jowls. I stooped; made a cup of my hands and cooled my glabrous scalp with what remained of the dirty water. But then a shock, like one that might have been engendered by an arachnid wearing high-heeled thigh boots abseiling down my back, jerked me to attention. The princess had run one of her steely talons from my nape to the root of my spine.

'It's not as if I ever asked you to go all the way, Duane.'

'Don't you get it yet? Zombies don't fuck.' Her hand withdrew; the tail retracted. I saw in the mirror that she had turned away and was studying the scum that had accumulated under the long, red fingernail.

'And such a *beautiful* zombie.' But her ironic banter was unable to conceal the bitterness of her frustration. I threw the towel into a corner and walked into our sleeping quarters; the princess followed, prim and businesslike. Avoiding my gaze, she quickly pulled on her scapular, then, skipping about the splinters of glass that still littered the floor, brought out a plate and cutlery from our travelling chest and set the table for breakfast. As I watched her extricate her trophy from the icebox and place that grinning, blue-visaged *memento mori* before me (removing, with a flourish, the brainpan that she had thoughtfully sawn through at the same time as she had separated head from torso), I focused on the great declivity of her eight-inch cleavage that so violently disrupted the folds of her tightly cinctured robe. One day, I thought, surely one day the absurd plenitude of that voluptuousness would breathe life into the little comatose man between my legs, the appendage that was just one more snippet of tissue kidnapped from the bodies of dead men who, unlike me, had been given no opportunity to ape the living; one day, surely; but not today.

I dipped my spoon into the exposed cranium and scooped the life-giving brains into my mouth, delicious, so sweet and so cold. My neo-cortex – the myriapod that contained the shattered remains of my personality – flooded with endorphins; I felt it palpitate with delight. Grafted onto the ruins of my original cortex, the fat mechanical insect to which I owed my life of serial resurrection, the parasite that had burrowed its way into my brain-dead head soon after I had been consigned to a body bag, cried out, greedy for neurones and receptors. As I studied the great, mottled expanse of my ulcerated thorax, a thrill of expectation coursing through me, the parasite shifted, extending its segmented body into my cerebrovascular system; and I recognised, in the first rush of manic pleasure, a rush that filled my body with work crews of rugged joy, the inception of self-repair. My chest's necrosis began to fade – the healing process, as always, ridiculously swift – gangrenous vesicles disappearing in a transformation scene that resembled time-lapse photography; and I studied the princess's insidious décolletage with renewed interest, reciting to myself, once again, the specious arguments of hope.

'Dress for me,' I said. 'I like it when you dress for me.'

'But my maid hasn't—' I sucked on the sticky spoon, then broke off a piece of the brioche that had accompanied my repast and fell to wiping the brainpan clean.

'Dress yourself. It's better that way.' The rush had

reached its crisis; from the pinnacle of that high I faced a
descent that, if at first gentle, would, in a few days, have me
nose-diving towards obsolescence. I tried to glide; find some
lift. In vain. Acknowledging my plight (at such times as this I
could always count on her submitting to my humour), she
slipped the monkish saffron from her shoulders and swept
back the curtain that shrouded the alcove serving as her
wardrobe. Resting her foot on a stool, she pulled on her
ankle socks, followed by her plastic sandals and greaves,
taking care to assume a *pose plastique* that suggested the
kitsch pin-up stance of a young woman adjusting her
stocking. Her homage to the idol of plasticity intensified as
she strapped on the polyvinyl lorica artfully embossed to
portray the curves of her naked torso. Running her hands
over the tight-fitting armour, she spun around, letting the
loose strips of the peplum whirl about her hips in a cheap,
flirtatious clatter of lamellae. More plastic followed:
vambraces, a plumed helmet, a holster which, normally
concealed beneath voluminous skirts, displayed, today, the
flintlock that she kept habitually buckled at her thigh.
Ready for combat, she placed a hand on her hip and
confronted me, grinning.

'Come and get it, you dead bastard,' she slurred,
somewhat drunk on the moment.

I spooned the last of the grey jelly between my
lips. My body was restored, but not, alas, my virility.
Undeterred, her eyes scouring each muscle of my body but
one, she slunk towards me, her cuirassed breasts oozing
from beneath their merciless confinement of schlocky
second skin. But now I looked away; stood up, casting a
long shadow over my suddenly diminished companion
(even though I was hunched over, the white plumes of her

helmet still only just brushed against my pects); walked to the window; pulled up the smoked cellophane and squinted down into the courtyard where a rat-monk was giving a group of schoolchildren a history lesson.

'It doesn't matter,' said the princess. 'I mean, it's funny really, but' – she snorted with the effort of containing a laugh that seemed to have been scored for an overture of pure hysteria – 'but it's not even as if you remember what it was like.' I heard the complaint of bedsprings as she sat down to compose herself, the inhibiting, yet at the same time exhibitionistic armour squeaking as it reluctantly accommodated itself to her refractory flesh. 'I'm sorry. And I *do* get it, Duane. It's just that I sometimes find it hard to accept. I want you. I want you bad.'

'You're right, I don't remember,' I said, casting her a cursory glance. She brushed a wisp of hair from her eyes; smiled, conciliatory. I returned my attention to the courtyard.

'It must be nice not having a past. I wish *I* didn't have a past.'

'A past? But I do. It's just that I have inventories rather than memories.' I had a flashback of falling through a cold, azure sky, of a dream of dark streets spangled with inhuman eyes. 'It's all so, so *borrowed* – so confused.'

'Atlantis?'

'Sometimes. Sometimes, there's this feeling of loss, of having left something behind which I know I can never recover. But apart from that—'

'Nothing?'

'Nothing.' But was it the missing dates of the past that most disturbed me? I could live without a past; as the princess often averred, a biography with its pages torn out was preferable to one that had been defaced; it was the dead future that froze my blood, the knowledge that the calendar ahead had been anonymously struck out; the knowledge that I was without potential. Outside, the sun threw its daggers of light against the walls of the whitewashed dorms; I screened my brow with my hand. The monk had seated himself between two great stone phalli that flanked the arched entrance of a stairway cut into an artificial hill ~ a scale model of K'un-lun Mountain ~ at the top of which stood the peristyle and altar dedicated to The Rat. 'Nothing,' I repeated, 'nothing beyond the experiences of the last few years.' I placed a digit to either side of my forehead, massaging the temples.

'Your own selfhood's in there somewhere, Duane Duarte. Don't give up on it. You've come this far.' Invasive thoughts percolated down into what remained of my cerebrum. In a starburst of inscape ~ the revelation died, showering sparks, almost as soon as it had ignited ~ I was transported to a riverside bar where I drank rice wine with a mysterious beauty who was inviting me back to her home…

'The guy you killed: who was he?'

'A soldier. Just a soldier. A regular, I think.'

'A moment ago, I felt him pass right through' ~ I put a hand to my solar plexus ~ 'right through, like a ghost. It's always the same, after I've finished eating. My body becomes … haunted.'

'That's real bad spiritual dyspepsia, Duane.'

'Yeah. But the soldier. His death ~ was it hard?'

'Naw. Easy for me. Easy for him. Did my usual routine. Hello, I says. *Well hello*, he says. I'm a nymphomaniac, I says. *Really?* he says. You want to come home with me and get your head lopped off? *Sure,* he says, *like, there's simply nothing I'd like better.'*

I turned the skull around so that it faced away.

'Maybe I don't have a self any more. Maybe I'm whoever I've just happened to eat. Maybe I—' But 'I' didn't exist. 'I', the 'I' that endured in the neural net of the artificial being that sustained me – who was he? She? It? Countless voices shrieked inside my head, begging for release from the dank prison of my consciousness. But I needed their energy. If I was as dead as they, I was my own shrill prison's keeper; and I consigned the voices to the depths.

'Cathay made you, Duane. But what can be made can be remade.'

The children had formed a circle about the monk. He was explaining to them the origins of the perverse, telling how, thousands of years ago, when the Earth had been bathed in radiation issuing from the catastrophic melt-down of a series of parallel universes – the cataclysm historians call The Abortion – the lost, wandering souls of those alien worlds had merged with their counterparts in this, our world, changing them, clandestinely, but utterly. The children beamed; they had heard this tale before. *'Living on, but not in, this plane of life we call "reality", the children of the perverse hid themselves amidst the Earth's multitudes, unrecognised, their faces turned from those who would persecute them, for though their souls were alien, their flesh was as other flesh. But the day came when the children of the perverse walked proudly into the light and made themselves new bodies to set themselves forever apart from mankind. Bodies that celebrated animality! And some of the confabulated were called Birds, some Cats, some Wolves and some—'* The monk cupped a hand to his ear.

'*Rats,*' chorused the children, with delight.

The princess joined me at the window, her head resting on the firm, orthopaedic support of my biceps –' biceps that had been grossly inflated by symbiotic *quid pro quo.* If my parasite was demanding, it also gave much. Health. Vitality. And strength. 'Let's go outside,' she said. 'My maid is late. I want' – she extended her hand and made as if she were running her claws down a bungling ancillary's cheek – 'I want to rebuke her.'

'Mrs Herzog,' I mused, 'doesn't care for a life of celibacy.'

'Old horror's probably creeping back from some all-night session with those wretched trishaw drivers she likes to hang around with.'

'*And the tribes of the perverse,*' the monk continued, '*began their journey East, an exodus which brought them to the wastelands left by the War of The Liebestod, where the hordes of the old Khans had been besieged and destroyed, there to rebuild the cities of the Orient in their own image, never again to fear the censorious magisters of the West. But now our enemies once again persecute us, even though we have shown them that we too can be as civilised as they. Once again, children, once again the skies grow dark…*'

I pressed my face into her piled, frost-white mane and inhaled stale musk and the base notes of cigarette smoke, cloves, incense and opium. Taking a step backwards, holding her at arm's length, I allowed myself a peremptory scan of her over-the-top pulchritude, the creamy embarrassment of riches that spilled out of that bright red carapace cut high on the thigh, so low – so gibberingly low – on the neck. I cupped her left mamma in my great scoop of a hand (which, despite its inhuman size, still struggled to meet capacity) and hoisted it to reveal the yellow star of the Annamese Resistance, until then eclipsed by the shadows of her buxom overhang. As soon as she had received her dress uniform from the field commander in Hue the princess had had her maid stitch her coat of arms above that five-pointed symbol of oriental defiance. I traced my finger along the contours of the star, and then up, until it met the scroll beneath the bar sinister of the escutcheon. '*Who, if I cried, would hear me amongst the angelic orders?*' I read, translating the Thurn and Taxis motto.

'Nobody, I guess,' she said. 'But then, that's angels for you.' I kneaded the back of her neck, ran a fingernail down her spine, like she had done to me, earlier, when we had performed our bathroom *pas de deux*, but with the difference that there was now a tacit understanding that I would rein in before coming to the lover's leap of no return. Squeezing the upper half of her hindquarters, my hand toyed with the scaly root of the tail that issued from her coccyx.

'You'll dress for me again, sometime, won't you? So long as you dress for me I think I can–' Can what? Overcome? Endure, I thought.

'Sure, sure. Dressing up. It works for me, too.'

'Such lovely clothes. Silks, plastics, leathers, furs–'

'Duane,' she said, suddenly. 'We're going to die, aren't we? Atlantis is coming and I'm frightened. I know I shouldn't be. But I am. Frightened. I'm frightened of death.'

'I can't believe the living are ever really afraid of death. It's only when Cathay dragged me back screaming from the void and turned me—' Into a cipher of its own impotence, I thought, it was only when I became one of the living dead that I truly feared the void; but I was wary of articulating my self-pity; the princess surely found me pitiable enough. I looked out beyond the courtyard, across the airspace I had tasted, knowing the brief freedom of incorruptibility, just the other night, looked out to where, far distant, the suburbs hugged the foothills – those mounds of useless tek stripped from the city's heartland – foothills that counterpointed the heaps of buried artefacts that dotted the city itself, graveyards wherein lay interred the superstructures of broken skyscrapers, broken technologies, broken dreams. 'I need some air.'

She broke away, pulled her saffron robe on over her armour – a prudent rat, she, my little upper-crust mongrel, that armour imbued with enough dirty tek to stop a sword thrust, if not a musket ball – and opened the door. I garbed myself in my own tent-sized robe and followed, a cadaver who had just checked out of Henry Frankenstein's Health Farm wearing his swankest winding-sheet.

The stairs were set flush against the outside wall of our lodgings and were designed for beings of more modest proportions than I; I descended, a kamikaze, powerless to match the princess's dervish-like departure. Swaying, tottering, as if I were attempting the suicidal feat on a unicycle, I finally slipped on the penultimate step and made a pratfall into the yard. I picked myself up to the gleeful applause of the schoolchildren and walked out from under the panoply into the glare of the late morning sun. In the centre of the courtyard, a bronze tripod, its bowl smouldering with incense and ghost money, seemed to intensify, by way of evoking paragnosis, the autumn's uncommonly humid atmospherics. The princess was far ahead, leaping the concrete stairs that wound up the hillside towards the peristyle. A little girl had left her school friends and trailed after her, first hesitantly, then, giggling, with slavish enthusiasm, calling, '*Miss Frenzy, please, don't go, please don't go!*' The children parted at my lumbering approach, looking up at me with open mouths. Their laughter had been stilled; and some had begun to cry. The cross-legged monk shifted, allowing me to pass between the tall, phallic monoliths, his tranquil, almond eyes (inherited from those settlers who had interbred with the region's aboriginals) reassuring his charges that the bogeyman would not tarry. Holding the hem of my robe aloft, I pressed on with the pursuit. The princess had by now acceded to her little admirer's pleas. Together, hand in hand, they reached the final stair; and then they disappeared through the propylaeum and over the lip of the summit. Too heavy to be a sprinter, unable to shift gear, my muscles laboured to propel the warrior's bulk of my body up the gradient. By the time I too had reached the synthetic plateau the two ratgirls, senior and junior, were seated by the basalt altar that stood at the centre of the peristyle. Backs against that slab of funereal stone – a black, sacrificial table engraved with incomprehensible calligraphy – they seemed like two siblings at a picnic, two little girls destined to be accosted by a lewd intruder. About them lay a sea of junk.

'I'll be a big rat like you some day, Frenzy. A big, buxotic rat with white, white skin.'

'Well, I'm not really a one-hundred-per-cent rat like you, you know.'

'*Really?*'

'I'm more like half a rat. But where I come from the people call us goblins.'

'Tell me about when you were a little girl, Frenzy. Tell me about the castle.'

'Castle Duino, you mean? My home? It stands near Trieste, overlooking the Adriatic. Trieste, Venice. Ah, they're all in ruins now. Poisoned, decayed. If war desolated the East, it left the West with a victory just too, too Pyrrhic.'

'Trieste? Where's that?'

'Europa, darling.'

'Cathay,' she recited, counting off the continents on her fingers, 'Atlantis, Afric, *Europa*.'

'That's right.'

Lewd, intrusive, I squatted next to them, staring between my feet at the ground-up machinery that constituted the dust. The child edged nearer to the princess, her fingers groping amongst the discarded circuit boards and microprocessors as if seeking out a comfort blanket or doll. 'You want to know about the Princess Frenzy? Her mother was raped,' I said. 'A ratman crept into her bedroom one night and—'

'That's enough, Duane.' I offered her protégée a cathode-ray tube as a peace offering; she withdrew, menacing me with gritted, needle-like teeth.

'Did your mother die?' said the child. 'Did she die in ecstasy?'

'Of course not. She was human.' She looked down big-sisterly at the pouty rat-child, still peering at me with half-lidded eyes through a protective screen of black ringlets. 'But procreation is such a bore. Simply everybody is arguing about it.'

'Did they argue about it when you were little?'

'What I remember best about when *I* was little was that I saw things other people couldn't see. I was barely out of the cradle when I could see fairies. Then the wraiths of those who had lived in the castle long ago. Explorers from parallel worlds. As I grew, I came to see angels. And then at last, the dreams of the orcs – the rodent people, your brothers and sisters, darling, my cousins, if you will – who lived beneath the ruined cities and the mountains that bordered our domain, and who were waiting, waiting for their day to come...'

'I'm glad *you* could come, Frenzy. To Cathay.'

'I had no choice, poppet. The humans who were my family – I'd always frightened them. So I got into the habit of wandering away. And one day I didn't come back. No place amongst humans for a goblin princess.'

'Were you alone, Frenzy?'

'Not quite. The angels came with me. The angels of Duino.'

'I don't believe in angels.'

'You should. They're everywhere. But they're invisible. Even rat people have trouble seeing them, sometimes. But *my* angels – they seem to have deserted me. Or perhaps I just don't see as well as I did when I was a little girl.' I again tried to present the rat-child with my gift, the icon of another age.

'There's no need for you to fear,' I said.

'No, he won't hurt you,' added the princess, letting the child rest her head against her bosom.

'I don't like the monastery, Frenzy,' she said, trying to ignore my attentions. 'I want to have a boyfriend, like you do.'

'Perilous thoughts, little one. Perilous.'

'I don't care. I'm a rat. I'm happy being a rat. I want to die in horrible ecstasy.'

The sun had achieved its noonday height and the arena of worship, littered with the remains of bleached electronic consumables, shimmered with convection. About the perimeter, statues of rats, upright, rearing into the sky, their rain-worn bodies wrapped in lengths of tattered saffron, seemed to be closing in, outriders for an imploding world. Again, I proffered the cathode-ray tube; and this time the little sister took it.

'It's broken,' she said.

'It's all broken,' I said, looking about at the centuries of accumulated junk. And then I looked out over the valley to where the mist had been burnt away from K'un-lun Mountain; narrowed my eyes, tried to focus on something beyond, a land that might offer true restoration. 'Even the wrecking-ball that crashed into the Earth all those thousands of years ago – the perverse – even that's broken. That's why you're in a monastery. The perverse is dying.' The child picked at a loose wire.

'Can't you fix it?'

'The Earth? TV? The perverse? I'm sorry,' I said, laughing at the child's naïveté, a certain maliciousness bubbling beneath my skin like a counterpart to my more generalised corruption. 'After The Abortion—'

'*After The Abortion,*' recited the child, '*dust and par, par, par—*'

'Particulates,' offered the princess, 'noxious particulates released by the cataclysm.'

'*Began to settle across our own universe, gradually obscuring the cosmic code.*' The child allowed her new toy to fall to the ground.

Lost forever, the secrets of the cosmos; no path left for retrieving knowledge, now, once it had been obscured by physical laws which had no currency in this world. The dark cloud of Otherness blanketed all. The age of induction was over; we lived in an age of grimoires, a knowledge-hoard that was being squandered, misused, discarded by the priestly castes to whom had been entrusted the future of the cognisant Earth.

'After The Abortion, when the alien souls grafted themselves onto those Earthlings they had chosen as their soul-mates, everything, they say, was frozen. It was as if history had come to a stop. After the middle of the twenty-first century, Man's sum of knowledge was atrophied; and ever since, it has become obscure; all life has become a slow decline.'

Perhaps there had been a sadness in my pedantic utterances, utterances prompted, I would guess, by the remnants of my encyclopaedic conditioning; but the child's suspicions, her instinctive fears, seemed allayed; for she leant over, reached up and stroked my bald head, little painted fingers playing with the scars and rivets that decorated my scalp. *Why so sad, zombie?* I asked myself, *Why so sad?* I was – or had been – an Atlantean, a man from the glittering towers that had survived the Liebestod, towers that, if fated to succumb to the entropy that racked the whole world, still ran down a coastline that stretched from pole to pole; an Atlantean, I told myself, from a civilisation that was the proud contradiction of Cathay, mirroring Cathay's decline in the inverted image of its own ascendance. The kernel of my being should have been doped with optimism; it was the princess who was the *natural* melancholic. I looked at her;

tried to smile. Princess Frenzetta von Thurn und Taxis-Hohenlohe (the 'goblin princess', the peasants who gathered beneath the gates of her castle had called her), child of a principality where the invisible enfolds the visible; Princess Frenzetta from the old, dark, haunted lands of Europa. Atlantean, Europan; optimist, pessimist? These days the princess and I seemed equally susceptible to morbid attacks of the vapours. 'Pick-and-mix,' I said. 'That's our culture. We have DNA technology – or at least, *some* of us do – yet we're unable to reinvent the rifle. We have radio–'

'But not television,' said the child.

'Sometimes I think it's not merely the fact that the axioms and the equations aren't there. I think they are, even if we can't see them. It's that they simply *don't work*. They've become' – I looked down at my hands which, in a few days, would again become gangrenous, at last to rot, the flesh falling from the bone – '*corrupted.*'

'Pooh! Knowledge is cumulative,' said the child, correcting me, 'you take away the foundations, the whole building collapses. The equations work all right. But not for us. Because something inside us doesn't *want* them to work. The par, par, par *particulates* have, have–'

'Skewed everybody's perception,' said the princess. 'And inclination. And orientation. Perverse. So perverse.'

'It's just like in *The Snow Queen*,' said the child. 'By Hans Christian Andersen. A very evil man makes a terrible mirror. And those who look into the mirror see, not themselves, but an ugly, wicked distortion of themselves. And then one day the mirror breaks and the pieces are blown all over the world. And it's like everybody, now, has a piece of the mirror in their eye. And it changes the whole way they look at things.'

The child's insight had unnerved me into silence. I looked away, avoiding her nasty, precocious eyes. On K'un-lun Mountain the white light of meridian haloed the jade palace in a necklace of weightless diamonds. How many skyscrapers had been eaten up, digested, transformed by that great, raised heap of technological detritus and moribund energy? K'un-lun, I thought, you are both monument to life and funeral pyre. The pleasure gardens were being prepared for this evening's banquet; below, at the base of its towering, man-made cliffs, the great portcullis that led the way to the necromancers' lair was opening to allow passage to a caravan of butchered men. Frenzy's hand closed upon mine.

'They're putting up a marquee,' she murmured, her eyes so much keener than mine, 'and there seem to be arrangements for a firework display.' The funicular railway ferried between ground and summit, laden with tribespeople, livestock and rice. Her black, expressionless gaze followed the progress of the slow-moving cars as they ascended and returned. But I knew, without turning my head, that she too was looking beyond, to some place that offered rebirth.

'We shall rise,' she said.

Later, on the Bund, at The Thunderbolt Vehicle Café, the little restaurant that I had bribed the proprietor into allowing me to use as my office:

'Yes, yes, my little bonbon,' croaked Mrs Herzog, downing a tumbler of rice whiskey, 'there's a good market for porcelain at the moment, especially the later pieces.'

'The aesthetics of hysteria,' said the princess, 'has always struck a chord.'

'We have porcelain in the chapel next to the girls' dormitories. It's hysterical, Frenzy, I'm sure it is. Why don't you help yourself to it?' The child from the monastery – the brat, I should say; I had conceived a jealous resentment of her – had accompanied us as we stole through the backstreets, stubbornly hanging on to the hem of the princess's robe, a seven-year-old maggot of our private commonweal. Her name, she said, was Lara. 'I could help you, Frenzy. I'm a bad girl like you. I am, really I am.' She pursed her lips, casting a prurient glance at the trishaw drivers huddled outside. This over-sexed maggot seemed eager to complete her life cycle.

'Seems to be taking after you, Mrs H,' I said, nodding towards the raggedy men, one, some or all of whom had probably rogered the filthy crone but twelve hours previously. But the three women – spring, summer and a particularly hoary if still horny winter – ignored me.

'The porcelains in the monastery are fakes,' said the princess, running her hand becalmingly down the brat's long hair. 'Supposed to be Ming, apogee of the potter's craft. Though some people go crazy about the Sung. Anyway, don't be fooled by the reign marks; it don't mean a damn thing as far as authenticity goes, there's so many good copies around. Fakes! Fakes! And quite, quite worthless, my sweet. Besides, you don't really want to be a bad girl, do you? Why should you want to leave your temple? I'm ten years older than you and *I'm* happy to live there.'

'But I crave insemination, Frenzy.'

'No, no,' cooed the princess, gathering the brat's head onto the cantilevered shelf of her bust, 'it doesn't have to be like that. It doesn't have to be like that at *all*.'

'Hey,' I said, 'if she's so itchy about reproducing, who

are we to stand in her way?' For my pains, I was rewarded with a contemptuous narrowing of the princess's eyes, black mascara confusing the perimeter of two liquid-midnight slits, delirious ocular engineering designed for goblin cities deep in the sunless, fun-less Earth. Volatile, they seemed to ripple like pools of petroleum, or like dark crystals lush and shot through with the breathlessness of mother night.

'The robbery, Master Revenant, address the issue of the robbery.'

The old dwarf – barely taller than our annoying if temporary foster child – dabbed at her cheek with a rag where three fresh scratches testified to the princess's dissatisfaction with her punctuality. In Mrs Herzog's case, the appellation 'dwarf' was not a taxonomic designation and meant only that she was unusually diminutive; she was human, and her bloodline had not been infiltrated by the heterogamous traits that had inspired those at Duino to call her mistress 'goblin'. But sometimes, the mythic resonance of her dwarfishness seemed to overpower reality, and both maid and mistress appeared to me like creatures from a dark, Teutonic fairy tale. A tale that I longed to hear concluded with a *happily ever after* ... I passed a hand over my eyes, as if trying to disabuse myself of some enchantment. Blinked; looked out towards the street. Hunched over the table, I was eager to hide the brute spectacle of my outrageous height from passers-by whose acuteness of vision might be sufficient to penetrate the restaurant's shadows. My robe offered meagre camou-flage; indeed I sometimes thought it accentuated my freakishness. Like Rodin's monument to Balzac, ungainly, fantastic, a curious onlooker might hardly believe that a man's form lay shrouded beneath its dirty, saffron folds. But projection left me enervated; it was unwise to leave my body more than once in twenty-four hours; my design compelled me to walk the streets in my fleshly configuration. Besides, it was necessary to be corporeal at the office; how else was I to meet and speak with clients?

'We will drive my deserters to the foot of K'un-lun Mountain at the appointed time,' I said. I would have to be corporeal tonight, too, as would Remarque and Stricker. They needed flesh to pilfer ceramics from the palace; I needed flesh to relieve them of their haul. 'They will be transported to the summit, proceed to the banqueting rooms, and, as subtly and as quickly as possible, use the cover of the crowd to fill their pockets with as much antique porcelain as they can – the later pieces made by the settlers, I guess we're agreed on that – just as if they were helping themselves to canapés.' The catering would include those special little tidbits, I thought, that revenants can digest; so nice to pretend, even for a little while, that you had a normal stomach. Let my deserters live the high life while they might.

'And we just bide our time while they rip the empire off?'

'As soon as they have a chance to make their excuses and leave we will collect them and make our way to the rat necropolis.'

'The entrance is nearby,' said the princess to the crone. 'The catacombs actually worm their way through the roots of the mountain. It was conceded to the rats by one of the early emperors, a rat himself, so they say.' She took out a pencil from her sleeve and sketched a rude map on a napkin. 'You go here, then here, then—'

'I know, I know,' said Mrs Herzog. 'Here, there. For how many years now? Everywhere. She had me drive her right across Europa, Master Revenant, right into the badlands of the East.' She pressed her walnut face to within an inch of the princess's own. 'Don't think you can hide out in that monastery for ever, young lady, not with a member of the walking dead at your side. Such things attract *attention*.' We both ignored – as we always did – the cantankerous maidservant's bibulous hectorings, happy to leave her, exhausted as she was after a few seconds of such bluster, staring at the bottom of her glass, eructative with nostalgia for that high limestone plateau rising directly from the Adriatic, The Karst; for the ancestral seat of Thurn and Taxis, Castle Duino.

'The rat priests will have made sure that the gates to the catacombs will be open,' I said.

'At night they're closed,' said the crone. 'Except to midwives.'

'I said the priests will make sure they're *open*. At least, they'd better make sure. I've paid them enough over the last few weeks. Once we're underground, we'll be clear. No one will think of following us into the necropolis.'

'Then goodbye to your deserters,' said the princess.

'I don't want them killed,' I said. 'They have a ship waiting for them. Passage North has been arranged. Once they've paid their dues, they can leave. I just want to make sure they deliver the porcelain.'

'Such a spoilsport.'

'I think my little bonbon is thinking of that ship for herself, no?'

'Well–'

'Not yet,' I said. 'A few more jobs, then–'

'Such an *honourable* zombie,' said the princess. 'To want to help all those poor deserters. Never a thought for himself.'

'You had better think of moving on, sir,' said the dwarf, 'the talk is all of how Atlantis is putting together an armada of airships to penetrate the city's force field. I feel we don't have much time left to us.'

To one side of the table was a fish tank, the dismal waters of which would suddenly flash with the fins of glittering, amber carp. Lara dis-embosomed herself; stood up; dipped her hand into the fishy filth, terrorising the tank's inmates like a cartoon kitty.

'Don't,' said the princess. 'You're not a cat. You're a rat.'

'Don't you like cats, Frenzy?'

'Cats are treacherous, spiteful girls.' She was gazing out into the street where a litter of slit-skirted felines was wiggling past, each tabby-cat featured superfem casting arch, insolent glances at the trishaw drivers and the other examples of human riff-raff that agglomerated in packs of salivating concupiscence along the sides of the street. They seemed more like the mechanical people that populated the pleasure domes and private palaces of wealthy merchants than like tribespeople of the perverse; it was the way they moved – like wind-up toys, each step a calculated pose – that conjured up images of automata rather than the self-modified, the scions of genetically-altered flesh; but they *were* self-modified, as confabulated as sharks, snakes, she-spiders and, yes, even rats; in many ways, they seemed the *sine qua non* of confabulation, the left-hand path in its most realised, evolved and perfect form. But this was something the princess could not admit; neither was it an opinion, if I expected to be in her good graces, to let fall from my own lips; the princess was insecure in her perversity and did not like competition. But, for now – unflappable – she retained her blue-blooded *hauteur*. 'Strange, how their ancestors chose to confabulate themselves in such a way. But no more strange, I suppose, than the fact that most of our ancestors chose female rather than masculine flesh.'

'Femininity is the quintessence of the perverse, Frenzy,' said Lara. 'Didn't they teach you that at school?'

'How do you teach a mystery?' I said, exasperated by the child's upstart comments. 'After The Abortion, when untold universes had been smashed apart, their ghost traces, infecting our universe, had urged those tainted by the disaster to conform to the erotic scripts of their alien soul-grafts. But, amnesiacal, trapped in the brute matter of their own existence, those infected could only imperfectly realise their pre-existent selves; the perverse, in this world, knowing itself through the dark mirror of mankind, is truly lost, and apprehends its former glory only through dreams, half-remembered myths, the visions of sexual outlaws and the insane. Through mystery.' The three females lifted their eyes, unstated mockery of my pedantries now, for them, second nature.

Skipping between street performers and peddlers, the catgirls looked over their shoulders at the tight-lipped contingent of Eugenics Police who‹were handing out leaflets that condemned unregulated coition while advocating monasticism; and then they were gone.

'Don't you dare,' said the princess. Lara had lifted a carp free of the water and was dangling it before her upturned mouth. 'Don't you *dare*.' The fish was rank, its convulsive vigour contrasting shockingly with its dead, tarnished scales and bulging, mutant eyes. I knew that stink, that rumour of mephitis: history, locked in a faulty refrigerator, slowly decaying, as surely as was I. Lara let the fish drop back into the tank, the brisance of its splash sprinkling our table with mire. 'Cats: they think they're so much *closer* than the rest of us are to the perverse's originals.'

'What do you mean, Frenzy?' said Lara.

'I mean they think that they've confabulated themselves to be perfect replicas of the denizens of that dead universe they call home. Whereas the rest of us—'

'Where *do* we come from, Frenzy?'

'Does it matter? We're lost, darling. Selfhoods alienated, against the grain. Beautiful. Strange. But lost. Cat, Wolf, Shark, Rat—'

'But Frenzy, you said you were only *half* a rat.' The princess, I think, had been tiring of her protégée for some time; intimacy, verbal as much as physical, was something she feared as much as she desired; now fear and boredom combined to reveal a less agreeable side to her haughty nature, a flick of her tail leaving the child – in the princess's revised opinion, a child now neither rat nor cat but impertinent, unalloyed *brat* – sprawling on the tiles, too surprised to cry, but with enough assuredness to quickly pick herself up, lift her robe clear of her ankles and scamper out of the restaurant, far, far from lady harm's way. Though no stranger to the confessional, the princess seldom brooked reminders of her mongrel status. It was a subject only I – the one person with whom she was intimately at ease – was privileged to address.

'Do you want me to go after her?' And throttle the

life out of the wretched chit, I thought, as my hands unconsciously fidgeted with a napkin, manipulating it into a garrotte.

'Why? She only spoke the truth.' Shakily, she lit a cigarette; looked about the restaurant, a flush of paranoia enlivening her cheeks.

'Is it troubling you today?'

'The part of me that's perverse? You make the rat side of me sound like something as commonplace as menstruation. But, yeah. It's troubling me. It's like it's always seeking its home. But home has been destroyed, hasn't it? It's an exile's soul, mine. Full of longing. And the crazy thing is it's always longing for death.'

A waiter served our meal: noodles, red pork and rice; and moon cakes. 'Talking of menstruation,' said Mrs Herzog, 'isn't your womb telling you it's a very special day?'

'The fifteenth day of the eighth moon,' said the waiter before departing.

The princess blew smoke in her maid's crevassed face. 'The Moon? Well, she's the author of all women's troubles, they say. She'll get you raped and eviscerated for sure.'

'Moon Festival,' I added, somewhat extraneously, surveying the food with distaste, unable to quite believe that, human and alive, I had been eager to consume such ordure. 'Tonight's banquet at the palace is in honour of The Moon.' The Moon, I thought, to which they said the spirits of dead tribespeople ascended to join with the ghosts of their ancestors. But how many of the living still tilled its artificial soil? The tribespeople condemned to lunar imprisonment in the twenty-first century – how many still survived, burning with the undiluted fires of the perverse?

'Could people really still be there?' said the princess, as if reading my mind. Mrs Herzog shook her head.

'Only bones and ruins are to be found on The Moon, my little bonbon.' It had been a prison, at first, a place of transportation; but after the convicts had established homesteads, tribespeople persecuted on Earth had migrated there out of choice, finding in its rugged environs a sanctuary. That had been before the spaceplanes had been grounded; the rockets, too, all technology that had ferried mankind to The Moon and beyond, even to the reaches beyond the Solar System, malfunctioning, its tek riddled with the fallout from The Abortion.

'Maybe not,' I said. 'Some say the machines that sustained life are still working. Maybe there *are* tribespeople there, living in a way we can only dream of.'

'No, Duane, the only way you get to The Moon is by dying.'

'A myth,' I said. 'A pretty myth. Still, there'll be plenty of brainwashed *wusha* at court being lectured on the nobility of *dying*.'

'For Cathay, you mean?'

'Their beloved, adopted home.'

'How chivalrous.'

'My deserters will blend in nicely.' The table fell quiet; but I think the princess must have continued to scan my death-drawn, moony thoughts.

'How many times do the necromancers say you have to die before you go to heaven, Duane?'

'One time too many, as far as I was concerned.' I raised my glass in a toast.

'To crime,' said the princess.

'To success,' said Mrs Herzog.

I put the glass to my lips, but forebore from draining it. 'Nothing can go wrong,' I said.

The coach-and-four roared along the pitch-dark tunnel, its lanterns jangling against filigree brass work to cast darts of yellow illumination across the racks of glass coffins that lined the tunnel walls. 'Faster,' I cried, leaning out of the window. The dwarf lashed the furious team of destriers with her whip. 'Mrs Herzog' – the pressure chamber of fear compressing my larynx into a singularity of over-punctiliousness – 'a little more application, if you please, I perceive we are losing ground.' The zealous crone, her tiny matchstick body obscured by a windblown frock that was little more than a squall of ghastly rags, raised a hip-flask to her lips, pointing ahead to the small disk of light that marked the termination of the catacombs, and then applied her whip with redoubled vigour.

'I always knew we shouldn't have come East,' she shouted, pushing her bonnet to the back of her head, 'I told the mistress nothing good would come of it. She only fifteen years old when she left home! But she had such *romantic* ideas.' The palace guard were nearly upon us, our barouche, with its iron chassis, thick oak panelling and decorative, rococo trim of pewter and electrum, no match for their fleet saddle horses. 'But she had always so hated Atlanteans. They reminded her of her family, I think. So censorious, so self-righteous, so repressive, so cruel! She'd wanted to kill them ever since she was a little ratling.'

I eased myself back into the carriage. Remarque and Stricker, huddled on the seat opposite, each clutched a blue-and-white Ming vase.

'All this just might have been worth it if you'd only helped yourself to a little more porcelain.'

'We had whole rooms filled with that stuff in Duino,' said the princess, pulling up the skirts of her billowing silk gown and unholstering her flintlock. 'I don't know where you get your hired help from these days, Duane, but—' A ball punched a hole through the back panel of the coach and opened up a small mineshaft between Remarque's eyes that glistened with a ruptured lode of blood. 'Now that's really bad luck. Isn't that bad luck, Duane? I mean, one stray shot and poor old Remarque gets hit in the old neo-cortex.'

'That's not bad luck,' I said, 'that's lack of foresight.' Since I had deserted I had had my own skull fortified with reinforced steel. I could no longer pass through a metal detector with impunity, but then I no longer wished to play the part of a walking bomb.

'Listen, Stricker, you armed?' said the princess. The younger revenant had been captivated by his former sergeant's newly-acquired third eye. Now he gave me his attention, his knuckles whitening as he tightened his grip about the vase, pulling it against the patriotic tin that honoured him for being such a stupid, servile son-of-a-bitch. The medals were stippled with beads of vomit. Stricker seemed ready to crack. Assessing him with a mixture of amusement and contempt, the princess sighed, turned, opened her door and steadied the flintlock against the jamb; discharged it into the darkness. 'Think I got one,' she said, fumbling with ball, wad and powder, quickly making to reload. 'Stricker, didn't you hear me – *are you armed*?'

'Of course he isn't armed. He's just come from the palace. They body search everybody who goes in.' Though not, of course, those leaving. It had been an equerry, acting on a tip-off, who, discreetly trailing my deserters out into the gardens and down to the foot of the versant, had alerted the guard and thus undermined my hubristic plans; if not for him, and the little informer who had betrayed us, we would have made a clean getaway. 'Hell, *I'm* not even armed.'

'I want to go home,' said the teenager in the ogre's body.

The princess tore at her encumbering dress; slipped off the leg-of-mutton sleeves; struggled to free herself of the bodice. She had attired herself like one of those rich courtesans who attach themselves to the fringes of court life. Waiting in the getaway coach at the ground station of the funiculars, as if for a secret assignation, and making a meal of her mid-Europan vowels, she had kept the guards at an apprehensive distance; the Empress Dowager was eager to woo neutral states into her camp and her servants were wary of annoying foreigners.

'Could you help me, Duane?' I spun her about, ripped the bodice asunder, buttons ricocheting against the polished wood and leather seats. She shuffled the flounced silk to the floor; stepped out of its calf-deep frou-frou; then, with a fevered presumptuousness, pressed herself against me and lifted her face. I grabbed her, squeezing her upper arms where her white satin evening gloves imperceptibly melted into her skin tone, pale as boiled milk; flexed, as if I were performing a beach-party trick, a muscle-bound, woman-hating display of callisthenics. Her shoulder blades closed like pincers; her lips parted, revealing the rows of tiny, pointed teeth; and she arched her back, breasts spilling over whalebone, the rouged areolae staring at me with drunken insolence, erect. Her corsetry was, with its bows and laces, its scintillant grommets of steel, quite admirable, I thought; but—

'You're not wearing your armour.'

'Oh, Duane, is that all you have to say?' I put an arm between her stockinged legs, my wristband snaring in her garters, chafing at her dewy thighs, and lifted her so that her cambered amplitude was level with my mouth. She threw her head backwards. '*Is that all, is that all?*' Outside, rushing past in mad agitations of light, a coffin, wiped clean of grime by a dutiful midwife, might sometimes reveal a face locked in transcendence; an abdomen exploded from within by the spawn-rage of the perverse; limbs twisted, broken, in the throes of a paroxysm that had been the fulfilment of a life's teleology. I released her.

'Well, it's – it's imprudent. Not to wear your armour – it's ... Never mind. You've left your entire wardrobe at the monastery – it's gone, gone – you do know that, don't you? I mean, even if we escape, how am I to get by, how am I to *survive* not being able to see you dress?'

'Dress, undress; undress, dress. Duane, you can make a girl dizzy.' She wobbled on her heels; then, recovering, nervously patted her powdered hair as if she had detected something feral worrying at her chalky, translucent roots. 'And what are you looking at?' she said, pointing the flintlock at the luckless, if still extant deserter.

'You shouldn't be making out. It's dangerous,' he said, talking more to himself than to my splenetic little aristocrat, 'a ratgirl can only have sex the one time. And then she dies in black orgasm.' He seemed to have retreated even further into the paralysis of his shell-shocked funk. 'The goblin has to cool it. Put her breasts on ice.

Freeze her clitoris at −273.15°C. We need her, we *need* her.'

'Goblin?' enquired the princess, her upper lip aquiver.

'Princess Frenzetta' – panic had suddenly burst through his introspection – 'please, please. Do. Not. Fuck.'

'Fuck? Are you crazy? Look around you, Strick. You think I want to end up like those little tarts out there? Inseminated? Killed by the intensity of my own pleasure? And then interred until my little baby rat gnaws its way out of my belly? Why do you think I hang around with Mr Duane Duarte?'

Stricker held out the vase.

'Take it. I don't want to go on with this. Let me surrender. I don't want to die!' The detonation resounded through the catacombs like the bark of some gigantic, perfidious bat abandoning a dismal belfry for better climes. Stricker had acquired a third eye identical to that of his friend. Grazing the barrel with her lips to leave the gunmetal with a souvenir of strawberry lipstick, the princess blew the promiscuous gases from the muzzle of her pistol.

'You were dead already,' she said to the corpse, bereft now of animation.

'No armour, no patience.'

'Well, aren't I the fickle bitch.' Stricker's eyes flipped heavenward, the pupils half-occluded by the sockets, as his consciousness was dissipated into the Great Inane; and then the massive body collapsed in upon itself, like a leaky balloon, the Ming vase slipping between dead fingers to smash against the bucking, turbulent boards.

'And no porcelain.'

'And no more of your get-rich-quick capers after this.

No more Albracca. Don't pretend you need more money, Duane. You don't. We're leaving.' An extracorporeal body – long, ringed and argent – was emerging from Stricker's ear. It was the first sight I had had of the genus that contained a précis of my original brain tissue; the parasite that gave the dead life. Wounded, the thing died before it could escape the doomed habitat of Stricker's trashed cranium.

One of our pursuers had drawn alongside. It was a sharkman, one of those who preyed on the partheno-genetic, oviparous females who followed the paths of The Bird and The Snake, kidnapping their hatchlings to serve as pleasure-slaves.

'I've never really understood these sharks,' I said.

'It's easy. they breed like amoebas. But they need to really have their brains fucked out before they can achieve division. They're clones, of course. I knew a snakegirl, once. She said once you'd fucked one shark you'd fucked them all. But then, they have these *great* swimming pools.'

The princess raised her flintlock, her forehead knit-ting as she realised that she had had no time to reload. Covering her, I ripped a door from its hinges and hurled it beneath the approaching blur of hoofs; stumbling, the horse threw its rider, the sharkman's steak-knife array of teeth set in a rictus of astonishment as he skidded along the tunnel floor, the chain mail covering his dorsal fin throwing up a strident precipitation of sparks. Another horse took the fallen stallion's place. High in its stirrups was a catgirl, one of those too-sweet adolescent fellatrices who reproduced by infecting human males with the generative viroids con-tained in their saliva. 'Give me that gun,' I cried, snatching the flintlock from the princess's hand. Our feline pursuer had lifted a metallic tube onto her shoulder. Something resembling a small octopus shot from its aperture, flying initially towards the team of destriers, and then, correcting its trajectory, towards me. I tried to shield my face, but I was too late; the missile's jelly-like body struck me full, enveloping my mouth and eyes, the suckers on its flailing tentacles adhering tenaciously to my skin. I felt the princess's hands join my own in the effort to peel the cephalopod free; heard her muted imprecations. As I struggled to break the seal of the rapidly congealing jell, I felt my stomach take the up elevator; the missile had probed and then invaded my left ear, an elastic string of gelatin trespassing across the body-brain divide, curling itself about my neo-cortex. On red alert, my sensorium contracted; I was again a homunculus, wrestling with the controls of a thrashing, out-of-control body. In my cold palace of bone, blind, deaf and dumb, I wriggled, eluding the tentacular hunter-killer's grip; and then, as I lost all contact with my corporeal self, I was outside, observing the pieced-together being known as Lt. Duane Duarte – his dinner jacket torn, a disgusting, mould-spotted blancmange obscuring his soapstone features – slumped across the seat of the barouche. The princess blinked; stared at my projection, trying to focus, her eyes darkening as she adjusted to the radio spectrum of my metaphysical flesh.

'We're in trouble, Duane,' she whispered. The coach had stopped; we were surrounded by palace guard. 'I think they have it in mind to use us as spare parts.' Mrs Herzog had been trussed and flung onto the laps of my two late renegades, deserters who had hotfooted it into the final oblivion. Skidding, its legs barely able to check the deceleration imposed upon it, a majestic stallion came to an uneasy halt by our side; behind its rider a small girl in monastic robes sat side-saddle, squinting at us with enormous satisfaction.

'I thought you were my friend, Frenzy. But you're not, you're not.' A catgirl climbed into the carriage, covering the princess with her musket. 'Half a rat! Half a rat!' yelled the little rat novice who had made us regret using her as an object of our despite. 'I told on you, Frenzy. I *told* on you. Don't you wish you hadn't hit me with your big, nasty tail?' My proud-hearted princess ignored the remarks with the calm with which she had ignored the intrusion; whatever secret shame she might feel at her compromised genes, the blood of Thurn and Taxis, at that moment – branding her cheeks with rosettes of pride – had allowed her to dismiss Lara's maliciousness with blithe disdain.

'Glad you could get out,' she murmured in my direction. 'Has that thing done for you?' In my astral state, I could not emit sound, but, over time, the princess had grown accustomed to interpreting my lips and gestures.

'If it had, I wouldn't be able to project.' The princess's eyes darkened, so that they resembled liquid onyx; deepened, as if she were trying to mount me on her retinal gallery before the barbarians came and spray-canned it with images loathsome and obscene.

The catgirl studied my discarded flesh, her gaze lingering at the urino-genital region. 'Mmm, I wonder what *he* tastes like,' she mused. 'Never had a revenant before.' A cat's sexuality, like a rat's, terminated, as did her life, in black orgasm; but whereas a rat was destined to die at the moment of her insemination, a cat's short existence was one of furious, insatiable debauchery, each encounter a building block elevating her to an eminence which, by the time of her late teens or early twenties, would allow her to die in a climacteric of terrible pleasure. 'Had just about everything else,' she continued, as if offering a footnote to my meditations. 'Well, I've *had* to. Had to infect as many men as I can to give my DNA a chance of survival. You understand?' She swept back an errant tress of her long, golden mane. 'What does *he* eat?'

'Brains,' said the princess; no small concession, this; she seldom deigned to talk to those grisettes who worshipped at the altar of *Felis catus*. 'Fresh brains.'

'Shit. I wonder how that affects the taste? Ingested products which contain a high bacterial putrefaction level create the foulest tasting semen by far.'

'I said *fresh* brains,' said the princess, ever loyal.

'Aboutonia, ascorbic acid, blood-group antigens,' continued the feline, high on a school textbook recitation of the contents of ejaculate, 'calcium, chlorine, cholesterol, choline, citric acid, creatine, deoxyribonucleic acid, fructose, glutathione, hyaluronidase, inositol, lactic acid, magnesium, nitrogen, phosphorus, potassium, purine, pyrimidine, pyruvic acid, sodium, sorbitol, spermidine, spermine, urea, uric acid, vitamin B12, and, and—'

'And zinc,' concluded the princess, no tyro in sexual theory, if wholly lacking in practice.

'We have to try to jump them,' I said, 'while this sex cat's attention is transfixed by my genitalia.' I thought: And before she realises that, despite its monstrous promise, that grafted piece of ten-inch repro machinery was bound to bitterly disappoint.

'Duane, is that a siren?'

'Who you talking to, sister?' said the cat.

'Not talking, listening,' said the rat to the cat. 'Cocksucker.' A sharkman jumped up onto the coach's lead horse.

'Oh, why can't you see him?' cried Lara. 'The zombie: he's standing right in front of you. Look, look!' But the cat-girl's big, startlingly green eyes were unaccustomed to the world of invisible things; and no one paid the child heed. The coach's massive chassis creaked and groaned. We were being turned around, *en route* for the blackest, most infamous dungeons in the empire: the lair of the necromancers who lived in the deepest levels beneath the mountain, as far below the rat necropolis as we were below the clouds. (They said that those who left the portals of that place were either those who were in boxes, or those who belonged in boxes. White-hot memories of birth trauma, when, ripped from the grave, I had been given new life, sizzled inside my skull.)

Lara's eyes were unwavering, even though her admonitions were ignored. 'They're going to take you apart, Mr Bogeyman. Cut off your arms, your hands, your legs. And then they'll cut off your head and saw it open and take out the nasty, slimy thing that makes you go! And you, Frenzy, they'll cut you up as well and use you to make other zombies!' *So treacherous, that child,* I half expected the princess to say, *a rat who has forgotten her nature and become quite feline.* But my companion remained quiet, staring at the roof, unperturbed by the murderous infant's rant; only the hooked tips of her pink, pointy ears – twitching – belied that she had not turned into stone.

'If *you* can't hear it, I sure can.'

'Hear what?' said the cat.

A shock wave oscillated through the barouche; debris bounced off its bodywork. A portion of the tunnel had caved inwards, blanketing our enemies in a coverlet of brick dust. Moonlight fell through the coach's window, the faces of the two girls blanched by a shaft of pearly radiance, the princess's skin transubstantiated, brilliant as the face of one of the angels that had haunted her childhood; a pearl beyond price. Above, the truncated remains of a skyscraper, only partly subsumed by the side of the mountain – a portion of which had been blown away – was exposed, like a ligament peeled clean of surrounding tissue. The whine of air-raid klaxons filled the catacombs, stabbing at my astral ears with a reverberant cry.

'Well, do you hear it now?' said the princess. 'Or is your hearing as dead as the rest of you?' Her complaint trailed off into a rasping cough as a sooty cloud filled the carriage. As the cat brought her paws to her clenched, smarting eyes the princess's tail transcribed a vicious arc, striking her opponent across the back. Disarming the stunned girl – the purplish wound between the cat's shoulder blades testifying that the princess's barb carried a full bulb of venom – she shouldered her out of the carriage. The pall of dust had thinned, blown to shreds by the draft flowing in from the cratered roof of the tunnel. Pulling off her evening gloves and kicking off her highheels, the princess picked up the fallen musket, swung through the doorless jambs and was at once outside, hanging from the panelling of the coach by three fully extended claws, the thick, red keratin digging into the ornate trappings. Lifting her weapon – its long barrel wavering precariously in her free hand – she fired a ball through the back of the sharkman; her spine contracted as she readied to spring; with one leap – the musket jettisoned, smashing into the glass coffins – she landed on the driver's seat, uncoiled and took the coach's reins, setting the barouche on a bearing towards freedom.

Once again, we were roaring down the tunnel, the clamour of the wheels like the noise of a fever about to break; but with much of the guard either smothered in masonry or choking on dust ~ I thought I heard the squeals of the treacherous rat-child pierce the mocking cachinnation of the wheels ~ we now pulled effortlessly away from the posse who would have delivered us up to those who, having raised me, would think little of exercising their prerogative of re-interring me in my grave; those who, discovering that a ratgirl intacta had been delivered up to them, would have surely tied her to a table and employed a series of ingenious sex toys to pleasure her to death.

'It's really happening,' shouted the princess. I floated off the floor, my energies monopolised by the task of keeping pace with the accelerating coach. 'People were always talking about how they might actually invade. But now they've arrived. Arrived in their big, bad airships over all those thousands of miles. And they've broken Albracca's force field! It's just like the Nam, Duane. The Nam all over again. It's really *happening*!'

Within minutes we had broken into the air; behind, the open mouth of the tunnel quickly shrank into the skirts of the great man-made mountain of K'un-lun. Before us, on the eastern bank of the Huangpu River, the slums of Pudong stretched out, littering the interstices of aboriginal glass-and-steel towers that rose like ancient monoliths across the Waigaoqiao harbour area. Breaching the shantytown, we thundered down avenues lined with scrap-paper shacks and hovels, the inhabitants of which made a livelihood out of dredging the canal-system of tributaries spoking out from Pudong into the countryside; several dredgers fell from their bamboo rafts as we cornered a little too recklessly, the coach momentarily tipping, flying along on two wheels to half-demolish a cardboard outhouse. And then, rounding an abandoned, rotting skyscraper, the harbour, moon-lit, shimmering with barges and junks, presented itself to us with a visual slap to the face.

The princess struggled with the reins until the four big war horses submitted, slowed and came to rest on the quayside. Steaming and stamping their hooves, they were the only living things within eyeshot to remain oblivious to the red glow that pulsated near the horizon to either side of K'un-lun. Far away, the central area of the paper city was crumpling in an epileptic seizure of flame, curling like litmus, blue to green to heavenly red. I looked up. Bisecting The Moon, outnumbering the stars, the darkness swarmed with kite-men who jumped from the bellies of the great Atlantean dirigibles, swooping to earth through bomb bursts that sent a hail of carbonised bamboo and confetti onto our heads. The princess had jumped down from the driver's seat and was likewise gazing upwards, but not at the aerial war machines and their payloads, but at *our* ship, a rusty, ill-appointed coastal vessel that had, over the years, made runs North for my burgeoning clientele. Sailors at the gunwales – human, unmodified – beckoned frantically for her to board.

'Most of the porcelain's smashed. Do you still have money to pay the ship's captain?'

'I always had.'

'Yeah. I guess I always knew it. But why–?'

'How can you arrive anywhere not knowing who you are?'

'We'll worry about the arriving later. Right now all I know is that we have to depart. And quick.' I was picking up radio messages, a jumble of transmissions signing-off, their broken cries rising into the banality of the stratosphere.

'*Oh my God, they're shooting children—*'

'*Get away, no, don't, don't—*'

'*Brothers and sisters still lost in Europa and Afric – remember us!*'

'*Remember us and revenge us, Oh tribespeople, revenge us for—*'

'*Brothers and sisters who are slaves in Atlantis – rise up!*'

'*Perverts, outlaws, the dispossessed, the insane – rise up against your hypocritical masters!*'

I turned to witness Albracca draw its last, laboured breaths.

The perverse had run its course. It had injected its convulsive energy into Cathay's civilisation until that civilisation, like all civilisations exhausted by the excesses of their own joy, had become fearful of the wellsprings of its life. Cathay had been a great empire; it had been history's sole haven for those who had explored the left-hand path, a magnificent experiment, a celebration of The Extreme. But time, satiety and fear had neutered its rapture; and I, who had been a cipher of its decadence, its fall, I who had been one of the caretakers of its self-destruction, I was all that was left: a quintessence of its sterility. Like those who had made me, I too was lost. I and the Princess Frenzetta. Lost as the tribes were again lost, thrown to the mercies of a savage Earth. Exiles, now, we would be scorned; we would be persecuted; we would hide; we would begin our struggle; until the renaissance of our desire could no longer be ignored or suppressed; and then there would be the beginnings, perhaps, of a new Cathay. The princess looked up at The Moon

longingly, divorced satellite where, some said, the perverse
still held court. When would be my renaissance? Lost, I
dreamed of potency, of a life that was more than a limbo of
longing, of confused, moony dreams of an unknown past.
The princess closed her eyes; spread her arms, as if she were
about to bay and beg for The Moon to descend and claim us.
What held us two together? The princess and the corpse?
Was it love or desperation? I thought of the men who drank
alone in the bars along the Bund, who muttered to
themselves, terrified of the prospect of dying alone and sick
in a cheap hotel; it was a foreboding I shared, not merely
with those hopeless men, but with the princess. '*I've always
known that I'll end my days in a cheap hotel*,' she'd once
confided. '*Abandoned, no friends, no family. Sick. Alone.*' We
clung to each other, she and I, to know that the cry
emanating from each of our sick, lonely hearts was not the
only sound to disturb the Earth's silence.

The princess untied her maid. With the tiny old
woman's assistance, she managed to wrench the jelly – by
now crystallised – from my face. I re-entered the rotting
shell of the *wusha*; felt sick – my flesh was beginning to
bubble with corruption – but I did not, for the moment,
feel alone. 'We *can* remake ourselves,' I muttered, as if
reading aloud from an Atlantean self-help book sub-
verted with lewd marginalia. 'We can give ourselves new
names. Or we can go without names. We can be people
disburdened of all ties, all identity. You were right, Frenzy,
it *is* good not to have a past.' I nodded towards the burgeoning glow of the firestorm. 'Albracca. Call it Nirvana
City. A place that reconciled pleasure and death. Capital
of the Earth's only non-repressive culture. Gone. We're the
lost tribes now. Us, and whoever like us still lives out

there. The big, sad decaying world is ours...' And who cared what it would bring? The nihilism I subscribed to seemed as relevantly applied to the future as to the past.

Fireworks burst above K'un-lun. Set off by this first and last attack from Atlantis, perhaps? Or by the lords and ladies of the perverse, to celebrate a dance of death? Tonight was The Moon Festival. Let every night, I thought, be such a festival, till a goblin princess and her cadaverous henchman find some way of loosing the bonds of the dying Earth and finding the ancient expressway to Luna's shores.

I cared enough, at least, to hope for that.

Boarding, that goblin princess, that first lady of rats, cast her gaze over the sailors; winked at me with a certain electrostatic minxishness that would surely one day work its sensual abracadabra. 'Would you like to see me dressed as a *matelot*?' she said.

'Not before breakfast.'

Reaching the deck, she ostentatiously tugged and fidgeted with her corset so that, in making a show of concealing her eruptive breasts, she at the same time revealed to the pop-eyed crew her lascivious inclinations. Bending to pull a silk stocking to the top of her thigh she smiled coyly at one of the younger sailors, her evaluation of his brainpan unnoticed, I think, by any except myself. Would the fatal assignation be concluded below while we were clipping through the Yellow Sea? Or in the open when a drowsy midnight watch would not notice her entice her prey into the shadows, there to cut his throat? It would be a good meal, I knew. My little nutritionist always took care to provide me with the very choicest brains.

'Breakfast? I think that can be arranged,' she said.

I would have to buy her more clothes.

LOST IN EUROPA

To the accompaniment of a far-off nightingale's song, lulling the ear with morbid lullabies, the dark water of the Grand Canal sent out its ripples to the ruined palazzi lining its banks, with only the occasional splash, the glitter of rodent eyes behind shutters and the tubercular coughing of our gondolier to remind the princess and me that there were others in the city, and that those others, like us, were *contra natura*, perverse; that, after crossing the world, we were shipwrecked in a one-hundred-percent non-human zone. A qualified ease ran through my limbs as the gentle rocking of our barge ~ its lazy oar dipping into the brine, a metronome marking the evening's warbled berceuse ~ beguiled my senses, oar and bird combining to make an opiate of liquid harmony; I knew, even though we were amongst our own kind ~ chiefly because, I think, we were amongst our own kind ~ that I could not afford to relax and succumb to that soporific music.

'And where can we dream of going to now that Cathay the Great is dead?' said our ferryman, reflecting the rhetorical gestures of the Baroque architecture that surrounded us. 'No hopes now of escape from this city of the lost.'

The princess cast him a tired look, as if her mind had recently completed a circumnavigation of her life's vicissitudes, a list containing checked-off entries that had begun in Thurn and Taxis and ended with our arrival, six weeks ago, in the Mediterranean, to be so uncomfortably near to the home she had rejected when little more than a child; a list torn, crumpled into a ball, pushed to one side, but one she could not entirely discard from her consciousness. 'Not many escaped from Cathay,' she reminded him, seeking another object of focus other than the nagging presence of her myriad worries. 'Those that survived the sacking of Albracca were rounded up and packed off to Atlantis on slave ships.' Her interlocutor was a wolfman, the close-cropped hairs of his wizened face as white as the princess's own coiffure, but with advanced years rather than genetic predestination. One of the confabulated most intimately related to the cats (the cats relied on such men to regulate their profligate breeding patterns), the spittle flecking his lips seemed to suggest that he was continually dwelling upon the glory of past sex-murders; indeed, he had treated us to some murderous reminiscences during our passage from the Rialto, and it may have been their lurid minutiae that had provoked the princess's current fit of pensiveness. It was clear, however, that, despite the Technicolor intensity of his still active long-term memory banks, the old wolf's stalking days were at an end. The towpaths of canals, deserted night-time wharves, abandoned warehouses, factories, shopping arcades, the moonlit shadows of monstrous bridges, the dark fire-escape riddled depths of alleyways … Ah. The poetry of those places – loci classic to sex-murder – flickered in his eyes; but however much his imagination might invoke those haunts of his youth, he would never again play a role in their scenarios. For he was very old. Very, very old indeed.

'I'm sorry, *maestra*, I usually have only myself to speak to. So few these days need my services. It was not as it was in the past, when I was a boy.' He stared, far out, to where the blue-black lagoon was coalescing with the sky's deepening azure. 'Like all my kind, my parents were human – some of the last to remain in the city – my father having been infected by a catgirl in his youth, as were so many human men in those days when human beings and the confabulated lived side by side. It is cats, of course, who are usually engendered when an infected human male lies with a human female. But sometimes a wolf is born to hunt and kill his feline sisters and so prevent them – voracious little creatures that they are – from decimating mankind's gene pool. I was fortunate; my parents accepted me; so many wolves are abandoned, or fall prey to infanticide, exposed on the typhoidal beaches of the Lido.'

'Accepted you? As what? A sex killer?' chipped the princess. 'A disease? A slayer of *petite filles fatales*?' The wolfman laughed, his throat husky with scrofulous blight. Had he detected, as had I, our mistress's human moiety rising to rebel against the rat nature that perpetually threatened to engulf it?

'We are all three of us perverse, *maestra*. We are all aspects of the left-hand path.' His laughter died, leaving a paternal smile in its wake. 'Ah, but there was good hunting, then, when I was a young man. I had purpose. I kept the promiscuity of my sisters in check. But as the humans left, so did the catgirls until, today, there are hardly any left at all.'

'The Atlanteans treasure cats as sex pets,' I said, more to the princess than the geriatric wolfman. 'It's just as well that, in this city, their numbers are so few. In abundance, they would attract the kind of attention that we, in Albracca, were lucky to avoid.'

'You talk of slavers, of course,' said the wolf.

'I do. Atlantis seems intent on either killing or enslaving the entire confabulated world.'

'Felines make such *natural* slaves,' said the princess. 'They can't resist the prospect of betraying their own kind. These days, wearing a human collar seems to be every little cat-slut's dream. Your gamekeeping skills, wolfman, are sorely missed. At least by *this* rodent.' She looked out over the mellow bay, her nose twitching, as if detecting the scent of a mouser in the contagion-tinctured air. 'Cats. Ha. They deserve all they get.'

'You don't like cats, *maestra*?'

'You *might* say I'm allergic.'

'Rats and cats,' I said, not wishing to expand on the princess's prejudices, 'you know how it is. Like the dead and the living. They just don't mix.' I placed a hand on her knee. 'Isn't that true, my sweet?'

'*We* mix, Duane.'

'Affirmative, rodent. Truer. Truest.'

'We got out of Nirvana City just in time, *that's* true enough, Duane my undead darling. We would have made two interesting specimens for the auction block, that's for sure.'

'Ah, they raid us too, sometimes, the Atlantean slavers. But it is as you say: there are so few of us left in Venezia that I think they feel that latterly it is hardly worth their time. You, sir, if I may say, and you too, *maestra*, you look like slavers yourselves, so richly attired, so nobly turned out. Not like we hand-me-down Veneti!' In anticipation of the ceremonials that awaited us I toed the sartorial line favoured by the Dux's court. My corrupt body – surmounted by a jaunty peruke – was swathed in richly embroidered brocades, my doublet and knee breeches, completed by white silk hose, having transformed me into the image of a Brobdingnagian fop. Every inch of the masquerade pinched and bit at my tomb-robbed flesh, robbing me, likewise, of my dignity. Complementing my guise, the princess was attired in an elaborate gown that, ranked according to the local fashion's indices of pain, seemed to outpoint my own wardrobe in its homage to the superfemininity of the eighteenth century: a mantua of black silk, the front of its skirt slashed in the shape of an inverted V to reveal an embroidered petticoat; the similarly slashed bodice, with its gap at the front filled with a stomacher decorated with a line of pink bows – whaleboned and laced behind – pushing her milk-white breasts so high that the painted nipples peeked above the neckline. Her hair had been piled into a powdered *fontange* and was surmounted by a high cap. The latest Venetian street-chic martyred its followers; and if her other efforts to please my reluctant flesh had, over the years, been deserving of beatification, her toilette, that late afternoon, surely elected her to sainthood, to gaze forever blissfully into the face of all that was *à la mode*. She shifted, attempting to ease the discomfort caused by the *paniers* which distended the dress sideways from the hips, studying, with cramped avidity, the meagre strip of dry land to which we were bound. 'All the rats in Venezia are such excellent swimmers, *maestra*,' said the gondolier, his red eyes flashing with amusement. 'I am surprised that you do not take more pleasure in the canals.' The princess lifted a perfumed handkerchief from her décolletage and held it to her nose, the boredom with which she habitually regarded the geriatric wolf tinged with extreme distaste. I pointed to the canal bank, distracting her with hope of imminent, blessed disembarkation before she added our ferryman to her global tally of victims; we had reached the entrance to the Grand Canal and were about to moor at the steps which rose out of the water to Santa Maria della Salute.

After we had pulled level with the dilapidated pier, I stepped out of the gondola, told the gondolier to wait and then offered the princess my hand. 'No long faces. Look about you. For a time, it will all be yours.' Choosing not to accept my proffered help, she cursorily allowed her gaze to take in the antique cityscape; sniffed; clambered out of the barge, teetering on her buckled heels, the expansive gown billowing in the breeze coming in off of St Mark's basin, the lagoon stained violet, now, as the rays of the setting sun fell, oblique, across the glittering rooftops. 'Come, your betrothed is waiting.' Unappreciative of my irony – somewhat too deadly, perhaps, for her taste – she arched a thin eyebrow, puffed out her rouged, candy-apple cheeks and walked past me, her chin held high, negotiating a passage through the flotsam and jetsam cluttering the half-submerged steps, worthless leftovers of those human ships the pirates of Venezia had claimed on the high seas.

'As soon as I get my dower I'll be abdicating, *tout de suite*. I'm exhausted, *exhausted*, I tell you, by this sick, sick charade.'

'This caper was *your* idea, remember?'

'Well, *someone* has to get the money to buy passage to Afric. What would you have me do? There's no stupid porcelain to steal in this godforsaken city, not that *that* was such a clever idea, was it?'

She advanced towards the portals, the *paniers* swinging to the rhythm of her robust hips, her tail sweeping to and fro across the mud-caked stones as if she were auditioning for the role of a street cleaner. And then, passing between the high columns of the basilica's façade, she was consumed by the black fires of holy darkness. I followed after, cursing at having lost eye contact with one who had too often flirted with darkness – though more often of an unholier variety than that which filled the Church of the Salute – one day, if I were not there to aid her, she would push her luck to breaking point and be at last swallowed by the world's angry, profane shadows for all time.

But inside – rows of candles burning from narthex to chancel – it was light, a lambent play of illumination that might have issued from a child's night-light; and the hosts of tiny, still flames provided a balm to eyes habituated to the needle-sharp rounds of the photonic battery of the setting sun, the last energies of which had cast my shadow – long, grim and menacing – across the worn flagstones and deep into the basilica's circumambient bowels, my entrance blotting the snapshot of the Grand Canal, St Mark's Square and the *pallazzi*, Baroque, Gothic, Byzantine, that stretched out to either side, framed in the doorway.

'Let me present my bodyguard, Mr Duane Duarte,' said the princess to the Dux. He stood a few yards in front of me, his condottieri to either side, shuffling, unsure of what constituted an appropriately non-lethal response, their hands fidgeting with the pommels of their scabbarded rapiers as they appraised the hideous apparition that had materialised out of the last rays of the dying day. I bowed.

'I am honoured, my lord,' I said. Dux Pietro

Bessarion, self-styled 'Principe Serenissimo', a King of The Rats, a Doge *manqué*, lording it over the Queen of the Adriatic, all but abandoned by its human populace after the long, Sino-American conflict known as The War of the Liebestod; completely abandoned since. Dux Pietro, I thought – resentful of the mime I was constrained to play – Dux Pietro, you uppity rodent, you got it *coming*.

'The honour is mine, revenant.' His tail, heavy with over a hundred gold rings, encircled the princess's waist, proprietarily. 'I have read much about your kind. And the Princess Frenzetta has told me more. The princess – you have been of good service to her over the years, it seems. For that you have my gratitude.' The Dux's condescension was as greasy as his bergamot-saturated wig. And as fake. Beneath it there crawled something anxious, clammy, unpleasant. Almost as old as our lupine gondolier – the males of the perverse were as long-lived as its females were ephemeral – my little adventuress's betrothed supported himself with an ivory walking cane, his gorgeously trimmed clothes, their majesty accentuated by their ruin, like the majesty of Venezia itself, those of a youth whose procreative energies he still affected, and not always, as this birthing ceremony was set to declare, to such innocuous ends. Just what was the source of that slimy thing that wormed in his soul, that unctuous flea that itched him for lack of expression?

'I am but a poor *âme damnée*. Thank you, my lord, for inviting me here on this most auspicious occasion. Felicitations to you, your family and your court.' I bit my lip, as self-conscious of the flowery excrescence of my speech as I was of the grotesquely ill-fitting clothes that covered my titanic frame; both speech and attire would

unseam, I knew, and leave me ludicrously naked if I were
to press their limitations. But at least, I reminded myself,
my wardrobe, transported intact from our sunken ship,
outshone, in its unsullied newness, the ancient, filthy garments of the tatterdemalions who surrounded us. Their
airs and graces, in this rat's nest of canals, sewers and
polluted stills, were ridiculously presumptive, insultingly
banal. I checked my pride; straightened, and, like a bear
in a pit, looked about, apprehensive. The courtiers –
hangers-on, sycophants, courtesans, pretty boys, freebooters, mercenaries, piratical entrepreneurs – undertook
an evaluation of the monster before them, the ladies
peeking over the tops of their fans, the men preening
themselves in shows of coxcombry, representatives of both
sexes attempting to appear fearless as they gimleted me
with their stares. But they did fear; I could tell; though, at
last, curiosity overcame their trepidation.

'Excuse me, my dear,' said the Dux to the princess,
unfurling his tail from her hourglass contours, 'excuse me
while I have a little talk with your *man*.'

'Man?' said one of the ladies, clucking her tongue
with distaste, her gaze travelling from the riveted
cannonball of my head to my velvet-slippered, la-di-da
toes. ''Ban 'Ban, Ca-Cali*ban*.' I ignored the harlot's cruel
witticism – as worthless as her moth-eaten trumperies –
and allowed myself to be escorted by the Dux into the
circular nub of the basilica, where volutes of incense rose
into the great dome above; there, taking my elbow, he
manoeuvred me towards the sacristy, still adorned with
the treasures upon which the city raised its credit:
paintings by Titian and Tintoretto, their graffiti-daubed
canvases secreted behind armoured glass; and there was

booty there too, a tech-horde of electronics which, if non-functional, was much prized by collectors in less uninhabited parts of Europa.

'So many adventures you have had during your journey from Cathay, eh? Only at last to succumb to a shipful of my brave goblins!' He showed me his teeth – little rows of fish-hooks stained black with nicotine – and placed his hand on an old monstrance which still contained the semen-filled chocolate wafers with which cats, when there had still been cats in this forgotten city, had taken communion. 'As I have said, I know something about revenants. I want you to understand that, since the Princess Frenzetta seems to place such importance on you as an employee, I have decided to retain you at my court.' I inclined my head.

'I am indeed fortunate. To continue to serve the princess is my only desire.' And then the thing that gnawed at his insides showed its face, supplanting his visage with its own: a green-tinted basilisk-face of jealousy.

'You have, what, a *heterograft*, here, no?' he said, pointing to the side of his head with the extended talon of a beringed finger, the membrane of white flesh covering the skull so thin that the bone seemed visible, burning palely like a taper within a rice-paper lantern. He grinned, nose twitching nervously, his two rows of black incisors grinding against each other with undisguised malevolence. 'It keeps you alive, *animates* you, but at a certain cost, shall we say?'

'It is as if I were a eunuch, Dux.'

'Yes. I thought so. You are devoted to the princess. But your devotion has never, *can* never be that of a *man's*, mmm?'

'I am her man but – I am not a man. I am not even alive. I am a machine fuelled by the life of others. I–' I held him with a look that I hoped conveyed pitiableness rather than a more genuine rage. 'I am nothing.' The Dux retracted his talons; ran his thumbs down the moleskin revers of his lapels; readjusted his wig; drew himself up so that his eyes met mine at no more than a forty-five degree angle, tics that, coupled with his understated minacity, seemed to complete a ritual designed to set his *amour-propre* back on its feet.

'I make you my servant, Master Revenant. It is the Princess Frenzetta's wish. She may consider it a wedding gift. A servant, mmm? No more, no less. I just wanted to make that clear.' He again took me by the elbow and, leaving that room of art, swag, sacred vessels and vestments, guided me back towards the guests. 'The princess has told me something about Cathay,' he said, he, who had lived in rat-shadows all his life, trying to impress me with a worldliness he did not possess. 'Is it true you were all living in monasteries towards the end?'

'Not all. Many in Albracca refused to conform. The Eugenics Police were never able to impose their regime on everybody. And anyway, the policy was always somewhat lacking in political will. The argument was that by aping the ways of Atlantis – or, at least, some consensus of "normality" – the tribespeople might be able to win a degree of support from Europa and Afric, support necessary for the facilitation of a conditional peace. But it never had much chance of success. Just before the city died, there was much about Albracca which recalled one to its legendary depravity.'

'I am enormously glad to hear it,' said the Dux,

smacking his lips. 'But with the East pacified Atlantis will turn its attention upon us, the tribespeople of Europa and Afric.'

'Surely, Atlantis is exhausted?'

'But its thirst for slaves is undiminished. And here in Europa, where so much lies in ruins, we last free men of the perverse must prepare ourselves; for Atlantis, exhausted or not, will most assuredly come.'

We rejoined the assembly to find it swarming about the trysting place of death and life that provided the rationale for its gathering: the mausoleum of the Dux's late bride. The midwives, detecting telltale signs with their brass, conch-like ear trumpets, had indicated that the exhumation should begin. Soon, the lid from the raised tomb ~ which had been carved in the likeness of a supine ratgirl ~ stood propped against a wall. The Dux took up position next to the princess, one hand resting on the translucent lip of the casket, a father who, no matter how many times he had previously witnessed such scenes, still betrayed the anxiety of one eager to be presented with a strong, healthy addition to his brood. I watched, intent, mindful of the fate that lay in store for the princess if our plans should go awry, my excessive height allowing me to stand back and view the proceedings over the prurient audience's heads, an audience of rats, in the main ~ this was rat city ~ but also one that contained a few sharks, a dragon and a she-spider; they all crowded about the exposed sarcophagus of Murano glass, the corpse ~ ravishing, petrified in the moment of ecstasy in which she had died ~ swollen-bellied with child.

A midwife stepped forward, a steel trocar in her hand, its thin shaft turning the intense candlelight that surrounded the tomb so that splinters of refraction played over the basilica's massive, curving walls. The Dux nodded, signalling that it was time to induce the birth; waved the crowd aside, so that, an aisle of bodies opening up, I was allowed forward, obliged to proceed to the place of honour just as the midwife pulled back the black, diaphanous shroud and slipped her outrageous, parturifacient instrument into the exquisite corpse's umbilicus, a geyser of clear, milky fluid arcing over the flagstones and spattering my velvet footwear. 'She was fifteen when I took her into my bed,' said the Dux to the princess. 'Francesca Camilla Vittoria Angela Pompilia Comparini. Fifteen. And it did not even then take long to bring her to the boil. Our nuptials were sweet, most sweet. You are seventeen, my treasure, overripe, if I may say. Your boiling point, I deem, will be considerably lower than that of your predecessor. But you look forward, do you not, with the same desperation, to the night when your cravings will at last come to an end?' The princess tilted her head in coy acknowledgement of her sex's fate; nodded, as if affirming her eagerness to experience black orgasm; and I hoped that only I could see that the aspect of maternal longing she affected was a sham; her leaden eyelids, drooping as if with desire, could not hide the terror and disgust pooling beneath, the alienating dread inspired by the one half of her biology which, self-preservative, would not permit the other half's death wish to force her into a consummation of her lifelong erotic delirium.

The courtiers muted their gossipy whisperings and then fell altogether silent as the distended abdomen of the Dux's late bride wobbled like a mound of vanilla jelly, a slit opening up between the navel and the pubic bone; the belly ruptured, two little hands emerging to fiercely push aside the elastic abdominal wall until the slit had become a crevasse, gouts of creamy, crimson-streaked afterbirth flooding the casket as the rat baby's head burst into the air, its dull, gleaming eyes, like two buttons of black polished stone, surveying its adoptive family with cool hostility, its mouth – already showing signs of a set of sharp little teeth – snarling with instinctive distemper. With a convulsive wiggle it bit and clawed its way free of its mother's womb at last to sit triumphantly astride the wreckage of the body that had died for it, borne it, been desecrated for it, like a malefic cherub allegorising Life-in-Death, a little plaster representation of the perverse that had recently been dipped in the bloody maw of the void. Then the entire abdominal wall burst apart to reveal the roiling mass of the vanguard ratling's brothers and sisters, a hubbly-bubbly stew of new life; the midwife poked amongst the gluten and black mucous, seeking a male amongst the dozen or so girl-infants. She gathered the baby into a shawl, wiped it clean of embryonic chemicals – acidic gunk that had burnt the skin from the midwife's right hand – and presented it to the father. The Dux raised the child aloft.

'A son!' he shouted. 'I have a son!'

It was the seventy-seventh baby deviant to be engendered by his loins. The princess, who had the dismal prospect of bearing his seventy-eighth, clapped her hands. 'Huzzah for the goblin child!' she yelled. 'Huzzah for the King of the Rats!' And then, one of her talons zinging from its sheath like the blue steel of a switchblade, she tapped her intended on the chest, cueing him to fulfil a promise made in the heat of preceding days when she had tormented him with her necessarily stand-offish coquetry.

'Will you be the godfather, Master Revenant?' said the Dux, who, in the confusion of his joy, had forgotten, it seemed, that I represented merely another, and perhaps somewhat extraneous addition to his retinue. The princess, unseen by her betrothed, winked a sly wink, winning the small purse I had wagered on the Dux reneging on his word. I salute you, I thought, my goblin temptress, I salute you and the efficacy of your wiles.

'Of course.' I made the sign of the pentacle over the baby's head.

'Your son could wish for no better protector,' said the princess. 'Nobody harms those entrusted to my *âme damnée.*' I tried to look as humble and as eunuch-like as possible; and though I could see that I would never entirely win the Dux's trust, it was enough that, eager as he was to humour the whims of his bride-to-be, he would tolerate my presence today and, more importantly, on his wedding day than that he and I should enter into anything like intimacy. Intimacy: that – along with cruelty, disingenuousness and cunning – was the competence of my companion; and I conceded to her expertise.

The Dux walked to the high altar holding his infant son before him. The princess and I followed, a raggle-taggle of courtiers at our heels. As the Dux passed behind the lattice that enclosed the chancel he fell on one knee and passed the keeping of the child to the priestess who stood ready to officiate the baptism. The princess knelt by his side, I and the rest of the cortège adopting like poses of reverence in the area outside the railing. Above the altar hung a great cross, the crucified Queen of The Left-Hand Path rendered naked, writhing, nailed to the burnished metal, her crown of barbed wire testimony to the intolerance and bigotry of the human race. The priestess deposited the child on the altar's smooth marble surface; then she lifted her arms – her chasuble held to either side of her torso as if she were about to metamorphose into the bird whose zooplastic tissue she shared – and began the liturgy which would bring the baby boy into the fellowship of the lost tribes of the perverse.

'Dearly beloved, forasmuch as all men are conceived and born in sin; and that our Saviour Lilith saith, None can enter into the kingdom of God, except he be regenerate and born anew of Water and of the Holy Ghost…' The voice droned on, my eyes flicking from side to side to study the restless but submissive bodies, regenerate, born anew, that hemmed me in. I wondered how many, if circumstances should so demand, I could take out before their sheer numbers overcame me. 'I beseech you to call upon God the father, through our Mistress, Lilith, that of his bounteous mercy he will grant to this Child that thing which by nature he cannot have…' The priestess picked up the child, genuflected before the altar, then turned. 'Merciful God, grant that the old Adam in this Child may be so buried, that the new man may be raised up in him.' She proffered the boy for my inspection, her downy limbs quivering as I met her eyes, a fabulous bird fluttering in the face of captivity. She stared back, insolent, as if throwing out a challenge to see if the unnatural creature who had blasphemed the presence of her God – this revenant, this zombie, this abominable patchwork of rotting meat – could articulate the necessary response.

'Ludovico,' I mumbled, remembering my brief. 'Ludovico Pietro Giovanni Raphael Giacomo Bessarion.' The priestess dipped a finger in a bowl of chicken's blood and painted a five-pointed star on the infant's forehead. 'I baptise thee In the Name of the Father, and of the Daughter, and of the Holy Ghost. Amen. We receive this Child into the congregation of the tribes of the perverse, and do sign him with the sign of the Pentacle, in token that hereafter he shall not be ashamed to confess the faith of Lilith crucified...'

The Dux stood and took the child from the priestess's hands. The guests hummed with discreet murmurings of congratulation.

'He is regenerate, grafted to the body of the perverse,' said the Dux, as he allowed well-wishers to poke and prod the infant while launching cooing assaults of idiot delight.

'A beautiful child,' agreed the princess.

'A beautiful ceremony,' I added.

'An *exotic* ceremony, yes, Master Revenant,' he said, smug with the novelty he had introduced. 'The birdgirl is from England. They needs must practise their faith underground, there, hiding still from the authorities.'

'Too many humans, alas, in the Dark Island,' said the bird, her sentence ending in a twitter of song. 'They steal our eggs. Burn our nests. But, Lilith willing, the perverse will prevail.' Her ruff bristled, a display ritual claiming a territoriality that, the perverse yielding, these days, rather than prevailing, must serve only to fan the fabulous plumage of her imagination.

'Of course it will, of course it will. Thank you, my dear' - the priestess acknowledged his compliments with a demure smile - 'you are most welcome in Venezia.'

'I am to officiate at your wedding, *signorina*,' said the priestess to the princess.

'How nice.' My mock-mumsy aristocrat pinched the baby's cheek, a maternal gesture that her confabulated genes, pre-empting her future, would only allow her to enjoy as a surrogate. She tilted her head back, as if about to bay at the hidden stars; instead, looked up at me; smiled, mischievous; and then refastened her attention on the Dux. 'Do you remember when we first met, my love?' The priestess stepped back, throwing her robes about herself to conceal the nakedness of her white, marabou-like down; turning about, she retreated towards the altar, her hindquarters jiggling with the ostentatious sexual exhibitionism of a feathered showgirl; the conversation was taking an intimate turn. 'The time has gone so quickly.' The Dux's eyes misted. And other members of the congregation followed the priestess's example, removing themselves from our immediate presence.

'When I first lifted my telescope to better see that vision of pulchritude I had espied on the fo'c's'le of your doomed ship, then, then—' His voice cracked. 'I knew that I must have you.'

'I was frightened. Your pirates had killed all my crew.' And killed our chances, I thought, at least for the time being, of locating the spaceplane we had heard was still being operated out of North Afric by Venezia's piratical competitors, the Barbary Corsairs.

'Your crew? They were human. My rats had orders not to harm any who might be perverse.'

'And you have been so kind ever since. The house you bought for me—'

'Nothing. The city is filled with empty houses.'

'The jewels, the clothes—'

'Such magnificent clothes,' I intervened.

'And of course,' added the princess, eyeing me with a warning to keep the lanes of conversation clear lest there be some disaster, 'the infinite honour of your hand in marriage.' The Dux's face had become streaked with tears. He put a hand over his old heart.

'Tomorrow will be a wonderful day, but a *long* day, my beloved. Let us say goodnight now. I have much to prepare. Perhaps some of my condottieri could escort you back to your *pallazzo*?'

'My bodyguard will look after me.' He bent to bestow a kiss. She pulled away, giggling.

'Bad boy,' she whispered. 'Do you want to kill me before my wedding night? You have less than twenty-four hours to wait. Be patient, Pietro.'

'Of course, of course. What was I thinking?' What indeed, I thought. Don't let anticipation put too much strain on your ticker, Dux. We don't want you dead before you make your vows, matrimonial and financial. He turned to me. He had become short of breath. 'Make sure you look after her well, Master Revenant. I shall send for you all tomorrow, quite early. The ceremony is at noon.'

'The household shall be prepared,' I said. 'I'll brief the princess's maid on what is expected of her.'

'Bodyguard, major-domo. My revenant is going to be *such* an asset to your court.' The Dux, who seemed to have forgotten that I had recently become his youngest son's godfather, awarded me a chill smile, the extent of the favour I perceived I would ever receive from him once he had taken his pleasure of my partner in crime; but it was we – our partnership cemented in mass destruction, genocide, plague and rape – who would smile last and longest. 'Goodnight, my lord. The birthing was most satisfying. I will sleep now and rise with the dawn to make myself fit for your caresses.' A string of saliva hung from the side of the Dux's mouth to collect in the cleft of his long, pointed chin. I strode towards the basilica's doorway, a wedge that was no longer an overexposed daguerreotype but a long banner of blackness, a dark canvas pricked with a multitude of stars.

The gondola nosed through the canal's soughing, soporific currents, our wolfman half-dozing at the oar, his extreme age, if sinking his attention below the waterline of consciousness, still providing a reflexive homing instinct which allowed him to pilot us towards our destination despite apparent insensibility.

'How old do you think he exactly *is*?' I said, studying our ferryman.

'Old. Older than my betrothed, even. But not as old as some of the wolves I met out East. There was one who claimed to remember the first days of The Abortion.'

'Impossible,' I said. 'That would mean he'd clocked up more than two thousand years.'

'Wolves live long, Duane. It has to be that way. There are so few of them. And there are so many cats in the world. The perverse is wise.'

'Even so—' But the princess had ascended her gilded soapbox; she would brook no interruption.

'He'd say, this wolf, that during the first days, before the tribespeople had modified their flesh, not everybody knew that a cataclysm had destroyed the universes that are, rather *were*, contiguous with our own. People infected with the souls of that annihilated multiverse thought they were just born, well ... *strange*.'

'Perhaps they were right,' I said. 'Perhaps The Abortion is just a myth used to explain our own reality's innate perversity. Perhaps all along the aliens have been our own true selves.'

'Oh, wax philosophical as much as you please, Duane. You might not have any memories, but the rest of us perverse creatures do. We were born, not just *strange*, but with afterimages of our previous lives burnt into our brain cells.'

'Such is conventional wisdom. But I have an unconventional perspective. I'm like those first tribespeople myself. I mean, like them, I was human before I was confabulated. I have a foot in both camps of the Earth's sapient life. And I think humanity and the perverse aren't so very far apart.'

'But you don't *remember* being human, Duane.'

'But you do, Frenzy. Part of you is still human. You must know what I mean.' She frowned, her tail swishing under the seat, as if it sought blind, instinctive and with a life of its own, for vermin, the juicy entrails of small mammals as much her chosen diet as ice cream, nougat and éclairs were the preferred regimen of a cat. 'In you,' I said, pressing my point needlessly, the devil in me seeking her humiliation, 'in you is embodied mankind's left-handedness, the screaming desire to be *au contraire*. But, conversely, the perverse half of you enfolds humanity.'

'You're saying the perverse is *humane*?'

'I'm saying,' I said, worried my banter had been a little too relentless, 'that you're a fine person. A good person, Frenzy.' She tossed her head, proud and untamed.

'I am not *humane*, Duane. I am perverse. Very perverse indeed.'

'Of course you are.'

'Bite on it, dead man walking. You're not funny.' I stared at the bottom of the boat and kept my peace. But it wasn't long before I began to think upon the Dux, a stab of jealousy reaving my heart as I contemplated the two of them, my princess and the anile wretch who would be her spouse, together, hootchy-kootchying in the marriage bed. I looked up, my frown now matching that of the princess; stared out over the lagoon, wondering that so many rats – for this, like all cities on the Adriatic, had been overrun by the princess's kind – had chosen to live here, where there were so few subterranean homesteads, so few cellars unflooded, sewers and underground service tunnels that still contained air. But there were qualities to the city – its typhoidal stink; its rat-like ambience of wet, dark, scratchy terror – that doubtless compensated, in the rodent mind, for having to live above ground.

'Do you really think that the old lecher could bring you to orgasm?' I said, fixated now, nay, tormented by thoughts of nuptials, sweet foreplay and fatal deflowerings.

'I'm an orc, for Christ's sake. *Anybody* could bring me to orgasm.' But only a rat could impregnate you, I thought.

'The Dux is a rat chauvinist.'

'Sure. He believes purely in rat-on-rat sex; most ratmen do; the black orgasm of the female of his species would otherwise be to no purpose; his species needs must thrive.'

'He seems jealous of me,' I said, who was unable to fend off those stabs of jealousy – incessantly real-time, vicious – that punctured his own heart and churned within his empty bowels.

'Oh, he's such an arse. But your, how shall I say, your *flaccidity*, Duane – it has reassured many of my admirers, you know.'

'And the fact that I'm dead.'

'And that as well, of course.'

'It's just when I follow after you and see him touching your hair, your breasts–'

'It's not vagina he's after, Duane. He can have any tart in Venezia. It's my title. My thousand-year-old name. Pietro Fancypants is just a jumped-up little pirate, like all the lords and ladies in this feculent Nowheresville. He wants the sheer *class* an alliance with Thurn and Taxis can bring him.' She looked out across the moon-stippled water, scanning north-east towards her ancestral seat, the invisible psychodramas flickering behind her nocturnal eyes – so like slivers of smoked glass – perceptible only by way of the feedback that agitated her slim, tapered ears, her brows, lips and fay, upturned nose. Whatever was being enacted there was for an audience of one; I was rarely allowed access to anything more than programme notes, hints of a love-starved childhood filled with memories of prejudice, betrayal, fear, a drama that had terminated in a Last Act wherein our heroine flees to Cathay to have her revenge on those who had so misused her. 'I don't really like being this near to home. Lots of bad memories, Duane. Lots, lots.'

'It stands on the Bay of Sistiana, doesn't it?' I said, trying to cheer her. 'Castle Duino, I mean? Mrs Herzog sometimes talks to me about it. It sounds – beautiful.'

'I don't want to talk about Castle Duino. I don't want to talk about what's past. As Mrs Herzog says, What's done's done and it don't profit to make a deal of the doing. I mean, do *you* like to talk about the past, like, when you were made?' I felt my brow crease, involuntarily; it was true; talking about my earliest days in the laboratories of the necromancers always forced a lump of hot iron into my throat. But I was determined to prove the princess wrong. I swallowed, loosening that neurotic, molten ore from my larynx.

'There was a surgeon known as The Candyman. He was the one who supervised the transplantation of my brain into my new body. Or what was left of my brain. Most of it had been diced up and used to programme the neo-cortex. The Candyman was the one who taught me to speak again. Taught me how to walk, to think, to fight. And he taught me about the perverse, telling me I was now one of its creatures, just as he was.'

'And he was?'

'A dragonman,' I said. 'All the necromancers were dragons.'

'It's the control they enjoy. Sex in the head. They reproduce by—'

'Dragons reproduce by making revenants,' I said. 'As well as other, nameless things. I know. I know how much they like to confabulate others. Especially if it's without their consent. Control. Yes. He taught me that as long as I was a good boy, I would get my candy.'

'Fresh brains?'

'Of course.'

'And if Duane darling was a *bad* boy?' Like a blinding jag of lightning, a flashback seared the mangled engrams of my mind, photogenes of my infancy as a monster rekindled by the princess's minxish teasing; I was suddenly back in the necromancers' lair, a chained bedlamite, rattling the steel links of my confinement like a pantomime ghost. The Candyman tweaked his remote and the vermicular parasite inside my skull began to writhe, buck, its exoskeleton pressing against my optic nerve like a malignant tumour. Outside the gleaming bars of my cage, cyanic waves of plasma rose and fell between the wires and coils of my tormentor's Frankensteinian array of machinery as he strove to mould me into his puppet. 'Ah,' sighed the princess, a told-you-so glint in the corner of an eye that, with nightfall, had been fully eclipsed by a fuliginous pupil. 'You see, there *are* things you don't like to talk about. I tell you what, I won't ask you about The Candyman as long as you don't ask me about Duino. Fair?'

'Okay,' I conceded. 'The past no longer exists.'

'Past, future. To hell with them. We have to concentrate on the *now.*'

'Yeah. About how we're going to burn your friend, Dux Pietro.'

We passed under the Rialto Bridge and drew towards the left bank and the Pallazzo dei Camerlenghi, the sixteenth-century Lombardesque construction that we had chosen as our home out of the many offered us by the King of the Rats. Nearby, a great spider's web strung across the canal recalled me to the fact that the Rat King enjoyed the loyalty of many who followed other paths, and that his coffers were the richer for it. We would, in making off with the dower he expected to recoup after his marriage's consummation, be robbing not just him and his band of piratical rats, but the whole city of Venezia. The she-spider that hung from the web – a long-limbed girl clad in leather, a close-fitting mask covering the entirety of her face – surveyed the approach to her sticky, silken boudoir, listening, patiently, for the telltale buzz of an approaching insectman who, lured by her maddening scent, would tonight be ensnared, tortured, raped and eaten for the mutual fulfilment of their symbiotic lives. The web, shot through with moonbeams, cast lozenges of lactescence onto the surface of the dark canal. Our gondolier had snapped out of his trance, his gaze following my own as I concentrated wistfully on The Moon, our eternal but silent goddess. 'Could it be that they really *are* still alive, do you think?' said the princess. 'The descendants of all those tribespeople they transported to the lunar concentration camps during the twenty-first century?' The gondolier steered the barge so that it came to rest flush against the embankment. 'They say the air is almost all gone. That the fields are barren, the animals dead. If I could only ask my angels. I see them sometimes, you know, Duane, I see them flying through the night, out over the lagoon or passing through the city.'

'Still alive? Maybe,' I said, trying to ignore this talk of angels which always turned my spine to ice. 'And if life's hard on The Moon, at least they have their own world.' I stepped out; the princess followed, lifting her voluminous skirts so that her creamy silk hose glistened with moonlight so rich that its opals of soft brilliance seemed ready to curdle and further contaminate the already miasmic air.

'The Dux will send some of his men to collect us tomorrow, but please come to the wedding,' said the princess to our ferryman, risen from his self-hypnotic state and blinking after her as she stepped warily through the slurry, the hem of her gown, no matter how much she struggled to prevent it trailing, bespattered with mud. 'You'd be most welcome.'

'Thank you, *maestra*,' said the wolfman. 'The ways of the rats have always fascinated me. I only wish I had one of my sisters to bring along. A cat, as comely as she was treacherous and vain.' With a disconsolate salute, he pushed his barge free of the quayside; soon, with a mechanical ease, his body swaying to the rhythm of the oar, he was almost out of sight, his head drooping as once again, lulled by the lapping, morbid currents, the calls of night-birds and the automatism of his own languid exertions, he had elevated his consciousness to its former, transcendental disposition, somewhere between deep sleep and omniscience. I looked at him, a faint tremor of affection distressing my otherwise affectless innards, the wolfman, with his failure of potential, his end-of-the-road monologues on love and death, mirroring the double whammy of my own death, my own robbed potency. We stood in the shadows of the pallazzo's threshold. I rapped my knuckles against mildewed wood; Mrs Herzog opened the doors.

'I'm just going upstairs to repaint my face,' said the princess, giving me a cursory pat on the forearm – I suppose it was meant to reassure, to signal that, as ever, she was there to sustain my body's integrity – before pushing her maidservant into the house, my rat-aristocrat's inbound trajectory a flurry of rustles, flounces and imperiousness. I too entered; dawdled awhile to watch my little friend leap up the stairs to the first floor, dragging the crone behind her as if the old woman were a rag doll she were taking to her playroom; turned, decisive –

tonight was not a night I could afford to indulge myself in ogling the rites of female frippery – and passed into the ground floor room, the one facing the canal, which I had made into my study. The room was well-stocked with furniture, though much of it still lay covered in sheets; the ruin time had visited upon the room did not make the divestment of its sundries an enticing prospect. Settling myself into my favourite chair – one of the few pieces I had permitted to reveal its ruined nature – I turned up the oil lamp that stood on the escritoire and picked up the book I had selected from amongst the thousands of volumes that lined the walls: Giovanni Giacomo Casanova de Seingalt's *Histoire de ma fuite des prisons de Venise*. It had amused me to have reaffirmed by such a source that not only was Venezia's technology at the same level as at Casanova's time, but that the cultural mores that informed his Venezia – extravagant, dissolute, overly-refined, cruel – seemed so often to find a curious, distorted echo in the city wherein I and the princess found ourselves temporarily ensconced. I was rereading the account of the imprisonment (on spurious charges of spying, probably motivated by cuckolded husbands) and the escape of Casanova – self-styled Chevalier de Seingalt – from the lead-lined roof of the gaol of the Doge's Palace. It was, of course, an account of particular relevance to the princess and me given the contingencies that might be visited on us tomorrow. To ascend, as if lighter than air, above the rooftops of Venezia. To freedom. Yes. The Chevalier was an inspiration. Much was to be learnt from his career as lawyer, librarian, librettist, spy, gambler, violinist, and the administrator of the French lottery, from which he had made a fortune; for he was a charlatan *par excellence*, duping those at court with his numerology and cabbalism, advising ladies on their love lives and health; and all, of course, for profit. He sounded like my sort of man. I stuck my nose deep into the musty pages of my ancient tome. No one had ever escaped from the Leads. But at the stroke of midnight, on 31 October 1776, Casanova tasted freedom, with the assistance of a fellow prisoner, Father Balbi. It was All Saints' Day. And tomorrow, the day of the princess's wedding, would be All Saints' Eve. When I had told the princess, some weeks ago, about what my reading had turned up she had insisted to the Dux that their nuptials be postponed until Halloween. The poetic appositeness had, the princess averred, promised our enterprise good fortune.

There was a knock. 'I won't be long, Duane,' called the princess. 'Will you be all right?' I *harumphed* an assent; heard the door slam, to be followed, some seconds later, by the sound of our coach's wheels clattering over the alley that connected the canal with the streets and alleys that lay behind the *pallazzo*; not the state coach of Thurn and Taxis which the princess had stolen on fleeing Castle Duino; that had been destroyed when our ship was sunk by the merchant-pirates of Venezia; but a little black phaeton which we had rented from a local dealer. And to where was that coach ~ its cacophonous retreat shifting into silence ~ bound with such urgency? To the ghetto of cheap dives and bordellos that grew like papillomata within the city's diseased vitals. My concentration destroyed, as it always was, usurped by the anxiety that always plagued me during the princess's excursions into night-town, I put my book aside; held out my hands, studying the mottled backs, fluted with tendons and livid veins. Toying with one fingernail, and then another, I soon had a collection of aborted keratin deposited in the folds of my lap. Playing with one nail a little too vigorously, I discovered the index finger to which it belonged was less than perfectly adhered to the metacarpus; I abandoned my self-destructive pastime; left the finger hanging by a thread of cartilage, the wound leaking a foul corruption. I leaned back, letting my head fall against a wing of the chair; and then I drifted into sleep, dreamless for the most part, though sometimes images of The Candyman would soundlessly invade my undeathly peace and mock my pretensions to liberty; it was a particularly scarifying image of his face in close-up, glimpsed as he busied himself inserting plugs into the jacks beneath my scalp, that roused me to wakefulness. I didn't know how long I had slept – hours, I suppose – but jerked to consciousness in a fit of explosive galvanism, I knew that it had been no necromancer, but rather a mouse who had stirred me from my slumber; the princess had returned. Calming myself – holding onto the table that, startled into a kind of pseudo-epilepsy, I had nearly upset – I listened as I heard two pairs of feet attack the creaking staircase in the hall, drunken snickering stilled by whispers of maidenly concern, as if the princess were acting out the role of an errant daughter taking a man to her room without wishing to alert her long-suffering parents that she was about to carve yet another notch into her bedstead. I held my breath; but the house had returned to its earlier silence. Guiltily, I again studied the backs of my hands, twin maps that each confirmed the course my body was taking, a route which would take it over the edge of the world to free fall through the outer spheres of the unknown until it crashed into nothingness. The princess had, for my sake, taken upon herself the risks of foraging for my special dietary needs; I ponced off her seductions – how else might I subsist? A creature such as myself was not designed for the kind of undercover mission in which my companion had so often distinguished herself. I had, in the past, at the zenith of newly-restored health, presented myself as an Atlantean fighting man (Special Forces, I would say, to explain my enhanced bulk); but I could never, would never pass for a gigolo; only the princess possessed the necessary seductive gifts to induce a man or woman to part with their money, time, freedom and life. My meditative shamefest was interrupted; a scream escaped through the cracks of the floorboards upstairs like the whistle of a bubbling kettle, increasing in pitch as it waylaid second after second of agonised time. There was a dull thump as my food fell to the floor of the princess's boudoir. I held my hands up to the light of the oil lamp, suspecting that my putrescent flesh, oozing hyalin from the pores, had attained a uniform translucence and that I would be able to see the steady flame through the opaque windows of my epidermis. It was not so; but I still trembled.

I would, I told myself, soon be feeling much better, thanks to The Candywoman.

The organ swelled, The Wedding March reverberating about the vaulted confines of St Mark's as bride and groom walked out into the afternoon sun between the main arch of the church's façade, the great balcony above, on which stood the Four Horses – symbols of the freedom and independence of the city, if also symbolic of the annals of its hated human past – lined with a crush of rats, sharks and she-spiders who showered the newly married couple with confetti, streamers and paper coins. I stood leaning against a column outside the entrance idly studying the decorative frieze of allegorical figures above me and wondering how the antique iconographies of the divine, like the encoded secrets of Nature, had become so contaminated by the alien invasion of the perverse as to be indecipherable. The original import of these sculptures and mosaics was, in our corrupted world, an unknown; only the perversion, the distorted reflections of a once authentic identity, remained, taunting us with its song of might-have-been. A seriate explosion of firecrackers punctured the spell of my enchantment, and I refrained from further attempts to interpret the lurid hieroglyphs of deserted faith; refocusing, I concentrated on the festivities in the square. The Piazzetta – that space bordered by the Doge's Palace, the Library and the South façade of the Basilica – was bedecked in readiness for Carnival, balloons and bunting festooning the sur-rounding walls.

I ran my hands down my ill-fitting shirt; snorted; made to join the revellers. The party was about to begin. Tables, heaped with drink and food, awaited the wedding guests, men and women masked and attired in the costumes of the *commedia dell'arte*, their confabulated bodies, disguised, having undergone a transformation that made them seem oddly human, as if, in putting off an alien grotesque for one that was rooted in this world, they had revealed that the perverse had never been separated by more than a hair's breadth from the so-called normative behaviour patterns of mankind, that rather than parallel worlds, the perverse had, perhaps, occupied an area of space-time that was not so much contiguous with humanity's own, but a transection of it. And what then, I thought, ramming my thought train into the buffers, rehearsing speculations that I had taken to airing – to myself, to the princess, to anyone who might listen – whenever I felt myself tumbling into the vertigo that constituted all contemplation of the past, what if there had never been a meltdown, a catastrophic disaster which sent the souls of our alien counterparts hurtling into our own world? What if we, all along, had been the alien, but had not known it? I shook myself, like a mastiff confined too long to quarters small, choking, insane. The last of the congregation had left the church. I followed the stragglers into the square, pulling myself up to my full height so that, chest-and-shoulders above all but the tallest of the milling rats, sharks, spiders, insects and other zoomorphs, I tracked the progress of the newlyweds towards the top table where, before I had walked halfway down The Piazzetta, they had seated themselves between the two massive columns which bore the lion of St Mark and the statue of St Theodore, their backs towards the quayside, the striped mooring poles and the sun-dappled, azure lagoon. I clucked my tongue, a half-hearted gesture that satisfied my need of self-mortification; I should not have allowed such a gap to have opened up between myself and the personhood of her whom, in both actuality and in dissimulation, I was sworn to protect: my goblin princess. I increased my pace, shouldering aside indignant revellers, who, turning and looking up at their assailant and seeing a bolted, riveted face looking down at them with amused contempt, let the opportunity of challenge pass.

Indignation, in this city of scum and cut-throats, was suitable only for those who held a flush hand. A wave of dizziness rippled through my head; I was hearing voices; and I knew those voices would not cease until I had finally assimilated last night's supper. The young man whose personality I had devoured, to what path had he belonged, I wondered? What life had he led, that he kept nagging me with his last remembrances of this world, spread-eagled upon the divan where the girl who had recently been caressing him was to be discovered holding a razorblade to his neck? I swallowed, both mentally and physically, forcing the residua of my as-yet-undigested meal into the fallow recesses of mind and gut. I ploughed on, cleaving a traverse between those that, leaping sideways, accommodated my disposition, and those that, truculent, stood their ground to be sent spinning into my slipstream by a sideswipe of my impatient arms. As I negotiated my roughshod passage I took out the mask that I had been keeping in my pocket and secured its ribbon behind my ears. A flimsy thing of black velvet, it emphasised rather than concealed, deepening the dark, shadowy concavities of my almost Neanderthal eye sockets, and making of the protuberant, encompassing bone high, black rims of twin caldera; no matter how ridiculous, how grotesque I looked, I knew I had to make some effort to enter into the spirit of the festivities; self-mockery, I consoled myself, need not be such an ignoble art if practised with love. The guests seated themselves, their attention given over entirely, now, to gluttony and intoxication. Drawing near to where the princess sat I had managed to contort my face into the semblance of a grin. Several ladies, who, lifting forks to their mouths, had been about to sample the stuffed quail, dropped their morsels back onto their plates, averting their eyes with horror. One of the youngest began to cry.

'Master Revenant!' called the Dux. 'The princess is without her bodyguard! It is remiss of you!' He looked about, winning, by his willingness to josh so forthrightly, so fearlessly with his wife's 'creature', the calculated, admiring regard of those who toadied for position. 'Most remiss! Please, please, sit yourself down.' I complied, a chair being drawn aside for me by one of the kitchen boys, an insect-clone with limpid, multicoloured wings that, folded, gave him the appearance of being already bound and gagged by the silken threads of a she-spider's mantrap. I sat, Mrs Herzog to one side, the princess to the other, the exuberant folds of my goblin girl's white satin wedding gown rustling against my leg as I settled myself as best I could into the too-delicate, constrictive chair. That morning I had watched as her maid had enveloped her in the creamy magnificence of her trousseau; watched as she had pulled on one tulle petticoat after another, as if she were preparing to perform a dance of a hundred, no, a *thousand* veils; watched as she diligently applied her make-up; watched, watched, and hoped that the moment might not cease.

'The Dux is about to make his presentation,' said Mrs Herzog, a hand placed, with unpolished disregard for mannerly niceties, over her rot-toothed, machinating mouth, 'and surrender half his fortune to milady.'

'Queen for a day,' I mused. 'A bizarre custom.' If one, I thought, that was just waiting to be exploited. By us.

'*Principessa* for a day, at least. And not so bizarre. How else is the man – I mean, just *look* at the old rakehell – how *else* is he to attract a lady of quality into his bed?' Mrs Herzog downed a tumbler of neat gin and waved to a kitchen boy, indicating that he should fetch her another bottle. 'There has to be *some* compensation.'

'A generous dower compensates for being murdered?'

'It seems to have done on at least some of seventy-seven occasions. What? You doubt? But then you do not think like a rat, do you, Master Revenant?'

Some of the ratgirls sitting opposite, young women who would sometime, perhaps soon (their squires regarding them with hot looks of appropriation) share the fate reserved, today, for the princess, stared at me through the slits of their dominoes, sniggering to their comrades as if to demonstrate that they were unafraid and that I solicited their tears in vain. 'Quite the macaroni, isn't he, with his thin, buckled shoes, his big-buttoned coat and silly little wig with its simply *prodigious* curls?' The lady, whose prattle was imbued with the velvety insolence of a rich, well-bred but terminally nasty schoolgirl, would, I hope, not be unnecessarily delayed in finding a suitable matrimonial bed. Self-conscious, I put a hand to my peruke, wishing that, like many of the men present, I had chosen instead to wear a *tricorne*. A hat would have better camouflaged the indecorum of my cadaverousness. Mrs Herzog stared at her plate, spread with salted fish and cornbread, sighing as she always did, or so I surmised, when reflecting, whether articulate or mute, upon the injustice that had matched her beloved mistress with a zombie, and a sartorially-compromised zombie, at that. The princess's own headdress was immaculate and exuded a musky, rich scent that, due to my proximity to its cachet, seemed richer and more overpowering than when I had first greedily inhaled it in her boudoir that morning, ogling a rat at her toilette while that rat's maid cleared away the leftovers of the previous night's tryst. The giddy, superfeminine wig – supported by a wire frame – was at least a yard high, decorated with ostrich feathers, diamond-studded hairpins and crowned with a waxworks menagerie of prancing, silver mice; tiers of ringlets fell over her ears; and a chignon eclipsed her occiput. The Dux rose, the princess casting her maid and me a disapproving look, as if she worried that the ladies who shared our table might have overheard our deliberations; that her moment of victory might dissolve in the acid that dripped from the gossiping tongues of those jealous, conspiratorial sisters, all vying to be the next *principessa*. But it was not the women who gave me concern; it was the half-dozen condottieri who never left the Dux's side that posed the greatest threat to our enterprise. Heavily armed, they presented even an undead *wusha* with a martial challenge that would strain his unnaturally puissant resources.

'Gentlemen, ladies,' began the Dux, rising from his seat to address the crowd. 'Once again we find ourselves assembled to mark the occasion of an old man's pleasure, a young woman's death.' He gazed down, beaming at the princess; she covered her cheeks, as if to hide her blushes; and the crowd broke into happy applause. The Dux raised a hand and there was silence. 'In accordance with our custom, passed on to me by my father, by his father, even until when the Rat Kings lived in the sewers beneath the city, hiding, fearful of the human inquisition – ah, but they were happy days, were they not, when we had the darkness as our own

and caves and tunnels to rejoice in! – I hereby, *ahem*, extend
all the privileges of my rank, all the wealth of my coffers
and rule of the city itself to the Princess Frenzetta von
Thurn und Taxis-Hohenlohe, as long as she shall live. And
know also that today this beautiful virgin has bestowed on
my family an alliance with a bloodline that predates the
cataclysm which gave us life. Henceforth, Venezia and Thurn
and Taxis stand as one! As united as are our souls with the
perverse issue of The Abortion!'

'Much he'll get out of it,' muttered Mrs Herzog, her
insurrectionary words drowned by the cheers that
resounded across the square, sending clouds of pigeons
twittering across the Basin and towards the Salute. 'Thurn
and Taxis? Been nothing in those parts for years. Not even
enough of a population to sire so much as a brace of
playfellows for my mistress when she was a little girl. Just
the goblin people, waiting for us last humans to move on.
Coming in the night. Burglarising the castle.'

'And worse,' I said.

'And worse,' agreed Mrs Herzog, tipping another
tumbler-full of mother's ruin into her mouth, a thick
rivulet of rubiginous liquor coursing down her hairy chin
to stain her frock, a bundle of rags that she averred were
her 'best'. I raised my own glass in imitation of the Dux as
he and a multitude of extras prepared to bring this
particular scene to a close with a hearty, if ironic toast to
the princess's health. Composing herself, the princess rose;
placed a gloved hand over the hand of the Dux as he
offered to escort her to her doom. 'That's it, then,' said the
crone, as the couple stepped back from the table, the
condottieri closing about them in a protective phalanx,
'they're off to the bridal chamber.'

'So soon?'

'Bastard wants to get his hands on the goods as soon as possible.'

'But the dower—'

'She has the dower. It's a formality, Master Revenant. None of the Dux's brides actually get to *spend* their newly acquired wealth. So nothing gets signed. Or handed over. But you're going to change all that, of course, aren't you?'

'Of course,' I said. 'You know I am.' The princess's hand closed tightly on the Dux's, as if to reassure him of her commitment, or to hint of sensual promise. To the sounds of an epithalamion sung by a choir of squeaking rat-children who had stepped onto a podium nearby, they made to leave, enclosed on all sides by the Dux's personal bodyguard. 'But you've got the balloon standing by, just in case?'

'Think positive.'

'I'm proof positive, Mrs H.'

'Then you'd better follow them, post-haste positive, revenant. And if you let any harm come to my little bon-bon then I'll—' I got up, disdaining to hear the midget out, and trailed after the departing bride and groom, a scrum of warriors packed about them, like cotton wool about china, screening them from harm, zealous mercenaries who marshalled their bejewelled tails to the syncopated beat of the happy couple's step, flicking them like fly whisks as if to warn of unhappy consequences for any who invaded their perimeters. The princess's tail, visible through a chink in the circumambient shield of ratmen, writhed like a serpent from the white froth of her bustle, and, I was glad to see, seemed altogether more subtle, alive, as it was, with the sinuosity of feminine scheming, than the swaying, dancing tails of her guard. The Dux looked over his shoulder; focused on me with reluctance; tutted, like a shopkeeper who has been forced to concede an unnecessary discount.

'You have *your* bodyguard, Pietro, why shouldn't I have mine? My revenant won't hurt your little boys.'

'Very well, my precious. Very well.'

'My lord, I do not think—' But the Dux hushed the objecting condottiere with an impatient shake of his jowls. Like an uncle about to play gallopy-gallopy with his favourite niece, he would let nothing distract him from the ride that lay ahead. Retracing our steps across The Piazzetta – the seated row of partying tribespeople clapping, urging us on to the beat of the brass band that had struck up with an arrangement of the overture from Verdi's *Un ballo in maschera* – we at last came to the main entrance of the palace, the Porta della Carta, a great doorway that stood next to the basilica. We proceeded, walking beneath its winged lion, through its gothic arch, across the courtyard, and, by degrees, up the Staircase of the Giants and The Scala d'Oro and onto the second floor, where we came to the private residential apartments of the old Doges, long since the preserve of tourists, museum curators, army generals, until, all human life vanishing from the city, it had been sequestrated by the ruling family of rats who lorded it over the confabulated who had made Venezia their pleasure ground. The Dux had almost broken into a trot, the princess desperately holding her teetering headdress in place as she was dragged remorselessly towards the arena of her violation, her heels scraping across the tiles, guided, perfunctorily, and, as far as the Dux was concerned, for a first and only time, through the Room of the Scarlatti, the Hall of the Shield, and then the interconnecting rooms called the Grimani Room, the Erizzo Room, the Room of the Stucchi and the Hall of the Philosophers. As the Dux and princess reached a set of doors separating the public area of the apartments from the palace's most private rooms – the suite that was to be the killing ground – the condottieri took up position on either side of the jambs. Tour over, the Dux came to a halt; bowed, surveying his bride with half-lidded, lust-eclipsed eyes; gestured to the princess – ever the gentleman – that she should enter first, as if he were a politic vampire enticing a traveller to cross his house's threshold. She complied; and the Dux, salivating, hurried after, slamming the doors behind him.

'No further, revenant,' said one of the guard. For a few moments I walked on the spot, dithering, my legs unwilling to accept that I was interdicted. I gazed up at the stupendous stucco-work, mosaics and bas-reliefs; and all the while my feet pedalled, useless, against the tiles, my mind concentrated on effecting the princess's and my own escape, the plan of action I should adopt after she had postponed foreplay and despatched her geriatric husband, thereafter to claim his wealth. If I did not kill the Dux's personal guard now, I would surely have to do it later; all others in the court, weak, sheep-like deviants that they were, would, I calculated, fall in with our new regime. 'Why are you here, dead man? You going to raise your mistress from the grave? I mean, you got some kind of special dispensation for that sort of thing?'

'Habit,' I said. 'I wait not out of necessity, but habit.'

'The habit of service? Or maybe you just been

panicked into ingratiating yourself with your new employer, eh?'

'I'm sworn to my mistress to do my duty to her to the very end.'

'Then better take a seat. The Dux takes a while to gee himself up these days.' Dry laughter rustled through the hall. How much time, I wondered, should I give the princess to slit the wattled neck of the Rat King? I looked forward to walking free of the palace – where a hundred other guards lurked – and establishing the princess as the *Principessa Serenissima*, lauding her virtues and generosity to the drunks in St Mark's Square. Amongst the people of Venezia – whom the princess would quickly win over by bestowing upon them largesse – we would be comparatively safe. Anxious, I pulled out my pocket watch, willing the minute hand to accelerate and compress my reluctant sentinelling into a single loud pulsation of my heart.

'Sit? No, I'll stand,' I said, readying myself while at the same time assuming a stance as unthreatening, as deceptively benign, as possible. I studied a fresco, trying to calm myself. It depicted Lilith on Calvary, the two kleptomaniacs who flanked her writhing, I thought – I was unable to suppress the blasphemy – with more voluptuous insistence than the Queen of the Left-Hand Path. I sent a silent prayer up into the rafters, willing it higher, until it was on its way to The Moon, that place sacred to the intercessor's teachings. *In Cathay we called you Ch'ang-o, in Europa, we invoke you by your old name of Lilith; still you remain the one mistress of our hearts, sworn to remain with us lost souls unto time's end. Grant me, now, the boon of your protection.* I also raised my inner voice to the princess's goddamned angels, whatever *they* were; just, like, in case they'd been following us, as the princess sometimes implied. But how does one petition angels? I closed my eyes. My heart no longer pulsed in the vast cathedral of my chest, like a great bell tolled by a deformed bell ringer, it throbbed inside my skull – a length of steel cable thrashing about like an electric eel within a fish bowl – the myriapod that housed my self-hood inflaming my cerebrovascular system, secreting juices that had already primed my sinews and muscle for the task I had set myself. I blinked; focused on the guards, trying to gauge their weaknesses, their strengths. The condottieri looked away, bored with the sight of me, as if I were a fairground attraction whose disgusting novelty had, over the weeks, worn thin. I was glad to escape their attention; collapsing into myself, I stared down at the floor in an attempt to hide the veins that had begun to bulge on my forehead; filtered out all visual distractions; and my consciousness, thus imploded, was assailed by a distraction more terrible than any bagatelle that threatened to greet my eyes; for, unable to resist, I took to imagining the princess inside the Dux's chambers, the Dux inside her, the self-conjured scene so disconcerting that, as has happened on other such occasions of spiritual turmoil, I stepped out of myself entire, leaving my body ramrod stiff – its hyper-tense state of alert allowing no kink or fold in its titanic frame – and still ignored by the guards. Unable to constrain my jealous curiosity – though it went against our plan – I floated through the doors connecting the hall with the inner sanctum, into an antechamber, and then through into the bridal suite itself.

'What the hell are you doing here, Duane?'

whispered the princess, shocked. Clad only in stockings
and heels she hung upside down from the four-poster bed,
suspended from its topmost rail by her tail, swinging idly
like a monkey frolicking in the panoply of a jungle.

'I don't think your lover is capable of matching your
gymnastics, do you, my little perversion of nature?' I
mouthed, taking care to clearly enunciate each word so
that the princess might comprehend the subtleties of my
dumb show. 'Where is he?'

'In the bathroom, he's—' At that moment the Dux
entered, his short wiry frame draped in a paisley dressing
gown; and he would have surprised us in the act of
intrigue – his rat eyes as acute and discriminating as the
princess's – if I had not, at that moment, withdrawn my
glowing, energy form behind the heavy, black drapes that
kept out the sunlight, like an interloping lover in a French
farce. Fidgeting with his cravat, he walked confidently
towards the huge bed, age no handicap for one who would
have to do little to bring his partner to a shattering, lethal
peak of joy. Inspecting the princess's inverted body with
amused contempt, he plucked an ostrich feather from her
hair and ran the plume across the apex of her bifurcated,
upturned thighs. 'Ohh,' moaned the princess, goose bumps
rising in a localised rash of pleasure across the depilated
mound of her *mons veneris*. 'Ohh, Aghh, Ee-ee! Ee-ee!' I
swung a punch at the curtain, entertaining the notion
that the glib violator of my companion's modesty stood
before me, my big fist passing through his jaw, not in a
hum of harmless discharge, but with the satisfying concussion that would have resulted if I were in my corporeal
shell.

'What was that?' said the Dux, who had perhaps felt,

by way of sympathetic magic, the stubble of his chin prickle in a conduction of energy.

'Just me, my love,' said the princess. 'You have me so *excited*.'

'I shall take you to the gates of hell and heaven, sweet girl. And then beyond. The magical mystery tour has only just begun.' I peered through a crack in the drapes and, satisfied that I was invisible to the Dux, pressed my lips to the opening so that the princess might interpret the silent agony of a cuckold restrained from exacting vengeance.

'My God, what's he doing to—' The princess shot me a look of disgust which was proportionate to the excesses of her orgiastic whimperings and moans; no pleasure there, I reassured myself, repeating the formula until the evidence of my ears was discredited by wishful thinking, always a standby for eunuchs in the rough trials of love. As the Dux bent over, sinking his tongue into the bald, buffed buttonhole between her thighs – too wet and glistening to be able to effectively corroborate my fond fantasies of her lack of enthusiasm – she put a hand on the back of the lecher's head, pulling him down, as if she would suffocate him in the petaloid folds of her sex. With her violator thus blinded, and deafened by the pressure her thighs were exerting against his long, pointed ears, the princess deigned to whisper peremptory instructions.

'It'll only take me a minute or so now to manoeuvre him onto the bed, and then I'll be able to get my hands on the razor I've hidden under the pillow.'

'My razor?'

'Yes, *your* razor. So what?' I didn't like it when she used it to shave her legs; this was worse, far worse. But:

'It doesn't matter.'

'I should think not.' I tried to wrest my gaze from the Dux, his bobbing head a magnetic North to which I was irresistibly drawn, as if to a frozen wilderness of lust; and if I was an unwelcome foreigner in that land, *persona non grata*, I refused to be deported. That land was my land. Yes sirree.

'I can't—' I can't *stand* it, I had wanted to say, before, tired, too emotional to continue my mime, I averted my gaze, unable to bear the horrible sight before me.

'Go away, Duane. Beat it. *Vamoose*.'

'What was that, sweet bride?'

'I said, Eat it, *Dux*.' I thought of the guards, how they would come rushing into the bedroom if the Dux, in his dying moment, should emit a single Ee-ee! that could not be confused with a rodent cry of ecstasy.

'Okay, okay. I'm going,' I mouthed, my lips once again pressed to the slit in the drapes. 'I just wanted to check to see if you were all right.'

'You're impossible, Duane. You know that I only care for—' She threw back her head, yodelled, her tail unsnarling from the rail of the four-poster so that the twosome, unsupported, collapsed onto the black silk sheets, the princess with her heels pointing at the ceiling, the Dux coming up for air. The princess's hand slipped under the pillow. 'Hurry, Duane,' she muttered as she pushed the Dux back into place. 'Don't worry, foreplay might take a few years off my life, but only coitus is actually going to kill me. And there's no way this slimeball's going to stick his teeny, meany *fettuccine* into *this* rat's snatch.' Blue steel glittered in her fist.

Behind the cover of the curtains I made my retreat,

floating sideways through the connecting wall, submitting to the taut pull of my umbilical cord and allowing it to wind me in. Wall and corridor telescoped, perspective disappearing into a bright dot that shone, intense, minute, behind my eyelids, before deliquescing into the light of the Hall of the Philosophers as, re-established inside my physical body, I rolled my eyes, sending them on an orbit of their sockets, looked about, flexed my hands. The condottieri were as I had left them, my excursion – which had left my titanic frame in a state of terrific inanity – seemingly having gone unremarked; but the guards were aware of *something* amiss. The sudden termination of the soundtrack of moans and hollahs that had issued from the bridal suite's echo chamber until a few moments earlier was, I knew, an indication that the princess had concluded her work; and though the condottieri were unlikely to deduce that homicide was its cause, the silence – a phonograph recording ripped from its turntable and smashed to the floor – was making them twitch. I knew, then, that I would have to conclude my own work with celerity. I walked up to the nearest guard, a thin, tall athlete caped and cowled in festive costume; the sword and pistol slung at his side, were, however, anything but ornamental; I kept my gaze fixed on his hands, wary of their obvious familiarity with that armoury.

'Do you have a light?'

'Hey, what do you know, the dead get to smoke, *incredibile*, eh?' My hand already raised, as if about to accept a match, it was a simple matter to fork my fingers and push them deep into his eyes until my much-chewed, crenellated nails had penetrated his forebrain. Retracting, I gathered him up with my other arm, allowing my

brain-begrimed fingers – I gave them a cursory lick – to seek
the pistol and pull it free of his belt. I had put a ball through
the chest of my second victim before the rest of the guards
had even recognised that the man I embraced was, like me, a
cadaver; unlike me, inanimate, with no prospect of joining
me in my elephantine ballet. Releasing my dance partner –
dead on his feet these last few seconds – I lurched towards
the remaining guards who had hurriedly formed a group
barring the doorway that led to the Dux, each man levelling
a raised pistol; but if my locomotion was elephantine, so
was my flesh; three detonations that would have been sufficient to kill a mortal penetrated no deeper than my jaun-
diced integument, the other, which might have perforated
the velum that covered my skull, deflected by the steel plates
behind which hid my squirming neo-cortex. As I came within striking range, I killed two condottieri by the inelegant
expedient of smashing their heads together; and though this
task was executed with as much precipitation as I could
muster, my speed – never my most valued asset as a warrior
– fell short of enabling me to protect my flanks and rear.
With curiosity, and some dismay, I inspected the haft of the
rapier that projected from my left upper rib, the corresponding blade, slicked with black ichor, emerging from the
other side of my torso. Curiosity was transformed into anger;
I recalled when, undergoing indoctrination in the necromancers' lair, I had been stuck full of needles in a test
designed to calibrate my pain threshold; and anger,
correspondingly, was transformed into action. I hit the
offending guard with such force that, with a shower of teeth
raining onto the tiles, my fist entirely disappeared into the
shocked rictus of his mouth and did not stop until the
knuckles had punched an egress through the throat, fingers

opening and then contracting, so that the spinal column momentarily tangled in my slippery grip as I withdrew, still enough humanity left in my frame, I discovered, for me to briefly empathise with the shudder of terror, bitterness and death that conducted itself along my forearm. My last opponent dropped his sword and, accepting his fate, lifted his cape so that it obscured his face, acknowledging, if unwilling to bear witness to the fact, that the horrors that had been visited upon his companions were about to come calling upon him. His neck snapped like damp hickory.

I looked about, as disgusted with the carnage as the Earth's teeming millions were invariably disgusted with me, the sight of me, what I was, what I might have been, my deadness, my unnatural quickness, my strength, my corrupted life. Dazed, I did not at first notice the small figure in the doorway; did not, at first, recognise that the girl with the high-piled mane of blanched ringlets and curls, the girl with the beauty spot high on the cheek offset by a streak of foreign blood on the other, the girl naked but for the white silk stockings and the jewellery clipped on to her big breasts and lovely, swishy tail – I did not recognise that here was the one, the only one, not to have turned from me in disgust.

'Duane?' said the merry widow. 'Snap out of it, Duane.' She let the razor fall clattering to the floor. 'What the hell is this?' She walked up to me and pointed to the rapier that transfixed my torso. 'Does it hurt?'

'No,' I said, blankly, like a little boy who has returned home to his mother with a pair of ripped trousers, afraid.

'Do you want me to oblige?'

'Please.' She grabbed the haft with both hands and

jerked the rapier free. She passed it through the air a few times admiring its balance; then she threw the filthy blade amongst the shot, broken, pulped bodies of the condottieri. I put a hand to my head; pulled off the peruke and massaged my pitted scalp in an attempt to soothe the tense, stressed-out parasite that shared and vouched for my existence. 'You have to address the crowd,' I said. 'Before the Dux's—'

'The ex-Dux's,' corrected the princess. I smiled.

'Before the *remainder* of your late husband's personal guard decide to check up on the afternoon's proceedings.'

'Quite. Your arm then, Master Revenant?' She knotted her own arm about mine, threading it through the crook of my elbow. We scurried forth, an incarnadined seven-foot demon from hell and his inamorata, the aristocratic beauty who sometimes liked to move amongst her people in the manner of a vulgar serving wench, stripped, dishevelled and with the smell of cheap scent, gin and semen engrained in her pores, a demoness *manqué*. With quickening gait, we backtracked through the palace. Through halls, corridors, libraries, chambers, we searched for a suitable spot from which the princess might address her subjects. At last we found a door which led to the loggia; stepped out onto the open-sided gallery and prepared to address the crowd.

I took out my pocket watch and was gratified to find that, despite certain unforeseen distractions, we had adhered to our timetable; walked to the balustrade; scanned the crowd, noting that Mrs Herzog had left her seat and was, I hoped, putting our contingency plan into effect, a fallback measure we had arranged should we, miscalculating the temper of the city, need to relinquish our claim to its gold and silver in favour of a prudent and speedy retreat. I cupped my hands to my mouth, sucked at the thick, diseased air and filled the bellows of my lungs, still a little sore after receiving such a recent sword thrust. 'The Principe is dead!' I shouted. 'Long live the *Principessa*!'

'Crude, Duane,' said the princess.

'Sorry,' I said. 'I do *so* hate ascribing false titles to your name. There's only one real princess between here and the Baltic, and that's you, Frenzy. Only you.' Ignoring my sarcastic, mock-sentimental smooth-talk, she crept forward; crouched; peeped over the edge of the loggia; straightened herself.

'Crude, all the same,' she said at last. 'But possessing a certain efficacious immediacy.'

'True.' Every face in The Piazzetta was turned towards us, mouths agape, wine spilling down shirt fronts, down chins, necks, bosoms; or else, with eyes screwed, drawing beads of suspicion, focusing on us as likely target practice, an arsenal of musketry empowering every citizen that enjoyed the late Dux's hospitality.

'Take pity on a poor, frustrated ratgirl!' cried the princess. 'A girl robbed of her fulfilment, of her ecstasy! A heart attack took him, my friends, a thrombosis that left him dead before he could lie by my side!'

'Ladies and gentlemen of the Serenissima Republic, by the laws of succession and inheritance, I hereby proclaim the Princess Frenzetta von Thurn und Taxis-Hohenlohe the rightful mistress and ruler of all the tribespeople of Venezia. Three cheers for the Princess Frenzetta. Hip, hip—' The last hip was no more than a whisper as I came to perceive that the mob was unconvinced, the cognisance taking what little air remained in my lungs. 'Should have brought the body,' I said to the princess, 'maybe they want some kind of proof.'

'*You never loved him, bitch*,' yelled some envious rat lady.

'We come to bury the Dux, not to praise him.' I laughed, nervous, self-conscious of my idiot frivolity, the unlikelihood of its winning the mob to our self-serving cause.

'Oh, let me, Duane.' She grasped her magnificent breasts; squeezed them, as if trying to induce lactation. 'I give you my largesse ~ a half of my late husband's coffers for the people of Venezia!'

'*We don't want your money, you double-dealing whore!*'

I sighed. 'Well,' I said, stepping back, as screams for our heads began to echo about The Piazzetta, 'I hope you're pleased with yourself. "All your capers are crazy, Duane," you said. "In this city we do things my way." I hope you're satisfied.'

'Put a sock in that rancid mouth of yours, Duane Duarte.'

'You just tell me how we're supposed to get our hands on our money without—' I pointed irritably towards the welling mass of bodies, simmering, like maggots over a fire; the crowd's discontent threatened to turn into a mêlée; pointed with a nausea rising in my throat, so that I spat out my contempt along with the bile from my rotting guts. 'Without *their* co-operation.'

'You, you *horrid* common man.'

'Common? You could do with some common-*sense*. I

must have been mad to go along with this, Miss Hoity-Toity.'

'Horrid, horrid. At Duino, all you would have been fit for would have been labouring, or scullery work, or, or—'

'At Duino? All you were fit for was to be the family joke.'

'Oh, I hate you! I hate you!' Her claws extended and she scratched at my chest, like a puppy trying to attract its master's attention by worrying at the door. As she discovered that her claws had little effect on my pachydermatous hide – Master Duane was determined to rub his puppy's nose in its own shit – she took to beating her hands against me, my chest resounding like a kettle-drum, or a jungle telegraph sending out warning of an attack by the natives. 'I am the daughter of one of the oldest and noblest houses in Europa. We were here even before there were rats and cats and wolves and, and ... We were here even before The Abortion. How dare you speak to me like that!'

'Your airs and graces won't buy us a spaceplane. How are we going to get off this damned piece of rock if we don't have any money?' A small group of tribespeople had gathered beneath us; some were beginning to climb the portico, one such – a ratman with a piece of sharp and deadly cutlery clenched between his teeth – having attained one of the capitals. An improvised platoon had lined up some way back, a row of muskets pointed in our direction. The situation was both ludicrous and grim. 'Get behind me,' I said. As the princess took in our present danger and rapidly complied a volley of musket fire struck me amidships, reducing my brocade to shreds, completing the destruction initiated by the princess's claws; I listed, almost sunk to my knees; and then rallied, pulling myself up, puffing out my chest with defiance. 'Where the hell is Mrs Herzog?' The ratman who, determined on revenging his Dux (for both he and the baying mob seemed to have lost no time in seeing through our charade and pinning on us the charge of murder); the same ratman who, pirate-fashion, clenched a carving knife between his teeth and was encouraging the outraged citizens of Venezia to storm the battlements, climbed over the balustrade and took up a stance indicating that he was ready for hand-to-hand combat. I should normally have laughed and swiped him clear, sending him crashing into The Piazzetta, or else picked him up and used him as a missile to dissuade his compatriots from likewise attempting to compromise our already somewhat precarious freedom. But I was aware in him only of a quizzical expression, and that only glimpsed peripherally as I looked beyond and above to where Mrs Herzog, leaning over the basket suspended from the balloon that descended over the rooftops, gesticulated, indicating that the princess and me should make ready to depart.

'Damn,' said the princess, 'it's still Halloween. I wanted to leave tomorrow, on All Saints' Day. I wanted to be like Casanova.'

'Too bad,' I said.

'I'm sorry, Duane.'

'Sorry?'

'Sorry I lost my temper. I can be such a Tartar, I know. I think it might be as you said. Maybe there never was a cataclysm. Maybe The Abortion never happened. The only aliens are our true selves. It's time I found a way of being faithful to what I am, Duane. It's time I owned up, time we *both* owned up to where this journey of ours is going to end.'

'No time—'

The ratman turned, unable to constrain his curiosity; aping him, the crowd also strained to gaze skywards; and an uncanny hush fell over the rioters as the balloon, expertly guided by the shrunken aviator at its controls, glided in until the basket came level with the loggia. I picked up the princess and lifted her over the lip of the basket; I was about to follow when, feeling that I had left some business unaccounted for, swung about and confronted the rat who had meant to duel with me. I raised my hand, about to knock his head from his shoulders, when the sight of his frozen, wondering countenance made me abjure the merciless instincts of the made warrior; instead of killing him I grinned, not unkindly, I think – as beneficently, at least, as a mishmash of a face such as mine could manage – and held out my hand; but I suppose I should not have been surprised if he would not, or could not shake it.

'No bad feelings, I hope. Our little gamble didn't work. You still have your money. And you'll soon find yourself another King of the Rats. Or perhaps a Shark King, or a Wolf King? Who knows? Keep a look out for slavers, okay? Have to move along now. Got to find a way to make some cash, get to The Moon. No more crazy schemes. No more dumb capers. The next show will bring the house down, you wait and see, it'll be that good. So long.'

'*Arriverderci*,' croaked the rat, still frozen like a statue celebrating astonishment; one more allegorical device in a city already lousy with symbols and icons and myths.

I climbed into the basket. Mrs Herzog opened the valve of the propane cylinder and a column of flame shot up, exciting the air inside the great silk bag; the balloon ascended with a violent jerk that sent the princess and I to the rattan floor. A trunk fell over, spilling silks, satins, lace and ribbons, some of which fluttered briefly in the thermal draft of our ascent before flying out into the clear blue afternoon like exotic fetishes – winged, living jujus, charms, mojos – released from a cage. I quickly struggled to my feet; but the city had already become unreal, a postcard that was becoming a postage stamp that would soon be no more than a microdot, black and acetate, flashing in the naked sun.

LOST IN AFRIC

Tanjah. Port of Demons. Of Maverick Flesh. Port of Heterotaxia. Of Paraphilia. Port of Flagellants, Necrophiles, Haemodipsomaniacs, Epicenes and other, unnamed and more extreme embodiments of outlawed desire. Tanjah, port where the Barbary Corsairs relaxed, indulged in the pleasures the city had to offer, an unspoken truce as uneasy as it was long allowing rival gangs of pirates to briefly forget their quarrels in a round of wine, feasting and dance.

It was the dance, of course, that captured my attention, and not the pleasures of the gullet – gourmand pleasures to which I was immune; for the princess was a superb dancer, her natural talent refined during various undercover missions for Cathay when, disguised in a sequinned bikini, a feather boa, or else nothing except a pair of thigh-high plastic boots, she had worked the go-go bars of Saigon. A year or so on, her gyrating hips and the undulations of her abdomen were still a spectacle that, if failing to inspire my nether parts, prompted my head to swim in delicious, fatal circles, as if I were drowning in a maelstrom of sherbet, a vortex of sensation that accentuated the light-headedness I felt as I sucked in great draughts of hashish from my hookah. She danced in Turkish cabaret style rather than in the controlled, refined Egyptian manner; the Turkish style was flamboyant, blatantly sexual, much given to leaps and a certain pelvic freneticism which forewarned of autoerotic overload; and at such moments I grew concerned for my *rat fatale*. It was a style, moreover, whose celebrants were invariably scantily clad. I approved of the princess's attire as much as I did her chosen terpsichorean idiom. The clothes had been donated by the café's proprietor; the luxury of approval, luckily for me – given my impecunious state – thus came gratis, like the tips we both survived on. But that didn't make my approbation less intense. I wished I had been allowed in her changing room to watch her strap herself into that jangly, chain-encumbered brassiere, the coin belt, the tiny *cache-sexe* from which hung the spangled skirts of diaphanous chiffon, which swirled now, as she camel-walked to my table, her bejewelled navel flashing beneath the oil lamps so that the Moor who was my guest began to burble, his concentration given wholly to that diamanté, cyclopean eye as he tried to stare it down, or else submit entirely to its scrutiny. The dance proceeded, the princess's body dissolving into a series of lithe, arrhythmic poses. Shock-stunned by that vision of rodent loveliness, the Moor's own body became rigid, spellbound, as if he were a rat himself, a rat in thrall, not to a fellow rat, but to a serpent. And indeed, the princess, after a month of frequenting the dives and bars of the Medina, had learnt much from the snakegirls who monopolised Tanjah's erotic trades. Standing, then kneeling, she performed arm ripples; the cobra arms, a roll that moved from the shoulder to the fingertips; the willow arms; with arms held above the head, swaying like thin, white branches. Springing to her feet, she treated him to a *hobba* – a twitch of her buttocks

– the coin belt chinking, its pretty disarray like a fountain of splashing, liquid metal; and then came a rib-cage slide, a drop; hip slides, lifts, drops and snaps, this particular subroutine completed with a coy, one-hip circle; a pelvic tuck followed; and then at last, adopting the Chinese shimmy, she ran, ankle bells tinkling, hither and thither across the floor. Coming to a sudden halt at our table the princess leaned backwards across its surface – a plate fell to the floor – her arms weaving sinuous patterns in the smoky air. Her belly quivered as she arched her spine, her shoulders resting on the tabletop, her legs splayed, her head thrown to one side, the flamboyant abdomen pushed upwards into the Moor's face. A thread of saliva hanging from the corner of his mouth snapped, a gobbet of spit making a splashdown amongst the chaos of doubloons that girded the princess's *mons veneris*. As the music reached its climax, she arched her stomach into a still more radical convexity, as if inviting the Moor to lick up his pre-senile spillage. Her eyes, upside down, regarded me with incongruous coolness; amusement, even; I reached out, touched the beauty spot which, like the crimson lips, set off the uncompromising pallor of her complexion and exalted coiffure. And then I ran a finger across her jagged teeth, the ten-day-old jerky of my flesh, bad and rank, smudged with traces of her violently red cosmetic. The gold circlet about her brow dripped with black pearls; gravity had dragged the lustrous gems into her hair, dotting that frosted fleece like flyspecks. With a suddenly punctuated roll of hand drums, the music stopped. The princess sprang up, accepted, with an awkward curtsey, the bill that the Moor nervously tucked into her *cache-sexe*, kissed him on the forehead and then twirled, acknowledging the applause of the café's clientele. 'She'll join us presently,' I said as she skipped through the tables and exited behind a curtained door. 'She just has to change.' The Moor emptied the dregs of his mint tea into his mouth, then took out a gilt cigarette case and lit up.

'I never indulge,' he said, nodding towards my water pipe. 'Not when business is to be discussed.'

'Oh, business can wait. First, pleasure, no?' He studied the glowing tip of his champagne-hued cigarillo and raised his brows, a slow *hut, hut, hut* of choked laughter indicating that he concurred. I bit down on the mouthpiece of my comforter, inhaled an epileptic amount of hash and blew a cloud of pungent smoke across the dance floor, crowded now with a troupe of acrobats. Sweat coursed down my scalp, the steel plate that displaced my cheekbone; dripped from my nose and chin. For a few seconds, I looked upon the world benignly, the massive draught having dispersed the vapours swirling in my brain, the oppressive miasma exuded by my own corporeality, just as the massive quantities of *eau de cologne* that I regularly bathed in relieved those nearby of having to endure my graveyard stench. Neither scent nor smoke screen, however, did much to distract those men who populated the surrounding shadows from a secret study of the prodigy in their midst; nor did it dissuade their women from capturing my image in their make-up mirrors, to be examined and dissected even as they presented me with their backs, cold-shouldering one who had been blackballed from Klub Photogenic. And how might I protest? They were riff-raff, humans for the most part, freebooters who hoped to make a quick profit trading with the confabulated; wild-siders who had travelled over the seas to feast with the legionnaires of the lost tribes. Profit and prurience; both added piquancy to their jaded lives. How might I upbraid them for acting in a wholly ignorant, but human way? Humans is humans. Though, I reminded myself, I had never topped the popularity polls of my fellow tribespeople, either; and tribespeople, if not as ignorant as those who followed the *right-hand* path, could sometimes be twice as cruel.

'How old is she?'

'Seventeen,' I said, careless whether the condemned man should or should not glean a few details from the princess's *curriculum vitae*.

'Seventeen? Old for a girl goblin. But—'

'But young enough for you,' I said, pre-empting his argument. 'What other kind of she-orc would condescend to lie with a human? Only an old maid, who can no longer hope to find death in the arms of the male of her species would submit to having her hymen ruptured by one whose flesh was unmodified. It is well to be realistic.'

'I suppose so. It is just that, after so long entertaining this one fantasy, of making love to one of her kind, I had wished that there had been the promise of more pathos. Now, if you could fine me a twelve-year-old, or say, a girl goblin of thirteen, then—'

'I hope you are not trying to back out of our arrangement?' He coughed, waving a stubborn plume of smoke away from his face.

'Of course not, of course not.'

'You are lucky that I was able to look after you the way I have. Do you realise how rare it is for a human to have such an opportunity as this?' His mouth creased into a dreamy smile as he doubtless contemplated the stories –

testosterone-high, swaggering stories – he would tell his friends when he returned to the Gold Coast. 'I mean, where you come from, there are catgirls a-plenty. But having sex with a cat – dammit, what human these days *hasn't* had sex with a cat? But your rat, your elusive, fuck-of-a-lifetime rat, well–'

'I know, sir, I know. You don't have to tell me. This has been my little holiday dream for some time. A *long* time. I assure you, once I am upstairs–'

'Once *I* introduce you to the lady then you conclude *your* part of the deal. You give me the information; I leave; you do what you have to do. Understand?'

'Yes, yes, I understand. It's very good of you to place such trust in the veracity of what I have to sell.' Trust? I thought. Ha. We'll make sure your information's *bona fide*, my friend; by the time the princess and I have concluded our interrogation, we'll know whether you're the break-through we've been praying for or whether you're just a horny, stupid bastard who's full of shit. But to run our little psychological profile he had first to be enticed upstairs to where the last of our money had bought a room for the night, the requisite tools and the management's silence. 'Shall we be on our way?' Why not? I thought. The princess would, by now, I calculated, have all in readiness. I got up; both the Moor and some of the diners at adjacent tables instinctively shrank into their seats as my shadow fell across them, like a portent of all they most feared in the perverse. I walked towards the door chalked with the word PRIVATE through which the princess had earlier disappeared. A human woman had taken to the floor to dance the *Guedra*; kneeling, dressed in the indigo-blue robes of the desert, her arms and hands carved patterns in the blue pall of smoke, sculpting nebulous images of insidious, drawn-out seduction. I turned my head to check that the Moor followed; he did, the mad dog kennelled within his trousers growling, yapping, prancing, tugging him towards an assignation that would soon make him regret pampering that spoilt, truculent pet. I held open the door; ushered him through; and, taking up the rear, made sure he ascended the stairs that led to the first floor landing. Once upstairs I grabbed his arm, leading him along the hallway to one of the three doors that connected with private rooms. I bent down on one knee and peered through the keyhole and saw that, within, the improvised anteroom to the afterlife had been prepared for the reception of my guest. I stood; knocked. A lazy, sarcastic voice emanated from beyond – the timbre was uncalled-for; if the Moor had not been so pumped up with lust, he might have recognised it for what it was, an invitation to perdition, and run – 'Come on in, boys.' I entered.

The princess sat astride a chair, a white bonnet balanced atop her coiffure, its gauze veil covering the top half of her face. A lace choker encircled her neck, a cruelly laced corset, her waist, pinching it into a waspish circumference of similar, neck-like dimensions and lifting the opulent, nay, plutocratic breasts into a critical mass that threatened an explosion of super-voluptuous bounty. The patulous, white-stockinged thighs delivered their indolent yawn with an arrogance typical of her super-cilious coquetry; and the hands spread across the summit of the chair's fluted back supported her chin with the insouciance of a young woman who had teased the life out of too many men to let even the wound where pity, mercy and forgiveness had been ripped out trouble her with an ache of conscience. Her sexuality, like the satins and silks in which she had gift-wrapped herself, was dazzling; all-justifying; I held up a hand to my eyes, not entirely in jest, to preserve what masculine sap was left in my mind from evaporation, like the last juices of a rain forest vaporised by the fell, forgotten weapons of the War of the Liebestod, the microscopic swarms of machines that destroyed living matter but left inorganic structures intact. I reached out; grabbed the Moor by a loose fold of his *djellabah*; pulled him into the room, opening the fingers of the hand with which I shielded myself to peek at the screaming vision of pulchritude seated centre stage, winking at him as if to warn – again, not entirely in jest – of the serious, the deadly serious pleasures that were to come.

'Sir, may I present to you Miss Frenzy, famed interpreter of the Oriental dance.' The Moor inclined his head, suddenly as shy as a schoolboy.

'You have a name, blackamoor?' said my rude little aristocrat.

'Ahmed,' he said, his hands fluttering like butterflies high on the scent of nectar, 'Ahmed Ben Ahriman.'

'Well, if you aren't just the Sheik of Araby, handsome. So, why don't you sit down, *Sheik*?' He moved towards the bed. 'No, not there, Sheik, not yet, at least. Sit *there*.' She pointed towards a long dining table. 'Underneath.'

'Underneath?'

'I like to play games. Goblin games. You'll humour me, I hope?'

'Certainly, Miss Frenzy. Anything you say.' He looked at me as if to ask why I lingered in his chamber of love.

'Yeah, I suppose I should be going.' I retraced my steps until I stood before the door, my gaze never leaving the scene of the Moor's entrapment.

'That's it, Sheik,' said the princess, ignoring my feigned retreat, concentrating instead on issuing our gull instructions.

'This table here? The one with the hole in the middle?'

'Just crawl right on under.' Obedient, he seated himself beneath the table, his legs pulled up beneath his *djellabah* so that his chin rested on his knees. 'Now stick your head through the hole.'

'Like this?'

'Yes. That's exactly right. You *are* a clever boy.' The princess got up and walked over to him. 'Close your eyes.' Holding him by the hair she extricated and then snapped shut the U-shaped halter that had been concealed within the plain of the table; as I heard it lock, securing the Moor in its stranglehold as if he were a miscreant held to ridicule in the stocks, I stepped forward and pulled up a chair, seating myself before the Moor's incredulous face. 'Scream if you like, Sheik,' said the princess, 'but nobody'll condescend to hear you.' The Moor's eyes, that had snapped open the moment the halter had snapped shut on his throat, burned with terror. He knew, now, that this was no game.

'He'll scream whether he likes it or not,' I said. 'Listen—' I spread my hands over the polished wood. 'You know, or at least, you *say* you know where we can locate a spaceplane.'

'What are you doing?' he said. 'There's no need for this. I just wanted to make love to the beautiful goblin!'

'So you thought you'd love me to death, eh, you lousy prick? Well, how does it feel to know that *you're* fucked?'

'We regret having had to dupe you,' I said. 'We would, in normal circumstances, have been happy to pay for what information you have. Unfortunately' – the princess had collected her handbag from the dressing table and was retrieving a hacksaw from the jumbled pack-ratery of its interior – 'we are penniless. Thus, your discomfort. It is the only way that, alas, I believe we can negotiate.'

'Penniless,' repeated the princess. 'Why else would a gorgeous piece of rat-meat like *me*' – she gave a curtsey – 'be working as a belly dancer in a nasty little bordello like *this*.' She dangled the hacksaw in front of our gull's eyes, allowing him to contemplate what lay in store for him.

'I can give you m, m, m-money,' stuttered the Moor.

'Collect your thoughts, please. Miss Frenzy here is about to perform a delicate surgical procedure. The space-plane. Think. You said you had heard tales of such a plane from the caravans that travel to the Gold Coast.'

'Tales. Legends. Of something left over from before the coming of the perverse. Something old, made of metal, that flies, higher than any bird, higher even than airships or balloons.'

'Where is it?' said the princess, pressing the serried teeth of her instrument of excruciation against the Moor's forehead, breaking the skin, the edged steel beading with blood.

'I think, in Dahomey—'

'You think?' I shook my head. 'No, no, that will *never* do.' The Moor emitted a high, pure, girlish scream as the princess began to saw. I covered my face with my hands.

Blind, I wished I could also be deaf, the princess, to go by the sound effects that accompanied the Grand Guignol being enacted for the greater benefit of the Moor's lucidity, making swift, sickening progress. As the screams abated, and the horrendous, grating noise of steel against bone ceased, I essayed a look. The Moor stared back at me, eyes glazed, the top of his skull in the princess's hands, a pink hemisphere of brain matter in full view. 'You must concentrate, sir.' I swallowed, less, this evening, with hunger than revulsion. 'I want to glean some facts, not hearsay.'

'You're oddly squeamish for one who's worked the slaughterhouse as long as you have, Duane.' She let the excised pate drop onto the floor. 'Alas, poor Sheik. But then, I didn't really know him at all. So – what the hell.'

'Leave the sad, bathetic Shakespearian allusions to me, goblin girl,' I said. 'Stick to the neurosurgery.' She walked to an open trunk and brought out a big, silver plate and a spoon; proceeding back to the table – dipping to peck me on the cheek before reassuming her position at the side of the human entrée – she leaned over, as if to treat the Moor to a display of her dark, fathomless cleavage. That shadowy rill between two super-voluptuous prominences: it was to be the last thing he would see. Positioned just below his right ear and using the spoon as a scoop, she deposited a portion of fresh, pink meringue onto the silver platter. 'Don't worry, Sheik, I know what I'm doing. I'm only taking a piece of brain that you can afford to lose.' She spoke true. The lovely dollop of neural fibre had been excavated from the vicinity of the optic chiasma, on the undersurface of the hypothalamus near the pituitary gland. If he had lost a cranial nerve, his cerebrum remained, for the most part, intact. He should have been thanking us. Instead, he chose to whinge.

'I can't see! I can't see!'

'As long as you can *hear*,' I said, my own qualms about witnessing this atrocity, in both aural and visual modes, overcome by the naggings of appetite. The princess served dinner, placing the meal between my fidgeting, outstretched hands, tossing the spoon onto the table with an involuntary tic of disgust. 'Now, where were we—' I picked up the spoon; tapped it against the side of the plate; grinned.

With a sound like the breaking of a giant's bones as he skydived into pavement from the top of an antique skyscraper, the door fell inwards.

'How boorish,' said the princess, standing akimbo in her blood-spattered lingerie, an indignant, fearsome if also pathetic sight, 'my partner was just about to dine.' A negress, human, and corpulent as a force-fed pig, fronted a squad of militia, some of them carrying black-market weapons that could have stopped even a revenant, no matter how effectively the first mouthful of spongy, coral-pigmented cerebrum had refreshed his working parts and invigorated his senses. Skipping forward, a stupid-brave cherry volunteering to go on point, the negress lifted her arm, an accusing hand pointed at the filleted head with such vehemence that I suspected lightning was about to flash from the fingertip and reduce the shocking, vandalised bust to ash.

'That's him! That's my husband!'

'How affecting. He just dropped by to share his thoughts. Strange, how he never mentioned you.' And he did share; the rush had peaked some moments before; but the afterglow left surety that what the woman said was true. She had probably followed him, suspicious that his night-time wanderings might not be as business-oriented as he had averred. 'You can have him back, if you like, *Hausfrau*. It's all right, he's been quite faithful. In fact, in his present customised state he'll discover philandering to be more difficult than it might have been in the past. Say *thank* you.'

'Oh, my God! What have you done to him, you bitch, what have you done!' The woman tore at her short, plaited hair and then succumbed to a jag of hysterical weeping. I looked at the princess and shrugged.

'Have you got any spare change to try to convince these guys' ~ I hitchhiked in the direction of the militia ~ 'to look the other way?'

'Fat chance.'

'I'm a respected man,' said the Moor, struggling against his bonds, 'a respected human citizen of Tanjah.'

'Ah, come on guys,' I said to the stony-faced militiamen, most of whom, like most of the power brokers in this city, followed the Way of the Shark. 'You heard him. A *human* citizen. We tribespeople should stick together.' One of the sharks stepped forward, a weapon similar to the one that had incapacitated me in Albracca staring at me like a big, cybernetic phallus. 'Oh yes, I know you, don't I, my beauty,' I whispered to the hermetic gun.

'I'm glad,' said the militiaman. 'Because we know you, Mr Duane Duarte. You're a revenant, aren't you? Not born to the perverse, but made. A convert, you might say. Yes, we even have a file on you. A very *big* file. But we're not prejudiced here in Tanjah. In many ways, you see, I *sympathise* with your plight. But it's as the human man

says. He really does carry some weight. He's sort of—'
The militiaman surveyed the ruined skull held in the
impromptu stocks; kicked the sawn-off brainpan across
the floor. '*Important*. A member of the city council, a
representative of human interests, from Atlantis to the
Near East. This is an International Zone, monsieur. I cannot make concessions to favouritism. I'm afraid I have my
orders.'

'A representative of human interests?' said my outraged aristocrat. 'Rubbish. I mean, Tanjah belongs to the
confabulated, not humankind. Or is trade all you care
about? The trade in booty and flesh that keeps Atlantis
smiling? Come on, Duane. Let's talk this over with some of
our people. Not everybody in this city cares about whether
some human gets de-brained.'

'Yeah,' I said, getting up. 'Let's go and get this sorted
out. We need to deal with things in a *civilised* fashion.'
It was all bravado, of course. Despite the militiaman's
strained effort at comradeship, I knew that what we had
done was illegal even by the warped standards of those
with whom we claimed consanguinity. Any full-blooded
member of the perverse would have been punished for
such a crime; and we, who were made, or who were half-
human, could not expect a plea for special consideration
to fall on anything other than cynical ears. 'No hope once
they take us to the Kasbah, but I think it fair to say,' I said,
as quietly as I could as the princess approached me, her
face conceding our defeat, 'that we enjoy a modicum of
rapport with our captors.'

'Mmm. These sharks *do* seem encouragingly anti-
human,' she replied, in a low, mousy whisper. 'We'll go
with them and, and ... *extemporise*.' Another militiaman

came forward; reached for the flintlock that protruded from her garter; took it and tucked it under his wide, scaly belt. She looked after it with self-reproach, as if she had found herself forced to give up her only child. I placed a consoling hand on her arm; it was a beautiful pistol, the barrel – attributed to Peter Opel of Regensburg – engraved with the Seven Deadly Sins, the stock veneered with carved ebony that enclosed panels of staghorn carved into floral scrolls, hunting subjects and numerous studies of Oriental maidens. The princess had sequestered it from the Duino armoury; it was one of the few things she still possessed that reminded her of her ties to the dispossessed, imperial houses of Europa. We held out our wrists and allowed ourselves to be manacled. As we were escorted through the door I turned to see whether the Moor was rejoicing in his liberation; I discovered he was not; moreover, still in the home-made stocks, his agonies seemed to have been intensified by having to submit to a harangue from his wife. 'Goodbye, Sheik,' called the princess, who had likewise turned, as curious as I was to discover the ultimate fate of the man of whom I carried an abstract in my veins. 'Love is a minefield. Next time, proceed with care.'

We were led downstairs and then through the kitchens, where the staff, overcoming their initial surprise and fear, soon gathered around us like autograph hunters. The militiamen pushed them aside with their batons and firearms. We exited into an alley off the Grand Socco; and as we did so a cloud of insect babies, recently hatched from a lacerated web that hung from where the alley terminated in a chaos of barbed wire and trash cans, buzzed about us, their delicate, multi-hued wings chafing at our exposed flesh. I batted them away, momentarily considering that the annoyance they caused the militia might provide cover for an escape; but the brood, almost as soon as it had attacked us, flew on, soon to settle in some dank area of the city to grow within weeks into men who would all compete with each other for the honour of servicing a she-spider. I spiked that notion of escape; I would come up with something else, later; but the princess had her own ideas. 'They're on their way, Duane. I just know it,' she said. With hushed breath, she called upon the invisible. '*Every Angel is terrible. Still, though, alas! I invoke you, almost deadly birds of the soul...*' But the air was as naked of divine beings as it had previously been swarming with insects. With pistols at our backs, we were herded into the street where an armoured wagon awaited to transport us out of the Medina, the plumed, bombazine-draped stallions – fit for the most luxurious of funeral hearses – stamping their hooves as if anticipating our demise, a drum-roll to accompany a walk to the gallows. We boarded the wagon; the thick, wooden doors slammed behind us; we sat down. Outside, a boy walked up to the single window that punctuated the gloom of our captivity; put his face to the iron bars.

'Something special, *mi amigo*? Something *perverse*?' And then there was the crack of a whip and we were on our way. In the cramped space I struggled to negotiate myself into a position that enabled me to look out onto the streets; saw the boy disappear into the confusion of parked camels, herb stands, fruit peddlers and stalls cooking lamb kebabs that surrounded the square. We thundered along the rue Sidi ben Raissouli. Above us, moonlit houses painted white and pale blue and purple stretched up the hill to the Kasbah towards the *porte-cochère* that was called Bab el Assa. Beyond that gate, walled off from the Medina, on the highest point of the city, was the palace of Dar el Makhzen. A complex of buildings that was the former home and citadel of the sultans, it stood in the centre of the Kasbah.

In a wing called Dar ech Chera were the law courts.

'Sit,' said the magistrate, in the suave tones of a ranking wolf.

'I'm not a cat, you know,' said the princess, 'I don't do all that obedience-school stuff.' The wolfman regarded her with cold disdain. 'Okay, okay, look – I'm sitting. I'm sat.' She lowered herself into a frozen surf of white fur, a circular rug that had been placed before the podium behind which the magistrate and his staff prepared to judge the extent of her guilt. Kneeling, thighs pressed tightly together, she reclined on her heels, the long stilettos of her shoes creasing her pale, exposed buttocks. 'There, is that better?'

'Ratgirls,' muttered the magistrate to the clerk on his left, 'they have no sense of propriety. Now a cat—'

'A cat understands the virtue of submission,' said the clerk.

'Quite so.' His brow furrowed, each wrinkle testifying that he was aware that a cat's submissiveness was but the flip side of her criminality. 'Name?' he barked, suaveness giving way to causticity, the bitter moodiness that gripped all wolves when they considered their hopeless love for their treacherous, feline counterparts. The princess looked askance to where my projected form glowed, an aureate spectre fracturing the little room's shadows, though on a frequency only her peculiarly sensitised retinae could appreciate. One of her eyes was bruised, her corset and stockings ripped, her bedraggled appearance testifying that she had undergone a lengthy and unpleasant interrogation; but her look was defiant; and her tail, coiled on the rug, its barb covered in a leather sheath, trembled, in agitations of menace, like a cobra that has had its nest disturbed.

'I am Princess Frenzetta von Thurn und Taxis-Hohenlohe. And if you send a messenger to my house – that is, Castle Duino – you will find that my family will be eager to open up diplomatic channels with your ruling council in order to overcome this misunderstanding.' The magistrate gave a wry smile.

'If a rat can be a sheep, then you'd be a black sheep, I suppose, Princess Frenzetta. I happen to know that your family refuses to have anything to do with you.'

'You've heard from my family?'

'Age?' asked the magistrate, with seigneurial disregard for her anxious query.

'Seventeen. I asked you a question, Mr Magistrate.' The wolf huffed and puffed. 'I'm not a black sheep, and I'm not a little piggy, either. Now what about my house?'

'An insolent girl,' he said, first to the clerk who occupied his right flank, and then to the clerk on his left. 'Insolent, insolent.'

'But not, magistrate, an insolence inflected by that rather charming brazenness we have come to expect from a cat.'

'Not at all, not at all. This one is unfamiliar with the rules of the game.' He folded his hands together and laid them on the table, leaning forward to communicate the zealousness of his disapprobation. 'Many young women pass through this room – you understand, of course, that my authority extends only to the female of the perverse; there are other courts for the arraignment of men – and not one species of young lady, fishgirl, snakegirl, birdgirl, etcetera etcetera, and yes *catgirl*, has ever given me so much difficulty as those girls who follow the Way of the Rat.' He settled back in his high-backed chair, seemingly refreshed by this verbal catharsis. 'Now let us proceed. Height?'

'What news do you have of my family?' The magistrate slapped his cheeks with the palms of his hands, the impact forcing his lips into a fish-like pout; and then, letting his fingers slip under his spectacles to press upon his eyelids, he sighed, tremulous, as if trying to defuse the ticking bomb set to rip apart his tear ducts.

'Your mother and father are both dead. Killed by' – he took off his spectacles; scratched amongst the papers he had before him; held one sheet close to his reddened eyes – 'by "goblins", it seems. The rest of your family – you had a sister and a brother, yes?'

'A sister, brother, an aunt and Baron Cassirer, my cousin.'

'Well' – he let the paper fall to the tabletop – 'they've all been killed. Castle Duino was overrun some years ago by a huge rat army that crossed the Adriatic from Albania. Europa – so many rats. A veritable continent of goblins!'

The princess's albescent skin grew so pale that it became almost translucent.

'Your family: they were bad people,' I mouthed, catching her eye so that I could offer some mute token of condolence. 'They rejected you.'

'They were *my* family,' she said. 'They were all I had.'

'You have me.' She lowered her head, meta-morphosing, suddenly, from haughty rat to submissive, slavegirl cat.

'I have you, oh yes, I have you, Duane Duarte. Someone I can die with, sick and alone in some flophouse in Nowheresville.'

'Who are talking to?' said the magistrate.

'Myself.'

'Well and good. Just hold that pose. That's right. Let your hair unravel and cover your face; and keep your head inclined towards the floor. Now, we'll try again. Height?'

'Four feet eleven inches.'

'Good. Measurements?' Giving up, it seemed, the good fight against the inevitable, and surely drained by the news that Duino, its bad fight having gone to worse, had at last been overrun by rats, the princess drew back her shoulders, the rope which secured her wrists behind her back cutting into her tendons as she flexed her shoulder blades with intense, exhibitionistic effort. The corset's stays creaked and then snapped, the whalebone conceding victory to the triumphalist breasts, super-abundant flesh bursting forth with a kind of fanatical fanfare in celebration of the doctrine of breasticular self-determination.

'34EE-22-35.'

'Ee-ee!' laughed a clerk, grasping the bib of his robe between the thumb and index fingers of both hands to make of it two conical protuberances of cotton. 'Ee-ee! Ee-ee!' Through a chink in the white shag of hair that covered the princess's face I saw a tear trickle down an inflamed cheek.

'You bastards,' said my lips, though there were none to interpret, 'leave her alone. All this cat stuff: name, age, height, measurements. She's not your plaything, she's a princess, a Europan noblewoman who deserves respect!'

'Ee-ee!' continued the boorish clerk, relinquishing the pantomime with the robe to clap upraised fingers to either side of his head in imitation of rodent ears.

'Quiet,' said the magistrate, for whom the equation of a rat's breast dimensions with her sexual war cry obviously constituted a tired joke. With sombre regard, he stared at the princess's jutting bosom, as if he were taking that proud, hubristic display of carnality into account as he prepared to issue sentence. 'I will now' ~ he coughed ~ 'read out the charge. Princess Frenzetta, you have been found guilty of kidnapping, assault with a deadly weapon and grievous wounding. It is the verdict of this court that you therefore be transported to Atlantis, thereafter to labour in servitude for the rest of your natural days.'

'What!' The princess's neck performed an involuntary whiplash, flinging her dishevelled hair free of her face. 'It was a *human*, for God's sake!' She looked at me, incredulous, as if I might confirm that a practical joke was being played.

'This city is overly concerned with things human,' I said, miming, my lips benumbed with a terror I refused to allow her to see. 'It's business, I guess. The transatlantic trade. No solidarity amongst tribespeople here.'

'That's comforting, Duane.' The magisterial panel ignored her; perhaps they thought, in her panic or despair, that she had taken to blathering to an imaginary friend.

'The prisoner will remember that she is *half*-human herself,' said the magistrate, with some satisfaction. 'The sentence, in such circumstances, seems entirely appropriate.' There was the sharp concussion of a gavel against wood. 'And now the prisoner may rise.' The princess acquiesced as a guard stepped forward and helped her to her feet.

'Nobody ships me into slavery,' she said as she was escorted towards the door. 'I'm the last of my line, the heiress of Castle Duino. Nobody—' But she was silenced by the vigour with which the guard – another wolfman – performed his duty, ushered out of the courtroom with a speed that precluded all attempts at protest while leaving her vulnerable to the sly pawings that were a guard's sole consolation for working a shift in the oubliettes.

I had been too long discorporate. With my fleshly body's exhaustion tensing my umbilical into a brittle towline that tugged distractingly at its astral *doppelgänger*, I relaxed, allowed myself to be reeled in, a rushed slide show of the icons of incarceration briefly entertaining me with its dismal flurry of bars, locks, cells, straw mattresses, naked candles and naked flesh. And then it was if I was a speck of dirt, a leaving of scum being whirled, clockwise, then widdershins, down a cosmic plughole. The maelstrom bottomed out in darkness; I was alone in the great bone castle of my skull, once again wrenching at reluctant controls, struggling to set my self in motion.

The giddiness subsided. I opened my eyes; sat up. Separated from the general population of the prison, my cell was disturbed by neither sound nor percolation of air. However accustomed I had become to the monastic confines in which I had resided while in Albracca, the austerity of my current abode – combined with its dampness, filth and gloom - reminded me that the grave that I had unnaturally cheated was, perhaps, about to reclaim me, and that jesting death was ready to have the last laugh. The tomb-like walls seemed anxious to crush, to wring the last drops of ichor from my big, hunched frame. Above, the cell's trapdoor revealed, through cracks splintered with liverish illumination, the observation platform; every half-hour, a guard's feet would resound on its rotting wood as his patrol took him to this lonely section of the dungeons. Stretching, so that I sat with my back against the slimy bricks, I unbuttoned my shirt and examined myself. My sweat-soaked torso was covered in fungi, so that it resembled marshland overgrown with teratoid mushrooms. I should, I thought, have made sure I digested more than a mouthful of my last meal; it wouldn't be long - given the exacerbation to my system wrought by my most recent bout of astral projection - before decomposition started in earnest. A scraping noise distracted me from my morbid introspection and I looked to the grille opposite. Partly obscured by straw, it occupied a space I feared too big to prevent one of the princess's animal forebears from intruding upon my privacy. I manoeuvred myself onto my hands and knees; crawled across the cell; and had just raised my fist ready to squash the invasive beast when the grille clattered into the cell and the tiny head of an old woman pushed its way through the rectangular cavity to look up at me, her mouth wide, toothless and stinking of gin.

'Mrs Herzog?' The dwarf wriggled, extricating her shoulders from the grim pothole; the waist and rump followed, oozing like a newly hatched grub; and then, with astonishing agility, she fell onto the floor and in the same motion turned head over heels until she stood on her feet. Covered in grime, black as a little, orphaned chimney sweep, the formidable minikin crossed her arms and addressed me with rustic imperiousness.

'I hope you're pleased with yourself, Master Revenant. My mistress is about to be sold into slavery and all because of this ridiculous dream of flying to The Moon! A dream *you* have infected her with!' She reined in her temper, conscious of the surprise and disorientation her appearance evoked and willing, at least temporarily, to offer assuagement. 'It's a trick I learnt from the princess,' she said, nodding towards the modest aperture left by the displaced grille. 'It's in her blood, to slither through the deep, dark intestines of the Earth. Just like the one who fathered her, a goblin who lived in the sewers and man-holes beneath Trieste. When she was a child, she often had me join in her games, wriggling through the castle's walls, under its floorboards and into its plumbing. She has that natural suppleness that the rodent people have. I may be old, but I still remember those days. And so does my body.' I brushed a little soot from her hair.

'You don't expect me to fit into *that*?' I said, pointing at the hole.

'Of course not. I came here because I've come to an arrangement with the Atlantean slavers who have pur-chased you.'

'You bribed them?'

'Don't be foolish, Master Revenant, where would I get the money? No; I made them a wager.' I squatted, in an effort to bring my eyes level with those of the decrepit maidservant's; but though I had lowered myself onto my haunches as far as I was able, I still looked down upon her from an eminence of several inches; I stooped further, in order to pry loose the facts – by sheer terror, if necessary.

'And what did you wager?' I said, a little frightened myself by the terrible images of putrefaction mirrored in the depths of her pupils, images that presaged my doom.

'You are something of a scientific curiosity to them. They are eager to see a demonstration of your worth as a fighting machine.'

'And what does that mean, Mrs Herzog?'

'It means that they wish to pit you against one of their best warriors to see what will prevail, the *perverse* or *normalacy*.'

'Weapons?'

'Swords.' I relaxed a little; without appropriate weaponry, no man, human or confabulated, was a match for a *wusha*; perhaps this wasn't such a hard bargain after all. 'If you win, you and the princess are released.'

'And if I lose?'

'The princess remains a slave.'

'I, however, would be dead.' I lifted my hands into the air, in imitation of a pair of scales, as if to weigh my options. 'But as the princess often reminds me, I'm dead already, so what the hell. The main thing, of course, is to free your mistress.'

'Of course, revenant.' She dipped her head and looked along the vent that offered a conduit to the outside world. 'And now I must inform Princess Frenzetta.' She gripped the sides of the ingress with both hands and eased her head and shoulders through the opening. 'Please remember to replace the grille,' she said, as her feet disappeared into the darkness. 'You will be called in the morning. Try to rest and gather your strength. My mistress's liberty depends on your prowess. Remember that.' I picked up the heavy piece of criss-crossed iron and replaced it in its original location. The rustle of rags, the slithering of greasy, old flesh in the vents and shafts that ran through the prison's ancient superstructure, died away and I was again alone.

I laid down to rest. And my sleep was undisturbed by nightmare. For instead of counting sheep, I had told myself, again and again, that any single Atlantean, no matter how heavily armoured, would, if he wielded only a sword, have little chance of defeating one such as myself; telling myself this had lulled me into a deep and almost peaceful slumber. If I did dream, I think it was only of the land where we hoped to find an absolute rest, a final sanctuary, a moony place of violet seas and pale-blue skies where, lazing on a beach, the soughing waves would tell me, again and again, that I was in paradise.

They were catgirls, mostly, since the demand for the pleasures they offered – as the sophisticated pets of rich women, or as the sex toys of men – meant that they brought something like $200 a head on the auction blocks of Ellis Island. As I passed, my shackles clanking on the concrete floor, each prisoner held herself flush against the chromium bars of her cell and purred in an irony of longing; but beneath the irony, beneath the mocking leers and the knowing glances, the shared folklore of what I was and what I could not give did nothing to alleviate each cat's want or modify the compulsive rituals of her desire; I sneered at them, returning their ironic assault with a regard that I hoped possessed a sting as powerful as that secreted within the princess's tail.

The princess. I had thought about her ever since we had been segregated at our arrival in Dar el Makhzen. Each face squeezed between the gleaming bars, each tongue tip orbiting an ellipsis of strawberry-red lips, recalled to me her detestation of her feline sisters; and my scowl – I entered into, I suppose, a kind of psychic union with her prejudices – intensified as I cast my thoughts to wherever she might be held, the viciousness of my hooded gaze driving the girls to the backs of their cages. There, they took refuge on their pallets or else behind garbage heaps of powder-puffs, lipsticks and tubs of rouge, the accoutrements of superfemininity that had been discarded by previous occupants, cats by now doubtless enslaved in Metropolis, New Charleston and Caracas, or else one of the cities in the deep, unsparing South, even unto Patagonia. Hissing at me from the darkness, their black skin blending with the shadows that lay to either side of the shafts of light that fell from above, a few of the braver prisoners ventured to address me.

'We know all about you, dead man. They're going to send you over the sea, far, far away, to pick cotton in the fields of Atlantis.'

'Maybe he'll be put to work in a chain gang.'

'Maybe he'll be put to work in the mines. He's got a little goblin friend who could teach him something about mines.'

'Maybe he'll get lucky. Maybe he'll be a houseboy.'

'Or even a butler. Tee-hee, won't he look funny dressed as a butler?'

'They say he's special. A marvel of engineering. He'll make quite a collector's item, don't you think?'

'How much for him, I wonder? A dollar, a dollar fifty?'

'Who'll give me two dollars, then?'

There was a scream. The heavily armed guards who walked in front and behind me stopped dead, their heads swinging ninety degrees to lock into attitudes of dislocated inquiry.

'Seems you brought the house down,' said one wolf-guard, sniggering.

'You never can tell,' said the other, obviously more experienced and bored by a phenomenon he had witnessed many times before. 'The strangest things set them off.'

'Never known the sight of a zombie to bring a girl to crisis.'

'Zombie? I've seen cats go critical at the sight of a *human*, would you believe?' said the man of the world. 'Who can tell what goes on within the fetid confines of a cat's brains?' His companion nodded in sage agreement.

Inside her cell, limbs entwined through its bars as if she were a soldier cut down while attempting to breach an enemy's barbed-wire fortifications, the catgirl who had seconds before died in the violent abandon of erotic fulfilment – her back and neck broken, her lips white with froth – fixed me with her sightless gaze, as surprised by death as she had surely been by finding that her orgasm, that had so long waited for her, like a stranger biding his time in the shadows of an alley where she regularly walked home from work, had been precipitated by one such as me.

'I don't know what you've got,' said the still-nodding guard, 'but it sure had an effect on *that* pussy.'

'Walk on,' said the other.

'*Don't know what he's got?*' Mimicked a disembodied voice, its feline owner lost to the darkness. 'He's got venous leakage. Erectile dysfunction. Pooh! He's a revenant. And that means the meat between his legs is as dead as the rest of him.'

'Ignore her,' said the guard.

'I have, dear boy,' I replied, whistling a little Eastern melody between my teeth. 'I already have.' And we proceeded down the corridor, this revenant trying to suppress a strange, welling sensation of pride at having at last, however inadvertently, brought a woman satisfaction. It was appropriate, perhaps, that the only woman I had pleasured had died of my attentions; I was a creature of death; the outcome could not, I told myself, have been otherwise. Still, my chest pushed against my torn, sweat-stained shirt, puffed up, as I was, with a grotesque narcissism, the conceit of a self-deluded, monstrously pathetic stud.

We left the rows of oubliettes behind and ascended a stairwell; it brought us, by way of several portcullises that were raised and lowered as we tramped from one stark, torch-lit landing to another – spiralling upwards through the prison's bowels – to the upper floors of the palace, offices that administered the trade in and out of the International Zone, as well as administering the city's seemingly arbitrary laws. Led into a suite – there was suddenly a plethora of people about, humans and confabulated alike – I was taken to stand before a high, imposing set of doors. A secretary – a catgirl who had earned provisional freedom, I suspect, less by office skills than by an obliging mouth – whispered into a voice-tube and then smiled, wickedly, indicating that I should be allowed in. The guards swept open the doors and, grasping me by either arm, urged me into the corporate headquarters of what, if the brass plaque outside had been correct, was the *Normative/Perverse Import/Export Co. (Tanjah)*.

'Good morning,' said the Atlantean seated behind the massive desk. Inlaid into the wood, in front of the blotter on which he shuffled and rearranged papers, was a mother-of-pearl scroll; the letters etched into it read *Admiral John Duval*. Great swathes of sallow effulgence fell from between the shutters of a jalousie. The Admiral, intent on studying a column of figures, chose to delay acknowledgement of my presence. I took the time to orientate myself. Outside, enclosed within Dar el Makhzen, was the Garden of the Sultan, a formal Andalusian affair with orange and lemon trees, palms and hothouses bursting with sickly flowers. The smell of jacaranda invaded my nostrils. Beyond lay the bay and the streets of the Medina, dotted with glimmering tiled roofs and minarets. There was a splash; an explosion of giggles. I craned my neck. Directly beneath the balcony, sharkmen clipped across a swimming pool, their dorsal fins flashing in the sunlight as they broke the surface in ritual mating displays; such displays were lost on their audience; for though the bikini-clad fishgirls looked on, admiringly, prone on platter-like sun beds, as if about to provide their confabulated cousins with a 'fruits of the sea' lunchtime buffet, I knew from experience that those mermaids' sexual interests were focused entirely on the human fishermen whom they lured to their deaths in the Straits of Gibraltar; for a fishgirl required human blood in order to lay her eggs.

'Take off his chains,' said the Atlantean, sourly, without looking up. The guards complied, the irons, removed, taking strips of flesh with them. I stretched, flexing my spine and muscles, so that the slaver might perceive that I would present an interesting challenge to any champion he might care to pit against me. A saluki lay on the floor, chewing on a dark-veined bone, staring at me with anxious disfavour and growling, softly. At last, the Admiral deigned to meet my eye. 'He is indeed a fascinating specimen.' The little woman seated on the sofa clapped her hands in agreement. Mrs Herzog had worked a sartorial transformation on herself during the night; from raggedy Thumbelina she had metamorphosed into a porcelain doll that might have figured in the nurseries of the long-dead crowned heads of Europa. Scrubbed, scented, she was attired in a little girl's party dress, a concoction of emerald-green silk that boasted a puffed-out bodice and a corresponding bustle, lending her the profile of a garishly-plumed pouter-pigeon. Her hat was enormous and adorned with peacock feathers and ribbons. She emptied what remained of her refreshment; with a tinkle of fine china, set her cup back on its saucer and then set both on the teapoy.

'You are not, I hope, reneging on our little wager?' she said. The Admiral laughed.

'My own champion is, how shall I say, also something of a *colossus*. He has my full confidence.' He turned to face me. 'You. Zombie. The guards have explained what is expected of you?'

'They have. And I expect you to honour your commitments should I win.'

'Impertinent,' he said, glancing back at Mrs Herzog, his laughter unstoppable now.

'Impenitent,' added Mrs Herzog, punctuating his cachinnation with a few titters of her own.

'Imprudent,' concluded the slaver, his laughter

disappearing as suddenly as it had arrived. 'If you dare challenge my word as a gentleman again you'll be taken back to the cells. And your goblin friend will have only a life of servitude to look forward to.'

'At least his manners suggest the appropriate fighting spirit,' said Mrs Herzog. The slaver lowered his head in gracious acknowledgement of her perspicuity.

'You too are human, Madame, even if you are from a continent whose garden has become so blasted, so overgrown with the weeds of the perverse that, that—' Words disintegrated in his mouth, unable to satisfy his appetite for vituperation. 'I trust you, of course, to fulfil your obligations, just as—'

'Just as I trust you, sir. The property deeds have been deposited in a safety deposit box to which' – she lifted and held out for inspection the key that hung on a chain around her neck – 'to which I alone have access.'

'Property deeds?' I queried.

'To Castle Duino,' she said, smiling and lifting her brows, as if gently explaining the perfectly obvious to a retarded stranger. 'I had them forwarded from Zurich where they had been put into safekeeping by the princess's family before' – she coughed, holding a tiny handkerchief to her mouth – 'before their unfortunate demise. The princess, of course, authorised the transaction.'

'I could, of course, have used considerable powers of *persuasion* to have those documents forwarded directly to me,' said the Admiral. 'And, for that matter, signed into my possession.'

'But then I would have made sure,' said the dwarf, 'that every remaining noble household in Europa would know that you had obtained your title by torture.'

'I should not normally care about such things,' said the slaver. 'Europa. What is its opinion to me? But—'

'But you are an incorrigible snob, like so many self-made men. Though you would make a career of denying it.'

'The truth is, Madame, that the title would amuse me. It would, I think, prove something of a conversation piece at one of those interminable dinner parties that I am expected to attend when back home. But really, here, in Afric, I care too little about such a trinket to do more than treat it as an excuse for an equally amusing wager.'

He was being disingenuous, I knew; like most slavers, he was both despised in his home continent and respected as no more than an *arriviste* on this more forgiving side of the world. He wanted to become the heir of Thurn and Taxis, and he wanted the inheritance to be one as scandal-free, as untainted by blood, as could be devised. The wager seemed to be as straightforward a one as could be expected in our circumstances. However, neither Mrs Herzog nor I had apprehended that he would take steps, ignoble steps, to weight the odds implacably in his favour.

'And to show that I am giving you more than a fair handicap—' He gestured to one of the guards. They walked to the doors; opened them. I looked over my shoulder. Slinking towards me, the princess, in chain-mail brassiere and *cache-sexe*, a long white cloak trailing behind her, sashayed across the parquetry, her high-heeled sandals tapping out the percussive signature tune of super-feminine artifice. Her face was hooded with a cowl; as she approached the desk, she threw it back to reveal that since I had last seen her she had been given opportunity to wash, apply make-up and reconfigure her towering coiffure. Passing me, I noticed that, beneath the cloak, a sword was slung across her back. With the rightful heir of Duino slain in battle, it would matter little whether or not I bested his champion.

'She doesn't have any part in this fight,' I said.

'Quiet, Duane.' Gathering up the cloak and her tail with one arm, the princess set her naked buttocks down on the desk's edge; crossed her legs; and, displaying two little serrated rows of calcium, smiled at the momentarily discombobulated slaver, whose pretensions to civilised discourse were in danger of being punctured by her arrogant, insidious coquetry. He glowered at her with suppressed rage and desire. 'I insisted on coming along, isn't that right, Admiral?' Turning to look at me, the smile dropped off her face, as if it had been a cardboard smile, held on by an ineffective glue. 'You don't know what they're throwing at you, Duane. *I* don't know. But it's going to be an evil business, you can count on that. You're going to need all the help you can get.'

'Oh, my little, foolish bonbon,' said Mrs Herzog. 'Why are you doing this?'

'Madame,' said the slaver, 'I give you the advantage. And you protest?'

'If the revenant prevails, but she is killed in the process, how can I be said to have won the wager? No, sir, *you* have the advantage.'

'The contest shall take place before an audience of impartial observers who will ensure that all will be done properly.' And to whom you can later appeal, I thought, if there are any questions about the hereditary rights of Thurn and Taxis having been exacted from their rightful owner by anything other than by mutually agreed terms, no matter how savage those terms might be. The princess's smile re-established itself, this time adhering tenaciously to her face as if it, a delicate, spiritual essence lovesick for physicality, could not brook the prospect of again being divorced from its mode of expression. So beautiful, those modest, yet razor-sharp little teeth; so much superior to the heavy, mangled arrays of the sharkmen who disported themselves outside, whose over-furnished mouths ~ filled with teeth that seemed the size of combat knives ~ made their speech like that of village idiots perpetually gargling with a full flagon's flood of hydrochloric acid; and so much more chic, too, than the neat little incisors of cats, whose cutesy fangs were fit only for those too lazy for real vampire work; but then I was a rat chauvinist.

'It's the only way out, Duane. They threatened to put me in the men's section of the prison, and I don't think I'd last long there. It's filled with ratmen, and to them, I'm just an engorged, walking clitoris begging for stimulation.'

'My dear, my precious,' babbled Mrs H, 'this isn't the way I planned things at all.'

'Things are never the way *we* plan things, Herzog,' said the princess. 'But remember Admiral, we play this little game of yours, we go free, no strings, okay?'

'I would have no reason to keep you in custody. Besides, the audience before which you will perform would be most unhappy if, should you win, you were not to be released. It would spoil their day.'

'And your reputation,' said the princess.

Reputation. There was more at stake here than reputation. Life, liberty, the pursuit of happiness; that was the creed that would justify my death and the princess's slavery should I fail my makers and prove myself to be less than the perfect fighting machine promised by my blueprints. Life, liberty; no, not for her; and happiness only for humankind; for in Atlantis, a confabulated slave could not hope, isolated amongst humans and denied the perverse, to bear the vicissitudes of her existence without succumbing to despair.

'*We're ready,*' we said, with uncanny synchronicity, like identical twins who, since birth, had grown strangely disparate in appearance, but whose minds and affections now enjoyed a rapport that had only been heightened by the years.

Now, and at the hour of our death, Oh Lilith, let us, I prayed, be as one.

The journey, by airship, to the plains and valleys south of the Atlas Mountains, near Hammadu du Guir, where the land merged with the Sahara, had taken several hours. With the sun ready to set, the air cooling, the princess and I found ourselves standing in the centre of a sandy amphitheatre carved out of the surrounding dunes. The arena – an expanse of desert some hundred yards in circumference – had been preserved from erosion by wind shields of polyurethane, the manufacture of which had, in this hot slice of the lost world, long been the secret of Congolese alchemists; a secret that, like so many others, would soon be forgotten, blown away by the winds of the perverse, lost, like all else. A high electric fence demarcated the combat zone from the bleachers. I inspected our audience, a multitude of white-sheeted men, women and children a-buzz like sandflies about to feast on carrion. And I wished I could vault that thrumming, deadly fence and tear the spines of each man, woman and child from their respective owners. As the sun sank below the sea of sand, the desert turning from yellow to turquoise, a corresponding sea of torches was lit, the encircling flames like waves breaking against a strand that we, shipwrecked, would be unable to reach until we had met and defeated the mysterious creature of the deep, our challenger. As drums began to boom, heralding the start of the evening's cruel theatricals, the princess unfastened her cloak, letting it fall from her shoulders to the desert floor so that she might more conveniently bathe in the luxuriance of the temperate breeze that, after the sun's demise, had blown across the desert. She drew her sword, a scimitar whose damascene sinuosity was lurid with reflected torch-light; she swung it, scythe-like, as if mowing down ghosts, her imitative tail skirting over the ground to send up a restive spray of silica.

'What do you think?' she said. I cast my gaze from the top of her high-piled curls, ringlets and tresses, over her small, child-like face with its single polka dot to linger at where the delicate workmanship of her clavicles was contrasted by the bold *alto relievo* of her breasts, decorated and emphasised, if only perfunctorily protected, by the two thin strips of glitzy metal links barely wide enough to cover her nipples; continuing my voyeuristic journey, I checked out the taut rib cage; found it without flaw; made an evaluation of the stomach, abdomen and hips, the white belly offset by the minimalist V of the *cache-sexe*, that, along with the little high-heeled sandals – plinth to long, slim, columnar legs so at odds with the compact body – seemed, like the tin brassiere, to accentuate her vulnerable, all-but-naked flesh by mocking its own pretensions of impregnability. I had saved the tail for last, like a morsel pushed to the side of a plate, the sweetest, stickiest, most scrumptious part, so that I might enjoy it now, sucking out its visual pith at leisure.

'I said *what do you think*, Duane? What do you think of our situation, our chances? I mean, any ideas?'

'What do I think? I think you look beautiful,' I said. Oh, what a tail it was; a snake charmer's nemesis, hypnotic, lethal, it wiggled and jiggled, ready to kill the man who would attempt to tame it.

'That's not what I implied, Duane. *I was asking what you thought about—*' Her eyes narrowed, looking past me, as she chose to focus on the distant dunes, the atmosphere of procrastinated rape that already existed between us hopelessly muddied by the hothouse tension engendered by my own ocular panning of the corresponding dune-like bumps and declivities of her contours.

'Fuck me.'

'You know that's impossible. Besides, this is hardly the time or—'

'Fuck *me*.' She was staring above my head, her eyes, now screwed into slits, cranked to ever more extreme attitudes of elevation, to focus where, upon what? I spun about and was confronted by an apparition that seemed, at first, to be a skyscraper on the march, a dark tower of steel and concrete breasting the dunes; still distant, we were yet forced into craning our necks in order to comprehend its altitude. The ring of fire opened up to allow it to trundle through an opening in the electric fence; the opening was quickly sealed; and the princess and I were left alone with the enormous monolith, its argent skin flickering with the red night.

'Well, fuck me, too.'

'It's a mechanical man, Duane. Like they had in Albracca. But bigger. *Much* bigger.'

'Something left over from the days before The Abortion.'

'We've been set up. There's no way we can fight *that*.' The locomotive building, nearer now, its delineations backlit by the wall of flame, revealed itself to be a legless six-armed robot whose body – it resembled a Hindu idol amputee; Shiva in a wheelchair, perhaps – appeared to be screwed to a gigantic sledge propelled by tracks of iron. The torchbearers began chanting a desert mantra calling on victory for the faithful, victory for the worshippers of the great totem, the angry, old tribal god that connected them with their diseased past. Did their lyric utterances celebrate the unknown forces that motivated that great assemblage – sixty feet of steel ligaments, wheels, cables and gears – and send it crawling across the bald plains of the Sahara? Steam gushed out of the groaning sledge's exhaust, the robot's arms testing the air, tentacles probing the louring night like a super-heavyweight limbering up before a bout that would involve knocking down a couple of fairground palookas. 'Is it intelligent, do you think?' asked the princess. I looked up to where the robot's torso – the cylindrical tower of steel that was peppered with portholes, searchlights and embrasures – met the ovoidal head, an elongated shell of translucent plastic surmounted by frog-like eyes.

'In the old days there were things called cameras. Machines used them to see by.' I pointed towards the innervated mountain's summit. 'Notice those things coming out of its top? Yeah, maybe our friend over there can see us in the same way we can see it. And maybe that means it can think, too.'

'It *can* think, Duane, look!' I let my gaze follow the line of her extended arm and saw that the robot's egg-like head – softly glowing with a strange illumination – contained a man.

'It's like what I feel when I return to my body after an astral excursion,' I said, studying the little man, the homunculus, sitting behind his control panel, wrestling with the wayward machine that lumbered across the sand. The turret-head revolved on its axis in a jitter of nervous energy as he played to the crowd.

'That's what we have to fight, Duane, *that*, not the machine. We have to kill the pilot.' I unshouldered the great broadsword that I had chosen from amongst the axes, falchions, sabres, lances, pikes and spears that had been offered to me by Admiral John, and tugged it free from its leather encasement, throwing the sheath aside. The princess tapped the edge of her own weapon against that of mine – *ching!* – then raised her blade into the air. 'Duino!' she cried, always one for the melodramatic flourish. And then she became still, her last breath left to fester in her lungs, left so long her next words threatened to be expelled along with the kind of graveyard miasma that would taint her breath whenever she would steal an impulsive kiss from my cadaverous lips. But when, after long nauseous silence, she did speak, there seemed to be a fragrance in the air, a smell of springtime and fecundity at variance with the dry, hot desert scent that parched my nostrils. And utterly at variance with death. 'They didn't forget,' she said to herself. 'Even after all this time, they haven't left me.' Imposing a tracery of black veins, a tear coursed down her cheek, depositing sedimental mascara *en route.* She breathed deep, refilling her lungs, ribs straining against the taut skin, bust oozing, in a congestion of voluptuousness, over the lean, metallic constraints of her brassiere. '*Every Angel,*' she cried out, '*is terrible. Still, though, alas! I invoke you, almost-deadly birds of the soul...*' She scanned the arena, her eyes focusing on a line of circumference beyond that of the visible horizon. 'They're here, Duane. Can't you hear them? The angels, they're here.' She kicked off her sandals; turned three-hundred-and-sixty degrees on the balls of her feet. '*Terribilita,*' she said. 'It's just like when I was a little girl. They're back, they're back! Ah, I knew they wouldn't forget me.' Looking up at the colossus whose slow but relentless headway had brought it to a halt some ten yards distant, the tentacle-like arms unfolding and making as if they were about to reach out and snatch us from where we stood, the princess broke into a run, charging the robot's engine of locomotion. The sledge seemed a suicidal objective for any improvised commando raid, even one carried out by a platoon of heavily armed soldiers; but for a small, lone, half-naked girl, that great iron boot with its huge caterpillar tracks, its hellish gouts of steam, its flame-throwers and cannon – an arsenal that had suddenly popped out of embrasures along its flanks – seemed to represent a particularly deviant and exotic excuse for self-immolation, and one she seemed perversely overeager to embrace.

'Duino!' I shouted, running after her, for, of course, I was a creature of the perverse, too. The crowd roared with appreciation. Accelerating, my long strides allowed me to overtake her within seconds; it was imperative that I shield her from the barrage of flame and artillery that was to come; though, taking the lead, I regretted having to forgo the delicious sight of her pendular hindquarters, framed in the T-shaped presentation display of her *cache-sexe*. Bidding that fabulous cut of girl-meat *adieu*, I prepared to say goodbye to life, such as it was, as I charged the sledge – cannon opening up, peppering me with grapeshot – happy that my last thoughts would likely be dominated by a stubborn afterimage of the princess's callipygian fundament. I jumped; clambered up the bevelled face of the broad, hydraulic scoop that had ploughed through the desert leaving a rill of disgorged sand in its wake. I felt the princess's claws snag in my trouser leg, ascend, talons raking at my disintegrating thighs to then grapple with my back as I myself made an ascent, struggling against the iron gradient. I pulled myself over the lip of the scoop, jettisoning the princess with a dismissive twitch of my shoulder muscles; as I did so I was blasted by a concealed flame-thrower; the princess hid between my legs. I dropped my sword; tore off my clothes, flaming cotton thrown hither and thither, falling through the air to litter the sand. Soon I stood naked, burnished with third-degree burns, my decomposing flesh fired and hardened as if by a kiln employed to turn out bellicose ceramics. The princess looked up, her gaze assessing, first, possible damage to my genitalia and then, with a giggle of relief that my impotence was not irreversible, the effects to the rest of my body, almost as golden, now, as my projected flesh, and crisp as a crust of baked pastry. She sighed with admiration.

'Sometimes, Duane, you're just too titanic for words.' I picked up the broadsword and smashed its edge against the barrel of the flame-thrower that guarded the ladder leading to the robot's cockpit. The muzzle sliced off; I grabbed what remained with my free hand and twisted the metal into a curlicue, the last drops of the napalm with which I had been sprayed, and which had fortuitously acted as an astringent to my flesh's necrosis, bubbling at the place where the sword had sheared across the fire-breathing orifice, powerless to wreak further damage. 'Cooly-cool, tough guy,' said the princess, her aristocratic fustian gone demotic, as was often the case when she was in Valkyrie mode. 'Now help me up and let's go get the jerk upstairs.' The robot's arms were trying to reach us, snapping their pincers like castanets; but something prevented them from railroading us into their flamingo. 'It's the invisible people, Duane. They're helping us. They're running interference. Huzzah!'

The broadsword hanging from my wrist by its braided leather strap, I placed a foot on the ladder – no more than a series of indentations scored into the robot's hide – and began to climb, as quickly as I was able. Clumsy, as I always was when faced with negotiating such fussy pieces of apparatus, the princess soon began nudging me, the cusp of her hair, stiff and hardened with what felt like gallons of lacquer, pricking my perineum. Her claws made her adept at such tasks as this; but it was essential that I lead; for should the shadowy regions ahead prove booby-trapped or conceal other defences – a cathedral whose machicolations might surprise us with an upturned cauldron of boiling lead – the shield of my dead flesh would be her only protection. I felt a judder; looked down between my arms; saw that the ground was moving and that we, clinging to the sheer face of the cylindrical tower like mutilated, quadrupedal bugs, were being driven towards the bleachers. The crowd, each of whom seemed to be holding lighted matches in the air, was baying for the bloody consummation of our lives, oblivious to the danger presented by the rampaging machine. The light from the banked rows of fireflies intensified, the sledge rumbling over the swells and ditches that streaked the battle zone, snippets of Arabic, French and English rising above the generalised, hysterical outcry; but the flailing arms of our mechanical opponent failed to engage, either through the incompetence of the pilot or, as the princess had claimed, by way of intervention of some invisible, perhaps supernatural power. Pitched from side to side by the unevenness of the terrain, we continued our climb, moving with more urgency now, as small-arms fire from the crowd resounded through the air, the occasional sound of a ricochet – deceptively benign, almost cutesy, like the sound of an orchestral triangle being struck – warning us that the rules of combat in this contest were fluid and liable to any reinterpretation that would facilitate our demise.

'Help us, angels,' called the princess. 'Help us, spirits of Duino!'

There was a commotion, not so much in the air, but felt at a deep level of the psyche, an intangible flutter of joy that lay forever round a corner I would be about to turn all my life, but never would until life itself had left me; it was a bird-like commotion, of wings beating, brushing against my soul, the scorched stubble of my body hair bristling at the touch of ghostly feathers, becoming transubstantiate, vibrant with the song that issued from those invisible creatures that saturated time and space, but were not of it. As if every vein and capillary of my body had been filled with helium, I rose, borne by an updraught of pure gladness; the princess rose with me, both of us transported, not merely towards the hatch at which our Jacob's ladder terminated, but, emotionally, perhaps spiritually, completely out of ourselves, with such suddenness that I struggled to keep my astral body from stripping itself free of my corporeal flesh, with a finality and irrevocability that would take it beyond the confines of this world, beyond time and space, and into the overflowing heart of a terrible Love. I burst through the trapdoor head first, for a moment blinded by the accompanying shower of splinters. Shaking myself, I raised the broadsword over my head, quickly taking in my surroundings: a bubble of plastic, its curving walls covered in some kind of weird tek, a thick, translucent felt that made the cockpit seem like a madman's padded cell, yet gave a panoramic view of the outside; a single chair; a control panel of knobs, switches and dials, and a viewing screen upon which was projected, with a miraculousness that froze my muscles with wonder, a close-up of the arena outside. The pilot had jumped up from his seat and was cowering against the mahogany panel. The princess flew through the shattered opening in the floor and, floating in a manner reminiscent of a principal boy suspended in a wired harness, settled beside me; I sensed the angelic hosts take their leave.

'Your friends – I never really believed in them.'

'Please, don't hurt me!' whimpered the pilot. 'They made me do it. I've got nothing against the perverse, really I haven't!' I swung the sword once about my head then brought it down in an arc that was intended to split the man's head from pate to shoulder bone. '*Nooo!*' The human jinked and the sword crashed into the panel, powdering the cockpit with fragments of wood, glass and plastic; the lighting – emanating from no oil lamp, but from some unknown source – dimmed, a thunderbolt zigzagging out of the wreckage left by my swordplay and towards the ceiling, a like jag of energy pulsing up the blade, its haft, my arm conducting it and the concomitant explosion of pain into my feet, the soles of which seemed to tingle horribly with chittering, insectile life; and then it was as if twin armies of super-powerful ants had decided to heave me off the floor and toss me against the padded wall. I slid, tranced by the long blade, stuck fast in the block of mahogany, oscillating with the residuum of the kinetic violence that I had briefly loaned it.

'Take five, Duane. He's mine.' The princess hopped two, three steps towards her prey. The human tried to repeat the evasive manoeuvre that had only recently bought him a few more breaths of life; he laughed, as if his laughter, pitifully child-like, might solicit a reprieve; but the princess, expert in parting heads from bodies, was high on adrenaline and remorselessly intent on her task. The scimitar zinged, cutting through the space that had suddenly become a borderland dividing his life from eternity; blood spattered my face, warm and saline; and a decapitated head rolled across the floor, coming to a grinning halt between my feet.

'Zero charm,' said the princess, evaluating the remains of the summarily executed pilot. She let the scimitar slip from her hand and fall across the dead body. She looked me over, a perfunctory damage assessment that seemed to suggest the opinion that I was indulging a hypochondria. 'So how do we stop this thing?' She kicked aside the head. 'You can save *that* for later. Right now you can help me get that sword unstuck and—' A tremendous concussion; her legs buckled; the cockpit tilted; and she fell, hair unravelling, legs pointed upwards in blunt erotic semaphore, by my side. The view-screen showed that we had crashed through the bleachers, the catapulted forms of hundreds of humans, their *djellabahs* billowing, flapping, so they seemed like white birds made platinum by moonlight, cascading over the top of the battering ram of the sledge's iron scoop, the topmost aisles of the grandstand almost coming level with the big frogs' eyes that provided the video feed, the shocked faces of the audience looking directly into our own.

'Is this what television looks like?'

'That's not television, Duane. My tutor used to tell me about television at Duino. No; television's finished, this here's all done with *mirrors*.'

'I suppose you had something like it at Duino too, eh?' I had grown a little tired of her habitual cataloguing of privilege. 'Like all the porcelain, the clothes, the gold and silver, the—'

'As it happens, we did. At the top of one of the castle's turrets was a little room. Not unlike this. You would look into a hole in the floor – just like looking into a well, really, but all silver and filled with light – and you would be able to see what people were doing outside, in the gardens.'

'What kinds of things?'

'Oh, Herzog at her *aqua vitae*. Herzog canoodling with the gardener. Herzog pulling up her filthy skirts and peeing in the flower beds. You know the kind of thing. There was never much in the way of entertainment at Duino.' Another tremor shook the cockpit, threatening to pitch us through the smashed, gaping hatchway. 'On your feet, Duane.' The princess, more agile than me, had already managed to stand, despite the giddy lurchings that had her staggering from side to side, like a prodigiously effeminate cabin boy who had yet to find his sea legs.

I rose; pushed down on the princess's shoulders, forcing her, for her own safety, to sit; stumbled to the control panel, where, wrenching the sword free from the cloven wood – the cockpit resembling an execution chamber, replete with executioner's block, instrument of death, dead bipartite body and theatrical splashes of blood on the walls – I experimented with a few of the intact switches, grabbing what looked like a joystick in an attempt to guide the behemoth through the bleachers and out into the uncircumscribed night. The faces that had fixed us, by courtesy of the viewing-screen, with looks of terror and supplication, were now pressed, screwed, distorted, against the glass, as if imploring us to let them in, streams of blood trickling down the screen in homage to the crimson, abstract expressionist extravaganza that decorated the cockpit's walls. Blinded by the countless victims that were splattered across my field of observation, like flies mass-murdered on the windows of a coach, I surrendered to recklessness and pressed the joystick forward as far as it would go. The robot made a series of hiccupy jumps, its engine screaming, its gears seemingly about to snap like desiccated bones. There was an earthquake-like rumble as scaffolding crashed to the ground, and screams, piercing and rising above the screams of the engine, screams that accompanied the cloud of dust that rose through the yawning hole in the cockpit's floor, reverberated through my skull, like a chorus of steam-driven dental drills boring into my teeth, my nerves, my brain. First one body, then another – alive, dead, it was difficult to assess – slid from view, some leaving a trail of scratch marks in their wake where fingernails had unsuccessfully sought purchase, the scored glass channelling rivulets of blood. Perhaps it was my stoked imagination, but one of the last faces I was to notice sliding down the glass, like raw meat slipping off a chopping board, seemed to possess an uncanny resemblance to that of Admiral John Duval. I contemplated his wide, staring eyes, his rictus and smashed teeth, but was unable to essay a positive ID, distracted, as I was, by something in my peripheral vision; I turned; the princess had crawled to the hatch. The dust had cleared and, prostrating herself, she leaned over the edge of the splintered wood and peered out into the darkness.

'We smashed through,' she said. 'We're leaving them behind. We're rolling out into the open desert.' I knew that what she said was correct, for the screen had been cleared of enough flesh and gore to allow me to observe that a great expanse of nothingness had opened up before us. The robot began to reel and lurch more violently now, as it moved from the combed plain of the arena and encountered the undulating landscape of the limitless sands.

'I don't know how to stop it,' I said.

'Well, it figures. I guess you messed everything up with that big dumb sword swing of yours. Have you any idea in which direction we're heading?' I stared into the black heart of the view screen, its upper portion spangled with a handful of stars.

'As long as we're moving away from the slavers, I don't see the problem.'

'You don't see the problem. Problem is, Duane, we're heading out into the Sahara with no food and no water. Problem is, when this thing poops out...' The answer, unpleasant as it was, was best left unsaid; and we both lapsed into melancholy silence.

And we travelled like that, without maps or compass, across a terrain black, endless, unforgiving, for much of the night. The inevitable came towards morning; our mechanical man ran out of fuel; stopped; and when the sun rose, playing down on the sauna of our bubble-brained domicile, we abandoned ship; climbed down to the desert, there to take refuge in the shadows beneath the sledge. Lying on our backs, the iron roof of the robot's lame foot above us, we closed our eyes, each of us silently acknowledging to the other that the prospect of rescue, though slim, was still potent enough for us not to waive the opportunity of conserving our energy. Death: it didn't seem so bad at that moment. Nor at that place, amidst a moonscape of nothingness, beneath an emptier sky. Nothing. It had often seemed good to be nothing, a man without a name or a home. The only reality at such times seemed a great silent joy, a skipped heartbeat of pure happiness, an annihilation of self which prefigured a flowing into the unspeakable name that was all. It was good to be lost, to be as nothing, a speck of sand; it was good to be alone and not alone, a waif of the desert. I held the trunkless head of the princess's latest victim under my arm, determined to share it with her, as one might a coconut on a castaway's island, when thirst became unbearable.

I had a dream: a storm was blowing, covering the desert in a blinding cloud of sand. Suddenly, I knew it was no natural storm. The silica that bit into my flesh was intelligent. I had returned to the days of The War of the Liebestod, that sandstorm composed of robots as small as our recent adversary had been big; smaller, even, than could be detected under a lens. The malefic little machines tore at me, stripping the meat from my bones. I was being vaporised ... And then, as suddenly as it had appeared, the storm was gone. And so was the desert. I was a little boy, running along a cliff-top path, high above the Bay of Sistiana. This country. It was strange. I had never seen it before. And yet I felt at home. Where were the angels? Playing on the cliffs, I had looked for them all day, and now no longer quite believed what the princess had told me. Last night I had known their presence, but it was easy to doubt; easy, too, to shy from their seduction. Only those who are truly lost will be found, they had whispered; only those without a name, home, family, friends; only those called wolf, cat, rat, shark and revenant; the outlaws, the perverts; only they will come home at last to know that life and death are one. The princess was beckoning to me from the window of one of the turrets. I turned into the shadow of the castle walls, slipped between a portal whose door hung from a single rusty hinge, and leapt up the spiralling stairs. Puffing, holding the stitch in my side, I reached the topmost storey. The little room – circular, and filled with fusty junk and broken toys – was a forgotten attic which we had made our secret hideaway. The princess gestured, inviting me to join her at the round, indented structure that glowed with mellow light. How pretty she was in her grubby pinafore dress, her plaited hair decorated with pink, childish ribbons. *I'm a pink girl,*' she would often say. *'Flesh-pink, shell-pink, salmon-pink, shocking-pink, hot pink, coral, carnation – it's all the same to me.*' The princess looked into the well of light; and as I too studied the limpid depths of that magic pool I spied yet another example of pinkness: Mrs Herzog's buttocks as she took off on a canter astride the supine body of one of the domestics. The princess giggled. 'Oh Herzog,' she sighed, catching her breath. 'Oh darling Herzog, Herzog, Herzog.'

'Herzog?'

The sound of a dune buggy stirred me from my uneasy sleep.

'Is that you, my little bonbon? Is that really you?'

I scrambled out from beneath the sledge. The princess's maid had dismounted from her steam-driven tricycle and stood gazing up at me, her tiny form eclipsed by the shadows cast by the train of camels and their Bedouin drivers, and by that longer shadow, mine.

.•

'You waste your time searching for a spaceplane,' said our host, the Englishman whom they called Prester John. 'Such planes no longer exist. But there is, I am told, *another* way to reach The Moon.' The oasis sparkled in the brilliant rays of the early dawn. I ate the last of my breakfast – not as fresh as I might have wished – the salver, wiped clean with unleavened bread, reflecting the brutish contours of my regenerate countenance, the disgorged brainpan, put to one side, serving as a goblet for wine that, out of courtesy accepted, was beyond the abilities of my constitution to consume. White tents encircled us, their flaps up, our host's slaves busying themselves with preparations for the coming day. 'Between the Earth and The Moon is a bridge. It seems, on first sight, a bridge like other bridges. But it is not one made entirely of cable and steel. It is a *ghost* bridge. Stepping upon it, a traveller is carried instantly to his destination.' Prester John had offered to help us in our quest. He was, he had explained, a human who, disgusted with his own species, had chosen to associate only with the confabulated, leaving his country – the Dark Island, now a mere handmaiden, as he put it, to Atlantis – to himself become a follower, albeit one with an unmodified body, of the left-hand path.

'Not a *literal* bridge, then?' I said. Prester John laughed. 'A matter transmitter?'

'Correct.'

'Who do you think you're kidding?' said the princess. 'Things like that have gone the way of television and the automobile. They don't function any more.'

'It's true, the bridge *doesn't* function. Yet. At least, it doesn't function as a *matter* transmitter. But it *does* function as a device that transmits energy patterns.'

'And where is this bridge?' I asked.

'Atlantis,' he said. 'Metropolis, to be exact.' The renegade human cast a studious glance over my body. 'I have never seen a revenant before. Your leg—'

'This one?' I said. 'Yeah, I know, the skin tone's not the same as the rest of me.'

'Almost like the complexion of a Moor,' he said, in wonder, as he reached out and touched the flesh that showed through my ripped trousers.

'The necromancers would try to go for a match, but sometimes—'

'Sometimes,' chipped in the princess, 'sometimes they'd use anything they could get.'

'From what I have read of your kind, you are distinguished by more things than mismatched limbs. It seems that you can project an energy signature of yourself out-of-body, yes?'

'I can,' I said, seeing, now, that the tack of our host's conversation was designed to tease comprehension from my reluctant brain. 'The bridge – the transmitter – do you mean that I could cross over it, *through* it, while in a projected state?'

'It seems not unlikely. There is a certain cabal of runaway slaves operating in the nether regions of Metropolis that would welcome your co-operation.'

'Why?' said my suspicious, prickly little aristocrat.

'It is they who have rebuilt the transmitter. They, like you, are trying to migrate to The Moon. And they would, I think, be keen to recruit a scout to test the way ahead.'

'It doesn't sound at all *safe* to me,' said the princess.

'I dare say it isn't. But if you really want to get off-world this seems your only option. With your help,' he said, locking his attention upon me, 'they could have their transmitter *fully* functional within months.'

'With our help,' I echoed. 'To what do we owe *your* help.'

'To the wonderful afterglow that I will experience after shipping both of you West. I *do* so enjoy confounding our mutual enemies.' I looked at the princess, she at me, an exchange taking place of kinesic disquiet.

'So, this bridge. How do we get to cross it?' she ventured, still staring into my eyes as if into twin crystal balls, unsure of what future, if any, was to be found there.

'First, of course, you have to *get* to Atlantis. If I might suggest—' He clapped his hands; one of his cats set a tray of dates and olives before us. The princess helped herself to the fruits, forsaking her crystal gazing to instead eye our host, her face creased with a mixture of low expectations and high concern. Could we trust him? Like our recent captors, he too was a slaver; but Prester John boasted that he only traded in the flesh of volunteers, cat-girls who came to him in order to renounce their liberty by an act of free will, who sought enslavement as they sought all things that brought them nearer to fulfilling their erotic destiny. Though his activities would have made him unpopular with the confabulated, especially the jealous, possessive men who followed the Way of the Wolf, he seemed, for the most part, to have trimmed his sail to the gathering wind of the perverse, and, in his own way, was loyal to it. Personal inclination, or entrepreneurial fore-sight? I didn't know. But I felt he gambled much on the wind of perversity becoming a storm; his allegiance to humanity had been wilfully compromised; his long-term safety lay in humanity's fall.

'What might you suggest?' she said.

'That you put yourselves into my hands. I have plenty of contacts in Metropolis. Both amongst humans and confabulated. I can put you in touch with the right people. People who share my dream of seeing Metropolis subsumed by the perverse.' The cat who had served us backed out of the tent, her gaze fixed demurely upon the ground. The princess looked after her, eyes spitting hatred, a ratgirl contemptuous of any tribeswoman who could so willingly become the property of another. 'Of course, you'd have to go in disguise. You, Mr Duarte, for instance, could, with a certain amount of make-up and the right clothes, pass for an Atlantean soldier.'

'I suppose I could,' I said, 'I've done it before. I tell people I'm Special Forces. It's the height, you see.'

'And you, Princess Frenzetta, you could pass, with the right clothes, a pair of green contact lenses and—'

'Oh no, I don't want to hear it.'

'A cat. You just need the right attitude. Of course, we'd have to do something about the tail.'

'The tail?'

'It could be docked. I have surgeons who—'

'Oh, no, no, no, no, *no*.'

'We have to make sacrifices, Frenzy,' I said. I could not suppress a grin.

'But a *cat*, Duane. It's too bad.'

'It's simply that the vast majority of female slaves exported to Atlantis *are* cats.'

'I would pose as your master,' I said.

'Yeah, well, don't get carried away, Duane.'

'I would pay all your expenses,' said our host. 'It always gives me considerable satisfaction to undermine the normative world, however so small or petty the triumph. To know that I had smuggled two such superlative examples of the perverse across the Atlantean border would give me a glow that would last for weeks. Please say you'll accept my assistance.'

'We will. Yes, of course we will.'

'*Duane!*'

Mrs Herzog, half hidden in the back of the tent,

began to sing a drunken *Lied*. The harem of catgirls who sat at the back of the tent rose; began to sway their hips to the music, their bellies undulating as the crone's voice mercilessly attacked our ears, like a threnody presaging war.

But it was to be another seraglio that, two months later, heralded our personal *Liebestod*, the merciless confusion of despair and happiness, life and death.

LOST IN
ATLANTIS

Act II. A garden in Pasha Selim's palace, Turkey. The sun is setting. At the back of the stage, the buildings of the harem; adjacent, the quarters of Osmin, the major-domo. Blonde, the maid of Constanze – both girls have recently been captured by pirates and sold into slavery – is warning Osmin to stop bullying her. Europan girls – even confabulated girls, she explains – are won by tenderness, not by the imperious demands of a human slave-master. She sings of the fall of Cathay, of how those tribespeople who have escaped enslavement will make their way slowly West, to liberate their brothers and sisters who have fallen prey to Atlantis. Osmin slaps her face.

I studied the princess with glances fitful and careless, unwilling to pay her the courtesy of direct eye contact lest those in the opposite boxes, or perhaps one amongst the audience in the stalls, should look across or up and discover an Atlantean man bestowing undue respect on the slavegirl who accompanied him.

'He's late,' she said. 'In his letter he wrote that he'd be here before the end of Act I.'

'Quiet, slave,' I said, rather enjoying our public role-play.

'Take care, Duane,' said she, the she-Spartacus lurking beneath her disguise surfacing with a flush of revolutionary ardour. 'I'm not some cat you can order about, you know.'

'But, my love, you *do* look it. And that's just as well, considering that so many men-about-town here have a catgirl accompanying them. Now, will you try to act the part, please? We can't afford to be unmasked.'

'*You* certainly don't seem to have much trouble getting into role, *mein herr*. Methinks Duane Duarte is beginning to enjoy being the slave-master just a little too much. Maybe it's the itsy-bitsy human bit left inside you.' On entering the box she had dissembled respect by ensuring that she sat a little back from me; and each glance I awarded her necessarily meant that my eyes strained at their orbits to fully appreciate her new-found feline charms. The turned-down gas lamp cast green tongues of irritable light across her face, counterpointing her green, darting eyes, the tint of their irises fabricated with ocular prostheses of stained glass. Her customary pallor had been relieved by a generous application of foundation, a thick layer of caramel that gave her the sun-kissed complexion of a pampered cat. Her hair had been dyed peroxide blonde, then streaked and pomaded, the mane vulgarly styled to fall down her back in a chignon of plaits and curls, in front, to terminate in a frisette that jostled with the inch-long spikes of her false eyelashes. The beauty spot had been de-emphasised; the lips, enhanced with collagen, treated with several coats of gooey, lustrous paint that made it seem as if she was disemboguing a mouthful of masticated plums, or else the remains of a small, half-eaten mammal. They were deep frozen in an insolent pout; lips from the bottom of the icebox; lips that promised never to melt. Her clothes? While in Cathay and Europa, and before our mis-adventures in Afric, she had always affected the mock

eighteenth-century fashions popular in those otherwise
disparate parts of the world. But here, in Metropolis, she
had adopted the look of an Atlantean woman, albeit one
who is an imported sex toy. Human females – if the public
mood could be rightly gauged from the letter columns of
the newspapers – had lately made a concerted hullabaloo
about the sartorial pretensions of cats, noting that their
overindulgent masters had made it difficult to tell a slave
from a mistress, especially when that slave was in her
Sunday best. At such times she was the *grande cocotte*;
and the princess, tonight, appeared one such creature.
There was, for the princess, of course, a wholly practical
dimension to her wardrobe. To be Atlantean was to abjure
the eighteenth century in favour of the nineteenth – say,
the 1880s – and cover oneself in a cuirass bodice and a
long, voluminous skirt bunched at the back into a bustle;
and the bustle, supported by ribbed, metal bands (working
on a pivot so that it was raised when sitting down and
sprung back into place when the wearer got to her feet)
gave the princess a fortuitously convenient place to
conceal her tail. The dress – its crisp, green *mousseline de
soie* matching her eyes and the virescent, gas-powered
illumination – rustled as she fidgeted in her seat, her
psychological profile showing as surely as the frothy hem
of her petticoats; and that profile revealed that here,
lacking only her dunce's cap, was a reluctant recruit
to submissiveness who would surely have been curtly
expelled from any school for slaves.

'Now, now, Frenzy, I *said* be a good little slave cat.
We've gleaned too many curious looks this evening.'

'The concierge at the hotel – she's got it in for us. I'll
put the horrid woman's eyes out, you see if I don't.'

'I was talking about the busybodies *here*, in the opera house.'

'I'll put *their* eyes out, too. What kind of people are they anyway? This is a *dreadful* production. Why, at Duino, we had—'

'Keep your voice down.' Several pairs of opera glasses were no longer trained towards the stage, but pointed in our direction. 'It seems we have to suffer a degree of attention here. But at the hotel? We'll move tomorrow. It's a rotten hotel. Even Mrs Herzog complains.'

'Yeah, about the fleas. That's pretty unusual. The fleas usually complain about her.' She sighed. 'But we can't afford anywhere better, Duane. We'll just have to stay put and try to act invisible.'

'Like angels.'

'Yes, my sarcastic dear, like angels.' It was true that we couldn't afford decent accommodation; especially, I thought, after paying out for this box; but our contact had insisted we meet in a public place that at the same time afforded a measure of privacy; an opera box, he had suggested, in the letter slipped under our door while we had been asleep; and the suggestion, in the letters that followed, had firmed into an implacable demand. 'Yeah, we'll stay put. It's a *survivable* hotel. Besides, there's so much riff-raff there we kind of go unnoticed, invisible or not.'

'*Shhh!*' said a voice from below.

The princess allowed her gaze to linger on my stern countenance; it lingered, I thought, for more seconds than decorum would allow, taking in the lava field of pocks and rills, as artfully concealed by make-up as my riveted pate was concealed by its wig, the massif of my shoulders

by a frock coat and cape. Circumspectly, I tapped my
ivory-topped walking cane on the floorboards, frowning
with disapprobation; remembering her script, she lowered
her eyes, though I suspected she still focused on mine – a
defiant slave, this – through the dark latticework of her
black, glutinous lashes. Uneasy with my own script,
finding that I enjoyed my part a little too much, I turned
away, avoiding the *faux* cat's clandestine surveillance;
looked down onto the gas-lit stage. Constanze was singing
her great aria, '*Martern aller Arten*', the most difficult
coloratura aria, they say, that Mozart ever wrote. She was
defying the tortures promised her by the cruel Pasha.
Death, she sang, would set her free. Conscious of the
despite of my own Constanze – her eyes, hidden behind
their artificial filters, pricking my nape with petulant
inquiry – I again beat out a muted tattoo with my cane, as
equally conscious of other eyes as I was of hers, the cream
of Manhattan's top-deck socialites becoming increasingly
inquisitive as to the identity of the anonymous giant and
his refractory slave.

    'If he doesn't arrive soon,' said the princess, con-
ceding to a whisper. 'We should go. Too many people. Too
much risk.' I tried to focus on her without moving my
head, a migrainous ache shooting across my brow as I
squinted, cornea buckling into unfamiliar attitudes, my
vision blurring with the effort.

    'I wonder' – my voice as hoarse as hers; I must, I
thought, distract her from imminent flight without
further aggravating the humans in the stalls – 'I wonder
whether I have any family out there? That would be
strange, wouldn't it? A member of my family, or simply a
friend, out there in the audience?'

'*Très* strange. You wouldn't recognise them, and they wouldn't recognise you. For heaven's sake, they'd probably call the cops if they *did*.'

'Maybe,' I said, the water draining from my eyes so that her low-cut bodice resolved into an image pin-sharp, even if its outline was still somewhat distorted by the violence I did my eyeballs. A small cross upon which hung the image of the crucified Lilith nestled in the fabulous fault plane of her cleavage; a bluebottle had made a temporary home there, too, crawling from that dark cavity to traverse a goose-pimpled breast before taking flight into the gods. The princess stooped forward, raised her lorgnette and studied the diamond-and-pearl saturated assembly.

'They look a despicable bunch. You wouldn't want to get to know them, believe me, Duane. Better for you that you were killed in action in the Nam and forgot all about these characters.'

'Frenzy, once upon a time I *was* one of these characters.'

'Never, Duane. Not deep down inside. I've always known that, whatever you might have been in the past, your soul was skewed from the day you popped out of the womb. Deep down, Duane, deep down inside, you were *always* perverse.'

The door opened; a sliver of light fell across the box; widened; became a wedge; and a man's silhouette performed a brief mime in its scalene brilliance. The door closing, its curtain swept back into place, we were returned to the comparative darkness afforded by the turned-down lamp. The man seemed to disappear, spirited away by the artificial twilight. Jerking my head one way, then the other, I suddenly found him unaccountably sitting to my right, lifting his top hat in salute, first to me, and then, bending slightly forward so as to peer around the imposition of my barrel chest, the princess. My masquerading goblin girl received him with her usual *hauteur*, her magnificent condescension translating itself into a single, raised eyebrow, sole emblem that she had noticed his presence.

'We thought you might have got lost,' I said.

'We are all lost, sir. Even we humans. The perverse runs through us all, a wild, violent river, taking us to we-know-not-where. I am Jules, your contact.' I nodded at his sage, cod-rhetorical words, humouring him; he had something we wanted; wanted bad.

'Prester John said—'

'Please, sir. Walls have ears. We must be careful. Now, are you ready to descend to the streets?' I averted my eyes; looked down at the audience. Down, much further down, through countless storeys of steel, glass and concrete, down through the great, jutting, miles-high verticality of this, mankind's biggest, baddest home; down from this eyrie of the rich and privileged who had forgotten what it was to set foot upon earth, sky-dwellers who had lived here, inviolate, for hundreds of years, ensconced in extreme altitude, immured from the horrors that nibbled away at their city's roots; down, down, yes, that's where we had to go. But after some weeks of living above the clouds I greeted the prospect of being summarily dropped to the forbidden depths with a new sense of disquiet.

'In the next couple of days, I suppose. But—'

'No; you must leave tonight. There is an old, disused

elevator shaft that is used by slaves that we in the underground help to escape. It is one of the few ways the streets may still be accessed. In a few hours the night watchman who guards it will be signing off from his shift. There is a small window of opportunity for escape during the change over. You must seize that opportunity and descend.' I exchanged a glance with the princess, suspicion vying with our more customary fatalism.

'How long will it take to reach the streets?'

'As I say, it is an old shaft. The machinery is extremely antiquated. The descent may take up to an hour. Perhaps more. But it really is a matter of just this one opportunity, sir. Another time might prove extremely hazardous. The streets are under interdiction.'

'I know,' I said, fatalism winning out. 'Yeah, okay. We'll go tonight. Now what about the map?' He pushed a hand inside his coat and pulled out a folded piece of yellow, dog-eared paper. He handed it to me.

'I will take you to the elevator shaft at once,' he said. 'Come.'

'Wait,' said the princess. She put her lorgnette aside and snatched the map from my hand. 'This will direct us to the matter transmitter?' She unfolded it and held it beneath the dull glow of the lamp.

'It will,' said Jules, our unctuous contact.

'And how do we know it will really lead us there?' she continued.

'We are eager that your friend journey to The Moon.'

'Oh yeah?' The princess drew a talon across the paper, tracing a route. 'They say it's dangerous down on the streets. I mean, *humans* don't go down there any more, do they?'

'Humans would not be welcome. But you, of course, are *not* human. Don't worry. The route we have devised for you is a safe one. Comparatively speaking. And we will be met by an expert guide. Why would we endanger your lives? You're vital to our experiment.'

'Experiment?' I said, placing my cane across my knees, ready to use it to coerce some truth out of him.

'To see if the restored transmitter actually works.'

'But you have tested it before, I presume.'

'Such tests give us little information, sir. We need to send an *intelligent* energy form across The Bridge. But it will be easy, I assure you. As soon as you enter the field of the transmitter you will be transported onto the surface of The Moon.'

'How do I get back? I can't cover more than a few miles in my projected body. I certainly can't fly back to the Earth from The Moon. And if I'm out-of-body too long my umbilical will break and my corporeal body will die.'

'After a set time, say, thirty minutes or an hour, the transmitter will lock onto your co-ordinates on the lunar surface and you will be recalled to The Bridge.'

'Thirty minutes, eh? I think I can safely say that I've been out-of-body for longer periods than that.' I looked at the princess. 'What do you think, Frenzy?'

'I think you risk having your atoms sprayed all across sublunar space.'

'I was told you were *eager* to go to The Moon. How else do you think you're going to get there? If the transmitter works, you get a free trip and we get confirmation that The Bridge has been successfully reopened. Think, sir. Soon we'll be able to send living matter through. We've had some success already. Dogs, for instance.'

'And?' said the princess.

'Well, you wouldn't expect a postcard from a dog, would you? Please: we've been up front with you about this. We would have sent through some of our own people. Lord knows, there've been enough volunteers. But Prester John really thought you'd be the ideal candidate, revenant. You're strong. I mean *really* strong. And best of all—'

'I'm dead. Yeah. I see.'

'More to the point you can project yourself as *energy*. At our present stage of development, if anything is amiss, you've got far more chance of making a round trip than any others amongst the tribespeople. It has to be a round trip, of course. We need to know what life is like on The Moon. How many people, for instance, are still alive up there. We want to repopulate Luna. We want to build a new Cathay.'

'Looks like I'll be going ahead with this,' I said to the princess.

'Okay, Duane. But as soon as they get this transmitter functioning for animal life – dogs excluded – we go *together*. Me and you, we're partners. No splitting up now.'

'I must admit, I'd like to see you tanning yourself by earthlight at the poolside of some big, abandoned lunar villa.'

'I've still got that chain-mail bikini.'

'Oh, oh, oh – my little goblin minx.' A discreet cough punctuated our verbal foreplay, delivering us from the tortures of Tantalus.

'Time to go,' said our contact.

'What about Herzog?' said the princess. 'She's back at the hotel. We owe her, Duane.'

'I know. But I think it might be a kindness to let her stay where she is. This isn't exactly going to be a pleasure trip, is it?'

'She'll be heartbroken. We've never been apart, not since I was a little girl.' Throwing master-slave etiquette to what winds wafted in the close, humid atmosphere of the opera house, I shifted my massive rump and positioned myself so that I might engage the princess in a *tête-à-tête*; placed a hand on one of her bare shoulders. It was huge, that hand, a five-limbed arachnid that attempted to reassure rather than threaten but whose stagecraft was insufficient to convince of anthropomorphic sympathies. The princess shivered, as if in gleeful anticipation of danger. And then she beat me to the verbal punch. 'But of course,' she added, her own symathies degraded so that she reassumed the persona of the cruel, animalistic child I was so familiar with, 'but of course a broken heart is such a *romantic* way to die. And Herzog has been in search of romance all her life.'

'You're a bad girl, Frenzy.'

'I know, Duane. But I'll always be *your* bad girl.'

'A sentimental rat, forsooth.' I was about to remonstrate that she should think again; backtracking to our hotel to collect her faithful retainer could not significantly disrupt our schedule; but, I thought, with so much sentiment, these days, bestowed on me – her monstrous, hopeless obsession – she had little, and *rightfully* little, to spare for anybody else. There was a ruthlessness to her love; it was a love that would admit no other into the sphere of its orbit; I was hers; and I gloried in being so possessed, in knowing that all was as nothing, whether it be sentient, inanimate, or otherworldly, compared to the jealous regard she had for me. I pitied poor old Herzog, left to languish in the less fashionable eyries of Atlantis, those stratospheric towers long since surrendered by Metropolis's smart set to the impoverished humans who were just above the level of slaves; but I was pleased, marvellously pleased that I might no longer have to share with her a portion of the princess's affections. At last, Frenzy was mine, all mine.

Jules rose, impatient to depart. 'There are people waiting for us,' he said.

'Why's a human like you in league with the perverse?' He tsked; he was, perhaps, one who was used to having his motives questioned; but he was not seemingly to brook having his loyalty impugned.

'There are *many* such as me helping the confabulated overthrow the despots of Atlantis. Not all humans are happy with a hypocritical regime that suppresses animality while enjoying the fruits of that animality's enslavement. The day is coming when the revolutionary forces of the perverse will rise up from the streets and—' The welling intensity of his voice, until then muffled by the orchestra's *fortissimo*, reached its climax; rang out, shrill and impassioned, through a sudden, unanticipated hush, the broken edge of his rhetoric cutting across the theatre like a knife slashing at a roll of limpid silk. And then there was the *crack, crack, crack* of a massed discharge of musketry. The smell of gunpowder was swiftly wafted to the heights of our box. I jumped up; leaned over the balustrade, my hands tightening on the brass railing as I saw that several men and women – all of whom were clearly confabulated – had run onto the stage from the wings. Their muskets were directed, as they must

have been but a moment ago, at the front rows of the
stalls, for several occupants of those seats already lay
slumped, presumably dead, their dickies and the bodices
of their evening dresses drenched with gouts of blood. Two
faces drew close, to peer, like mine, at the events taking
place below; and I did not have to look to know that each
face was as incredulous as my own.

'Your friends?' said the princess.

'I wasn't told,' mumbled Jules. 'The idiots must be
rogue elements, a breakaway party. They're acting without the authorisation of Revolutionary Central Control.'
The audience had shaken itself free of its state of stunned
petrifaction; panicking, they ran towards the exits, climb-
ing over each other, trampling those stragglers who
bottlenecked the aisles.

'Perv!' yelled the humans, not in accusation, as was
their habit; no, not as a prelude to pursuit and arrest; but
in the manner of those who warn of the presence of something supernatural, overwhelming, deadly. 'Perv! Perv!'
they cried, their faces blanched as they were forced to
recognise that demons and vengeful spirits really do exist.

'How satisfying to watch Atlanteans die,' remarked
the princess, dreamily, for a moment distracted from our
predicament by the comprehensiveness of the carnage
below. 'And the night's only just begun.' The terrorists had
reloaded and were again levelling their weapons at the
crowd.

'*The day of judgement is at hand, humans. For
centuries you have treated us with contempt. For
centuries you have hunted us, imprisoned us, enslaved us.
But the perverse has all the time been infecting your
homes, subverting your children. It has tasted the souls*

of your daughters, your sons. It has confounded the way you think, warped the way you perceive reality. And now the perverse is ready to claim its own!' Again, there was a staggered whip crack of gunfire as the rank of musketry plumed with smoke; and I noticed that, this time, the murderous fusillade was directed at the gaudily-attired *cocottes* who scurried after their masters. There were screams, moans, fatal cries that seemed almost like cries of pleasure as the slavegirls clutched at their punctured bosoms and fell beneath the feet of the stampeding throng. And the terrorists on the stage laughed as those who prided themselves on out-perversing the perverse – those treacherous cats – fell to confabulated righteousness. *'Down with taboo and restraint! Down with deferred gratification and the wholesale regulation of pleasure! Down with the sick ethos necessary for the maintenance of their despotic regime! Down with work! Down with sublimation!'*

'Such earnestness,' said the princess. 'Such plebeian enthusiasm.'

'When I was a boy,' said Jules, 'I was taught that such earnestness was evil. You, my teachers said' – he pointed a finger in the princess's face – 'were Eros, and I was Agape. I did not understand that to Be is to strive towards joy.' He closed his eyes, immersing himself, perhaps, in the past; and then, as if urgently recalled to business by a displaced memo, opened them again, looked the princess up and down, his tongue again tsking with fastidious complaint. 'You'd better get out of your disguise. These soldiers look upon catgirl slaves as collaborators.'

'And so they are,' said the princess. She pulled off her evening gloves, her nose in the air, grateful for any excuse to rid herself of her contact lenses, which, a claw unsheathing, she picked out of her eyes with the long, curved talon of an index finger, the eyes blackening now, like thimbles of water into which a drop of ink had been dispersed; and then she flicked those offending bright-green mementoes of her foray into felinity into space. But it was too late; one of the terrorists pointed to her from the stage, crying out, '*Up there! Cat slave! Traitress!*' Showing no trace of discomposure, she raised her hands in the air and presented me with the task of disburdening her of her cumbersome robes.

'Help me, Duane.'

'My speciality,' I said, and tore off her great, flounced evening dress with one motion of my hand. I threw the great mass of *mousseline de soie* to one side and took time out to watch her wriggle free of the wire-and-horsehair bustle, her tail springing free of its constrictive cage like a serpent piped free of its basket by a prurient charmer: me.

'Well, here we are again,' she said. 'Pursued by homicidal maniacs, the baying mob, the bloodthirsty scum of the Earth, on the run, our lives in imminent peril, all about to be lost, and me in my underwear.'

'Your highness,' I said, 'I simply wouldn't have it any other way.' She turned her back on me.

'If you wouldn't mind, Duane.'

'Not at all.' I put my knee into the small of her back, grabbed the laces of her corset and pulled them tight, cincturing her waist, until, relinquishing all resistance, it capitulated to the forces of superfemininity. She sighed with pleasure. I wondered that I had not fractured her ribs. 'Thank you, Duane.' I spun her about, the ridiculous plenitude of buxomness served up by the creaking stays meeting my downcast gaze with a frank and vulgar attempt at seduction. A musket ball shrieked past my ear.

'Please, we must try to get to the elevator shaft,' said Jules, tugging frantically at my sleeve. I ignored the importunate human. Stooping to plant a kiss first on one breast, and then the other, feeling, as I did – my wig slipping a little – her warm lips meet the cold, pitted surface of my naked pate, I let the world dissolve into its own tears, heedless, at that moment, of anything except the salt nectar that dripped from my companion's cheek, down her throat and across her mammae. I laid a hand on her right, silk-stockinged thigh, checking that the new flintlock that I had bought her was in place, its onyx handle protruding from a garter. I came up, reeling, no bathysphere of the libido able to prevent the bends that I always experienced when descending to such depths of desire, only to resurface with no hope of ever reaching the sea of sex's fathomless bottom.

'It seems we must continue with this later,' I said. There was another explosion of musketry, the screams that followed testifying to the terrorists' marksmanship.

Said the princess: 'Better later than dead.' I broke out of our clinch; picked up my walking cane and pushed it under my cummerbund; it poked through the skirts of my frock coat like a jaunty rapier; I swung about, pleased with the effect. I opened the box's door; hurried the human through; then, holding the princess by the wrist, followed, dashing into the outside corridor, a hallway empty – the occupants of the adjacent boxes having long since fled – and curving towards an anonymous perspective, its octagonal windows spangled with twinkling points of light signposting life clusters in the gas-lit city. The human sped before us; we took up the peripatetic slack, the princess yanked along in my wake, trailing from my hand like a pennant in the slipstream of a racing buggy. We rounded the curvature, travelling so fast, now, I almost expected to mount the wall, banking, all inertia gone; in the event, surprised by the glass-smooth expanse of marble that covered the lobby floor I defied gravity only by way of my improvised funambulism as my patent leather boots slipped and skidded across the ice-rink that had suddenly opened up before me. Half-falling over myself, I stumbled to the staircase, the princess dragging behind, like a drogue, stabilising my deceleration, the human already halfway down the steps that connected the lobby with the piazza. Hesitating at the top of the incline, I noticed that a squad of Eugenics Police – the special militia upon which Albracca had modelled its own Gestapo of sexual regulation – was massing at the edges of the square, taking cover behind advertisement hoardings, benches and shrubbery. But Jules had already begun to skip down the steps; and I knew we must not lose him. I bent over; placed one arm behind the princess's dimpled knees, another round her waist; then, despite her wriggles of protest, lifted her. 'I'm not some piece of meat, Duane. Partners, remember? Let me get a shot at them. I don't like this. I don't like this maiden-in-distress bit at *all.*'

'Get used to it,' I said, slinging her over my shoulder. I leapt, legs pedalling in the air, inhuman jack-in-the box and passenger describing an arcing trajectory that took them over the head of their human *confrère*. While in flight, subjective time dilated enough for me to appreciate the ramifications of our present dilemma: we were fleeing from fellow tribespeople of the perverse because, having identified the princess while she was in cat-disguise, they would likely kill her for being a collaborator; and we were fleeing into forces of discipline and order who would, seeing her stripped of her disguise, likely kill her for *not* being a collaborator. Touchdown. The soles of my boots crashed against marble, my reverie detonating in a fireball of decision, expanding gases dispelled – or so the conceit presented itself to me – through the pressure vents of my ears. For as I fell I had noticed that Jules had torn off his coat to reveal a parachute strapped to his back, and was, it seemed, ready to abort his primary mission. The poltroon had understood, I think, as quickly as had I, that our rendezvous at the elevator shaft had been hopelessly compromised; but that did not excuse his slippery inclination to hightail it and leave us to the mercies of Atlantis. If he would not take us to our destination, I told myself, I would have to take matters into my own hands. One way or another, we would descend.

The police cried out for us to stop; fired a volley of warning shots into the air. The would-be aeronaut, terror seemingly making him oblivious to the fact that he was likely to be shot to death if he attempted to cross open ground, scuttled past me, taking advantage of my befogged senses, the transient concussion precipitated by my fall. I straightened, a little unsteady; willed away the pain shooting through my impact-jellified bones. The princess wriggled free from my grasp; winded, hugging her ribs, she squinted after the human form sprinting towards the plate-glass windows that bordered the piazza and which gave way to the night. Before the police could reload their firearms

Jules had crossed the square and thrown himself against the glass. With a wet, percussive slap – like that dealt out by an Amazon to an unwelcome suitor – he bounced off, tumbling back over the guard-rails. Spread-eagled, a squiggle of blood decorating the marble floor where his broken body had come to rest (his top hat spinning like a gyroscope on the verge of collapse nearby), he lay motionless, staring at the chandeliers that scorched the cobwebs interlacing the high, stuccoed ceiling. The police again called out, a medley of megaphone-distorted voices warning that they would shoot to kill. 'Get behind me,' I said, crabbing towards the unconscious human. I grunted as a handful of ball-shot caught me in the chest, sending up a spray of black ichor, my shirt and cravat disintegrating, smoking with red-hot lead that had pocked but failed to penetrate my flesh. Those that are dead cannot die twice over; unharmed, I continued to move towards my goal, the princess crouched in my shadow, one hand hanging onto my belt, as if she sheltered behind a knight – or rather ogre – in armour, my pachydermatous skin absorbing the impotent firepower of the Atlanteans. But it was not until I was filled with enough lead to have me resembling a downed pheasant that I was able to crouch beside Jules's prone body and unstrap the parachute, to hastily refasten it – its buckles straining against my bulk – across my own back, the princess coming to my assistance as I found that my hands were subject to spontaneous swipes and flicks, my nervous system prompting them to try – quite impossibly, of course – to intercept the incoming missiles.

'Why, I ask myself, why oh *why* is Mr Duane Duarte putting on this parachute? And why am I helping him? You don't expect me to–'

'One round in the centre of that window, if you wouldn't mind, please, Frenzy dear?' The princess unholstered her flintlock, took up a kneeling position and, using a two-handed grip, aimed and pulled the trigger. The hammer snapped the flint against the L-shaped plate; a shower of sparks, and the powder in the priming pan ignited, sending a ball through the plate glass. The window cracked, spider-webbing with distress. 'Are you ready?' The combustion, its aftertaste thick and grey, roiled in my mouth, my nose like a wasp's nest angry with bonfire smoke.

'You're kidding. You're not serious.'

There was a crepitation of musketry, one that had the effect of making the bombardment we already suffered stereophonic; it corresponded, in its gnat-like worrying of my thick, shock-absorbent epidermis, to the worst we had been submitted to from the police; but this time it emanated from the top of the stairs. Some of the terrorists had broken out of the opera house; and we were caught in a crossfire.

'A *cocotte*,' shouted an insectman. 'I saw her in the theatre! A *cocotte* disguised as a rat!' No sooner had he delivered his brief *J'accuse* than he fell, drilled through by the police, his wings unfurling, but powerless to transport, tearing like the fabric of a child's multicoloured kite as he crash-dived down the marble steps.

'Ready or not,' I said, 'it's time to leave.' I scooped her up. Mindful of a decision having been made for her, and unable to enter into debate, she conceded to the moment's imperative and wrapped her legs about my waist. Another fusillade sent splinters of marble into the air, though whether the opposing forces of humanity and the perverse were firing at each other or had trained their combined attention on us, I could not tell; looking over the princess's head – she had pressed her face tightly into my pectorals like a little girl frightened of the dark – I was now occupied solely with the task of breaching the glass wall that separated us from the void. Putting one arm about my shivering rat, holding the other arm before me, I charged the window, one, two, three strides bringing me to the guardrail; I jumped, setting one foot on the rail's chromium horizontal, using it to lever myself upwards in an arc that had me diving towards the epicentre of the fractured plate glass. My arm broke the icy surface, a cold, numbing shock wave travelling up into my shoulder, jets of ichor from my lacerated veins spattering my face with a black, sticky oil, as if I had just crushed the ink sac of a monstrous squid; and then – feeling the barrier give way under the pressure of four hundred pounds of recycled muscle, sinew and bone – I was out, floundering in space, the sub-zero altitude and the thinness of the air paralysing me, so that all I could think to do was to hold onto the princess as, fighting for breath, the tissue at the back of my throat was ripped off by the extreme cold.

Above me, there was a secondary explosion, like an echo of the shattering thunderclap precipitated by the contact of my bulldozing flesh with the plate glass; it was immediately followed by a great *whoosh*! of escaping air as the great skyscraper had its breath sucked from its lungs; and I looked from side to side, desperate to avoid falling debris, my ears ringing with the screaming, cursing voices that called out from the darkness, each voice's owner, unlike the princess and I, having made a less-than-voluntary exit into the night. But I saw nothing.

If I had still been human perhaps my life would have flashed by. Instead, the lives of others, those who, over the years, I had consumed to sustain my unnatural existence, flitted through my brain like poltergeists, upsetting the furniture – all the familiar trappings of my sparsely decorated inner self – knocking on tables and speaking in tongues. My head buzzed like a jam jar filled with flies. Talk radio. But from no external source, this demon babble; rather, from the transmitter of my own desires, the violent want of a shrivelled heart that craved a life it could not have. Ignoring that disgusting chorale I tried to tune in to any signal strong enough to carry a whisper of my past, my true past, the intimated country that surfaced obliquely in my dreams, in unheralded epiphanies of everyday madness; the country where, once, I had been happy. Then, from deep within a Stygian pit of annulled love, I seemed to hear a child's voice call out; I knew that child, though I had forgotten his face and name; and I knew, with a simplicity that soothed me with a delicious peace, that I had only to descend into that dark pit and rescue that forsaken boy for all of my unreal life to be redeemed. I streamlined my body into the semblance of a missile; flipping my legs towards the sky, I careered headlong towards the streets, so far-off that I might have been viewing them in an orbiter, a rusted, antique, half-mythical orbiter re-entering the Earth's atmosphere, about to break up in flames. I screwed my eyes shut; bit down, pushing my decaying teeth deep into their diseased, gingival surround.

'Duane! Duane! What are you doing?' I felt five razor-sharp lengths of keratin drag swatches of necrotic flesh from my cheek. My neo-cortex, more cognisant than the corrupt brain tissue in which it lay, like a wise old caterpillar in a bed of rotting lettuce, wriggled and squirmed in panic; the princess wriggled too, a rat seeking egress from the sinking ship; but even if her struggles were ill-advised ~ given that abandoning ship would have proved fatal ~ they at least had the effect of alerting me to the peril of my autohypnotically-induced descent. 'Pull the chute, Duane! We're going too fast!' It was only after I had flexed my eyelids two or three times that I managed to ungum them, breaking the ice that sealed lid to lid with a triumphant splintering of tiny icicles that showered into the abyss like fairy dust. 'Duane, pull the fucking chute!' I shook my head with a vigorousness that both stilled the errant myriapod and the shrewish mouth of my fellow participant in free fall; we had plenty of time yet to enjoy terminal velocity. I assumed a skydiver's posture, legs and one arm extended, my other arm still clinging tenaciously to the princess, as she did to me, her thighs crushed against my hips in a travesty of the intimate congress we both longed for, but knew was not ours to enjoy. As she again buried her face in my chest, as if in acceptance of whatever doom might be meted out, I responded to our exalted, new-found habitat with an inverse degree of curiosity, glorying in the speed, the all-encompassing emptiness, the wind that stung my eyes and ears. Like a big, somewhat ridiculous prehistoric bird, I surveyed the lurid, overarching walls of the steel-and-glass ravine, a gully whose monochromatic, biomass walls dripped with strange vegetation. Below, its depths were interspaced with covered skybridges, a latticework of walkways, railways and carriageways whose gaping perforations of frozen, black vacancy received us as we plummeted towards a ground zero only the exiled, the outlawed, the lost, dared to trespass upon. Spinning, a toy helicopter out-of-control, I held my breath as we passed almost catastrophically close to a bridge, the gargoyles that projected from its parapets – the faces of cats, wolves, sharks, insects and rats – disemboguing rainwater and grazing my hypersensitised consciousness if not my cold, indurate flesh. I tried to assume command, piloting myself by means of my limbs. These makeshift rudders and ailerons, I found, lent me sufficient manoeuvrability to guide a path through the weave of girders and struts spanning the vortex that sucked us into the city's maw. Aerodynamically sound, I relaxed a little; took in the sights afforded by my whistle-stop tour of Metropolis. Lit squares in the surrounding hive of towers offered their *tableaux vivants* of domesticity; snapshots, filtered through stained glass; colour-coded brain cells of an Almighty Presence of Repression that, unseen, but immanent in everything, permeated all Atlantis. Tonight, the light show was epileptic, red, black, green, purple, gold silhouettes statuesque behind open blinds and drapes: a dinner party, candelabra suffusing the elegantly attired guests, vicious, self-satisfied smiles about to detach from the parent faces, fly about the room like rabid, foetal bats; a kitchen filled with liveried catgirls and wolfmen, parlourmaids and butlers who were about to serve at table dressed in the parodic, sartorial extravaganzas that befitted slavery; a gymnasium busy with those who lauded health – the health of those who monopolised the moral universe as a means of justifying their imperial power – working-out with prissy, self-flagellating rigour; the bedrooms where masters and mistresses played with girl-pets, boy-pets, thing-pets, hitching a ride on the left-hand path while simultaneously reviling it, this breed of humanity the most dangerous of the Earth's new carnivores, men and women who wallowed in self-hatred. To be an Atlantean was to be a sybarite, but also to be blameless; to indulge in a purity crueller, more despotic and more corrosive than the most outrageous of the many-splendoured appetites of the lost tribes of the perverse; purity, for an Atlantean, was the supreme vice. And it was indulged, shamelessly. I recalibrated my eyes; scanned, taking in more dark visions. A row of octagonal windows revealed, as if in a stutter of animated trans-parencies, a fashion show, female humans sauntering down a catwalk in ironic imitation of the sexual dis-play rituals of slaves. A bust-padded, calf-booted and ectopically bottomed young woman, suspecting, perhaps, that she was hallucinating (she stared, bug-eyed, out into the night and into the path of our descent), put a hand to her mouth, as if about to scream; but then laughed, probably dismissing us as an atmospheric anomaly; and, wiggling her bustle and waving a diaphanous scarf as the princess and I whipped past her field of vision, bade the *ignis fatuus* adieu. I looked away; studied the bleak perspective solidifying below, streets now clearly visible, dotted with fires and lantern light. We tore past a dirigible plying between some of the lower levels, these antique tenements carved out of the penthouses and rooftops of skyscrapers that were over a thousand years old. The princess and I had rented rooms in one of the hotels that graced these lower heights; I half expected Mrs Herzog to poke her head out from one of the flophouses' windows; and then, with the airship above us dwindling into an airborne cigar glowing at both ends, festooned with paper lanterns, we spiralled towards a glowing, jungle carpet of overgrown concrete and twisted metal, rising from the mulchy floor like rusted, ferroconcrete rampikes and gigantic, wilted iron flowers. I counted off the seconds. When I had reached to nine I groped for the ripcord; found it. I thought then, after I had tugged the cord two or three times, that the chute had failed; in a surge of panic I looked up; the princess, who still chose to fly blind, cried out with alarm; for as I crooked my head to peer heavenwards to where the sides of the ravine were lost, their definition smudged out of existence by altitude and the city's eerie, nocturnal glow, I was jerked, with indecent peremptoriness, between my legs; saw, with relief, the silk spewing into the sky, its white canopy soon bellying like a sail and becoming noctilucent, a personal moonlit cloud escorting us to the shores of a new world. The harness had split at several places of weakness, our combined weight confounding its ancient design; and though it held, it could not compensate for the burden we placed on the parachute itself, its umbrella unable to check the rate of our descent to the degree necessary to ensure a safe landing. There was the sound of snapping; shroud lines flew past my face, and we tilted to one side, converging on the empty, burnt-out shell that constituted the lowest storeys of a tower. I clung to what lines still attached us to the chute, twisting, struggling to prevent a collision. But before the sides of the ravine could claim us there was an additional rending of fabric; we were now hanging from the rapidly collapsing canopy – its gores tattered, ragged – by no more than a few threads; and we were sent nether-wards with a despatch that made all

other danger irrelevant. Stirred by our relapse into free
fall, the princess removed her face from the comforter of
my chest, glanced over her shoulder and screamed as the
urgent ground imprinted itself on her retinae, her claws
savaging my flesh with fright, her tail winding about my
leg. I pressed my ankles together; flexed my knees,
forsaking my redundant hold on the chute to concentrate
my energies on enclosing the princess within my arms as
securely as I was able. My cheek pressed against the top of
her head, the toxic aroma of her flamboyant mane compounding my dizziness. I looked down, frantically wishing
into existence a pond, a swamp, a feather mattress, a
trampoline, anything that might soften our landing. But
in the sudden calm, the transcendent stilling of time that
immediately preceded impact, all I espied was an avenue
of twisted iron and steel, a trough littered with the
detritus of the centuries, the dead might-tek blight-tek of
burnt-out automobiles, trams, nameless electronic
consumables, the scattered wreckage of things that once
flew, less nameless, though buried deep in my psyche,
things called helicopter, autogyro, plane; and on top of the
power junk, a glittering scum from later years, coaches
still yoked to the skeletal, flea-picked remains of horses
and cattle; broken swords, sheared-off trunks of lampposts stippled with crossbow bolts, the ossified corpses of
those who had fallen in street battles, their skulls polka-
dotted with ball, bodkin and brochette, slain bodies confabulated in forms that were new to me, specific, perhaps,
to mutations that had occurred only in bred slaves. And
over all fluttered a pall of scrap paper, shards of plastic
and the black pollen exuded by strange, uncatalogued
plants, a mélange gathered up into miniature dust storms

whirling about caved-in shop fronts, gaping windows, the mouths of alleyways, past which lay – as it lay everywhere – a curtain of mucous-thick shadow relieved by orange tongues of flame dancing from countless flambeaux and rushlights, that characteristic mode of illumination strewn throughout the recesses of the night-land's imbroglio, the wilderness that seemed a ferroconcrete metaphor for the Earth's psychosomatic decline. As the grace of time's suspension was revoked, the ground, with its terrible *chevaux-de-frise* of mangled machinery – the scree and rubble of an equally revoked past – speeded towards the soles of my boots, ready to impale them on its jags and serrations of buckled steel; the city vanished, like a theatrical backdrop suddenly blacked out by a gas leak, all my attention focused on the small, mentally spotlit segment of the street that was destined to be our rough, cruel landing pad. For the second time that evening my bones were set to be jellified by a terrific concussion.

I remember as little about hitting the ground as I do about my former life as an Atlantean. My knees had caught me under the chin, yes, and the big, fat vibrations that bit into my feet chewed their way rapidly through my legs, guts and brain, radiating out to be bounced, for all I knew, off the ionosphere, to rattle the teeth of those doomed to the unhappy reception of that scrambled music over all four continents of the Earth. And then there was only the night within the night, a maternal blackness hugging me to its oily teat.

The princess was sitting, her back against what, from pictures gleaned from history books, I knew to be a refrigerator. Its door hanging off, the mechanical icebox, with its promise of a land of wonder and plenty long since vanished from the Earth, seemed like a magic cavern inviting a small child to play within the nostalgia of its shadows; but my own child ~ my own little girl from Thurn and Taxis ~ seemed in no mood to have fun. Bruised, grazed, her stockings and corset torn, a heel hanging, broken, from one of her white, strappy shoes, I had regained consciousness to discover her furiously engaged in scraping a decal off the top of her thigh. The decal had substituted for the tattoo ~ an image of a rose and poppy, entwined ~ that it was customary for a slave-girl to have etched into her flesh as a badge of seigneurial proprietorship. I pulled off my wig, the little postiche I had used to hide the phrenological horror story of my bald, cicatrice-engraved poll.

'We seem to be alive.'

'How can you tell?' said the princess, wetting a talon with her tongue and reapplying herself to removing the mark of her servitude.

'Yeah, I suppose, for me, that's always been a problem.'

'A problem for all of us, Duane, to know where life begins and death ends.'

'Or vice versa.'

'Indeed. The angels say that life and death are the same thing. For them, at least.'

'Then there's hope for me yet. Maybe I'll wake up one day and find that all this has been nothing more than the dream of a man who's been mortally wounded in battle.'

'You think you're dead, bleeding and food for the flies in some paddy field in the Nam?'

'No, not really. But sometimes I think, or rather I

hope, that life, the true life, is yet to come. This life is so—'

'Like a dream? As if we had all decided to go to sleep in the middle of the twenty-first century and hadn't woken up yet?'

'As if we were dead, rotting in the grave, but still dreamed. Are your angels near?'

'I don't hear them. And I don't want to call on them unless it's absolutely necessary. My angels don't like being *presumed* upon, you know.'

'Enough metaphysics. Have you still got the map?' The princess reached into the plutonic fissure of her whalebone-engineered cleavage and extricated the crumpled sheet of paper. She held the map at arm's-length, at such an angle as to catch the meagre flickerings of coppery light that fell from a nearby building, intent on interpreting the lines, circles and arrows that constituted the route to the bridge between the worlds. I reached into my pocket and pulled out the compass I had packed earlier that day. I tossed it to her; she plucked it from the air, like a beggar-girl catching a spinning coin cast negligently at her feet. Setting the compass on a level surface – or such a surface as could be found; we sat amidst a clutter of rubbish, the ground unknown feet beneath – she glanced at the map; then at the faltering needle; again, back at the map. Puffing out her sugar-plum cheeks with exasperation she looked up, sweeping her hair into a high, weather-beaten haystack in an attempt to style it in the shape of its regular *fontange*.

'I think we head, ahhh – *thataway*,' she said, nodding in a direction as bleak and as unappealing as any other. Slipping one of her garters down her thigh, her calf, and then off over her ankle, she fastened it about her brow, employing it as an improvised bandeau to keep her chaotic tresses in some semblance of verticality. The haystack was transformed; but only into a Tower of Babel, struck and ruined by the hand of a God angered by a goblin princess's tonsorial pride. She faffed about with herself, determined to keep what remained of her once-magnificent toilette, her aristocratic chic a source not only of pride, but of strength. She stashed the map once more within the crevasse of her bosom and looped the compass's chain about her neck. 'You're very shock-absorbent, Duane, I must say,' she said, bending to rub her shins. 'Those legs of yours have got great suspension. They're sexy, too. Mismatched, but *sexy*. Sort of makes me glad I decided to enter into an unhealthy liaison with a walking corpse all those years ago.'

'Do you remember when—'

'I remember it all.' An adolescent dreaminess filled her eyes. 'They sent me and Herzog down from Albracca to stay with that NVA division in Hue. Oh, yes. And I remember when I was first ushered into the ranking officer's quarters and introduced to my first zombie. So big. So awe-inspiring. So *deceased*. They told me to look after you. They told me you were a secret weapon, and that my position was one of great trust. "*Bring back his head, Princess Frenzetta.*" they said, "*just make sure you bring back his head.*" Have I looked after you, Duane? I like to think I've been a good nursemaid. All those missions, you as a walking bomb, or else as a one-man commando squad, a beautiful and indiscriminate killer of men, women and children. I have looked after you, Duane, haven't I, haven't I?' A tear, polluted with its familiar black, cosmetic dye, ran down her plump cheek.

'This isn't memory lane, goblin girl,' I said, my harshness counteracting the sentimental tug I felt at my own tear ducts, 'these streets are trouble. All those fires,' I said. 'And no people.'

'No people we can see, Duane,' she said, wiping her face, her eyes once again hardened by contemplation of our prospects. 'Not even invisible people. No ghosts or fairies. No astral bodies or angels. And maybe it's just as well if whoever, or whatever, lives down here *stays* hidden.'

'How far do we have to travel?' I got up, stumbling, my legs still benumbed by the tremendous kinetic energy that they had recently soaked up, but uncoiling, now, like trusty springs, to once again propel me, as they had done so many times before, into battle. I held the princess by her arm as, unsteady as myself, but resembling more a new-born colt than a lame buffalo, she rose to stand by my side; stooped as I was, I let a hand brush idly against her thigh, its begrimed stocking laddered, so marvellous, with such strategically erotic regard. I drew myself up with audacious indifference for the opinions of any onlookers, relieved, for once, at not having to conceal the giveaway sign of perversity that was my height; cast my gaze along the route we would have to take; frowned. The road ahead was the mean, mulchy floor of a metal jungle. Negotiating a passage through its shifting thoroughfare of junk would be like trying to cross a forest of thorns, an enchanted forest such as had protected the Sleeping Beauty's castle. But no time for beauty sleep, for either my own too-beautiful princess or the ogre who attended her pleasure; we had to make the most of the cover of darkness. 'I said how far—'

'To the East River,' she snapped, wobbling as the ground undulated beneath feet already precariously balanced, one foot radically arched by a still-intact six-inch stiletto, the other hobbled by a broken heel, the balancing act now becoming extravagantly foolhardy, almost, one felt, about to be accompanied by a drum roll and a call for her audience-of-one to keep quiet. 'Don't ask me how many miles that is, because I don't know. But we'll be needing transport, I'd guess. We should start moving.'

'And hope,' I said.

'Yeah, against hope.'

Towards morning we came to the ruins of a hotel, its rooms – we seemed to stand at the level of its first or second floor – filled with masonry and the wrecks of yellow autos. I gestured to the princess to move into the darkness – shadows that swarmed like amorphous bats – and she complied, shifting beneath a lintel. The shadows were cast by the lights of the numerous, small fires that we had come to understand, during our recce of the streets, stood-in for street illumination in lieu of gaslight; and though we had not encountered any inhabitants of these depths, they were evidence of a degree of municipal organisation; but ahead – at what the princess, consulting her filthy map, assured me lay at the hub of a system of ancient thoroughfares called 42nd Street, Broadway and Seventh Avenue – was a locus of lambent radiance that vied with the city's top deck, where Metropolitans luxuriated in cloudless sunlight by day and an artificial cloud cover of luminescence by night. Day and night: it seemed less indistinguishable than irrelevant, here;

blazing torches ranged along the crumbling walls of the
cliff-like outcroppings, buildings unscalable except by the
most determined of mountaineers, were suddenly in such
profusion that all seemed to swim, in a convective
shimmer of orange, red and magenta, beneath a sea of
simmering, febrile blood. Music and the dark, shadow-
cast forms of dancers - stick-like, primitive cartoon
figures - signalled that, around the next corner, a
Walpurgis Night was in full, murderous swing. Projected
against the walls of the surrounding buildings, the figures
- gigantic, spectral, fluid - gambolled and cartwheeled as
unseen musicians slapped their hands - or so I imagined -
against steel drums, plucked at steel cable strung across
water tanks and ruptured boilers, blew a riff from a
collection of battered brass instruments, blue notes of
sexual longing oozing from their bells as they were
hoisted up and down to a 2/4 beat. Crosses - made from
the rotted timbers of pillaged architecture - rose out of the
morainic tek. And on each cross, nailed to its horizontal
by her wrists, hung a girl, her writhings correlating with
the manic, hysterical caperings of the partying crowd.
Other celebrants - men as well as women - were engaged
in complementary dances of death: chained in cages suspended over burning coals; swinging from lampposts by
their thumbs; or else tied to stakes and used as pin
cushions. The shadowy forms that bobbed and cavorted
along the sides of the soot-caked avenues - a lantern
show of alternating blacks and reds - seemed to recall a
wall painting in some cavern of primitives, wrested into
the present, parodied into a cruel, Bosch-like grotesque
and brought to phantasmagoric life by a team of mad
flipbook artists.

'So much pain,' said the princess, licking her lips, 'and so many people taking pleasure in it.'

'I don't think it wise to gate-crash. We aren't meant to end our journey here. Are we?'

'Aren't we? And what do we do once we've got to The Moon? Set up home, have kids, walk the dog before breakfast—'

'I thought you *wanted* to go to The Moon.'

'I do, I do. It's just what do we *do* once—'

'Live.'

'Are you so sure? We're perverse, Duane. For us, life's got to end in some kind of hellnight. Private, public – tomorrow's party will still culminate in death. That's the way it is. That's the way we're made. Love is our endtime.'

'And it'll be like this?'

'How else should love be?'

I stared at the shadow-play of the dancing figures, some borrowed memory surfacing of having once sat, as a child, before a makeshift screen in my village, behind which the puppeteers manipulated their two-dimensional leather dolls, telling tales of Rama and Sita. But that was a borrowed memory, the memory of just another brain I had devoured; I filed it away under *Guys I've Killed Out East/Miscellaneous*. The figures leapt, fell, convulsed and squirmed. Confabulated bedlamites – wounded, dead, or in the most ferocious of health, their orgiastic bodies burnished by the infernal flames that encircled them – they hollered, yodelled, the vocal accompaniment to their excruciations carrying over from the adjacent, but indiscernible street, a bestial screamfest that constituted a harmony of perverse joy. The ring of fire, redolent of my fight with the giant robot – so long ago, it seemed now, it

might have occurred in a previous life, far, far away in
Afric – was inviting us into its orbit; and it was as I was
inducing steel into my heart, resisting that Walpurgis
allure of sex-death, holding back a similarly excited princess as if she were a bitch in heat straining at the leash (to
ones perverse as ourselves, the perverse spectacle before
us a bait irresistible) that a sharp, sibilant whisper just
beneath my left ear made me flinch, as if a gimlet had
been inserted into the hinge of my jaw, and twisted.

'Welcome to Times Square.'

The interloper had a long, almost testicular face, his
golden skin covered in a fine network of glistening,
scrotal scales. Coincidentally, his expression – a con-
stipated grimace – seemed that of one who suffered from
permanent balls' ache, but who was determined to
disguise the desperateness of his congenital gloom. I knew
his path. Control, for him, was all. He was a dragonman.
The princess had spun around almost as sharply as had I
and now tapped her talons nervously against the butt of
her pistol. Perhaps it was an understanding that she was
without powder and ball that made her relax, or else dis-
semble relaxation; whichever it was, she assumed a
posture studiedly emblematic of carelessness, one hand
on her hip, the other supporting her weight against the
wall.

'We should give this little hellnight rumpus a wide
berth,' said the dragon, silkily. 'They're not part of *our*
faction. These people – they are but a mirror-image of
Atlantean decadence. They celebrate The Moon in the
manner ... in the manner of *barbarians*.' His red eyes
burned, tensile, feverish, reflecting the red night of Times
Square.

'Celebrate The Moon?' said the princess. 'Is it that time of year again already?'

'The Moon Festival,' I mused, for a moment unconscious of intrusion, or danger. 'We were supposed to be going to The Moon.'

'You still are,' said the dragonman.

'Whoa – just who the hell *are* you?' hissed the princess.

'He's a necromancer,' I said. And then to him: 'But I don't remember you being in Cathay. Did—'

'Did I make you? No; I'm no relation, Mr Duarte. And I'm no necromancer. I'm not even related to these people down here, the people who live in the basements of Metropolis.' He lifted his top hat. 'My name is La Gargouille. And I have been assigned to escort you to The Bridge.'

'Can you really get us to The Moon?' said the princess.

'We are organising a second exodus for the diaspora. We are building another Cathay. For you, and for all the confabulated. Except—' He drew a handkerchief from the breast pocket of his coat and held it beneath his nose. 'Except for certain, degenerative stock who have come to equate perversity with brutality.'

'You want Duane to test out your matter transmitter, don't you?'

'To see if I don't fly into a zillion atoms when you pull the switch, eh?'

'There are certain risks associated with every enterprise. You have taken many risks, have you not, simply to get yourself here?'

'It's no thanks to you we're here at all,' said the princess. 'Some of your people pulled a stunt in the Heights. Lots of shooting. Lots of police.'

'So I understand. But *not* my people, I re-emphasise. None of these' – he gave a little cough, muffled by the kerchief – '*people* are. Some of the confabulated down here are with us, of course. But most–' He patted his mouth fastidiously and then replaced the handkerchief in his pocket.

'Most are more lost than lost,' said the princess, casting a glance back at the crazed orgy.

'Quite,' said La Gargouille. 'They have their own agenda. Thus the attack on the opera house. To no end other than to vent their bitterness, to destroy, kill and revenge themselves on their tormentors.'

'Zero charm. Zero style. How did you find us?'

'We have contacts both in the Heights and on the streets. I knew you'd run into trouble and had had to make your descent without recourse to the elevator we had requisitioned for you. I theorised you'd be trying to follow the route on our map.'

'So we were,' I said. 'Until we came to *this*.' I thumbed towards the riot of flesh and cruelty, so like the frescoes, or collections of porcelain I had seen in Albracca, but given terrible life. The sight made me want to hide myself away once again in a monastery. Cathay, in its decadence had, perhaps, not been as soulless as I had imagined. But I did not like this dragon's talk of exclusiveness, his snobbery that spoke of a perverse élite.

'Let me suggest a diversion.' He began to walk across the street towards an alleyway that led away from the torture garden of twisted steel and twisted flesh. 'Come.' We stumbled after him, occasionally tripping over in our haste to make ourselves invisible from the partying crowd. When the walls of the alley enclosed us, our hands

and knees bearing the bloody signature of our pratfalls, I
stopped, holding the princess by the forearm.

'Wait, dragonman,' I called. 'I want to know exactly
where I'm going.'

'You're going to The Bridge, revenant. You're going
Moonside to become the new Columbus. How does it feel
to know you're going to be remembered in the history
books?'

'Guy seems full of shit,' whispered the princess. She
pulled the map out of her cleavage and held it close to her
eyes. 'Don't know where we are now, Duane.' She raised her
voice, intending that the dragonman hear her. 'We were
supposed to go through Times Square, not around it.'

'Then it's lucky I found you, yes?' called the dragon
over his shoulder. I pushed the princess before me; we had
lost one guide this evening; I was anxious we should not
lose sight of another, no matter how creepy I found his
utterances or how suspicious I was of his intent.

The alley gave way to a street that seemed identical
to the one we had recently left. All along its shadow-
haunted length was junk, trash – a midden of steel and
masonry. The bottom had fallen out of the world; this I
knew; and most of it seemed to have accumulated here. It
was the world's ripped-out stuffing; the stuff that would
no longer work, that could no longer work; the stuff we
would no longer *allow* to work, which we had turned our
perverse backs upon, like all things that lurked, accusing,
in the human past. For all the world was becoming non-
human. The confabulated had been only the froth on the
surface of a bubbling cauldron in which the genes, ideas,
values and habits of mankind had been brought to the
boil, cooled and then allowed to stand for over two

millennia. Other moulds, other fungi had accumulated besides us, exposed as that dish had been to a bacterium that had long ago wormed its way into objective reality, into what we had once called truth; a final reckoning awaited; no matter that the perverse was being enslaved; humanity would not out-survive it. I looked up towards the fabled Heights, the apartments, manors and penthouses where a breed of humanity lived who – masters and mistresses of the planet – thought themselves immortal, but would soon join the ghosts who populated the forgotten past.

'Your new Cathay – what is it going to be like?' I said.

'A civilisation without control mechanisms. Does that sound like a contradiction? Above' – he pointed towards the obscure heavens – 'society is mechanised, though its machine-like qualities are concealed by the luxuries and spurious freedoms of the Heights. For its inhabitants, desire is controlled, bought off by the pig-feed of style, comfort and the general anaesthesia of words, words, words, words, words. No pleasure for its own sake, say the Lords of Atlantis, the Good is defined by what is socially useful. Above: the apogee of Man's self-consciousness and his reason, the forces by which he has brought the world to heel.'

'And below?' shouted the princess, the dragonman's agility superior to both hers and my own, taking him over the tangle of garbage, debris and rubble with such alacrity that we were sore pressed to keep him in view.

'Below, pleasure is an end in itself. Self-consuming. Uroboric. A bright, but useless fire. If the perverse promises the overthrow of the Law, it offers little in return apart from the body's immediate gratification. But civilisations arise out of Death: dominion over Nature after centuries of forcing her, reaving her, killing her emissaries, until mastery is achieved. The perverse, such as it is, here, on the streets of Metropolis, lacks cohesion and order. It is not something we can build on.'

'And what should we build?' I asked, my naturally booming cadences, feathery with exertion, still resonant enough to echo off the alley's nigh-Himalayan walls, their paint-splashed sides wainscoted with a scree of pulverised tek, the night soil of those in the Heights who, as they ascended beyond the clouds, had taken to discarding the ballast of Man's intellectual history.

'A Cathay that represents a marriage between above and below.'

'Between heaven and hell?' piped the princess.

'Between sex and death. A non-repressive civilisation, its every thought, its every activity transformed into pure libido.'

'Sentimental bullshit,' quoth I. The dragonman came to a halt; lifted his hand, signalling that we too should stop. The princess's ears wiggled, as if itchy with aural nits.

'What is it?' she said.

'People up ahead.' Ignoring the dragonman's warning, I edged forward; the princess copied, taking cover behind my bulk, like an infantrywoman behind an armoured vehicle; it was a tactic that we had both become accustomed to; we assumed its *tango militaire* whenever we detected a threat. The dragonman remained frozen, like one of the shop-window dummies that projected, dismembered, from out of the barrows of glittering trash. Our breaths held, we attempted to enter into a conspiracy with the night's silence;

but the treacherous ground crunched beneath our feet like shale; lumbering brute that I was, I was not, I decided, designed for stealth, and released my breath; the princess looked up at me with practised exasperation. Forging on, we drew alongside our guide.

'Over there,' he whispered, nodding. Two men – wolves, dandified wolves in stovepipe toppers, velveteen frock coats, drainpipe trews and riding boots – were each pressing a catgirl against the cliff-face of a crumbling façade; the girls seemed to have little to fear, at least for the present; the wolfmen's attention was riveted, not upon their conscripted dates, but upon each other, as if they were lost in mutual admiration of their customised hirsuteness, their goatees, mustachios waxed and perfumed, their long, tapering, complementary sideburns glistening with brilliantine. 'All cruelty, all aggression, all destructive impulses to be transformed into the erotic,' said the dragon, high on theory, as the people of his tribe always were. 'See' – he held out a hand towards the canoodling foursome like a lab technician revealing the results of his latest experiment – 'the perverse has shown the way; but we must be faithful to its original, not the decadent gleanings that we find about us on these streets, or that, in quite another way entirely, was found in Cathay during its last days.'

'Dumb pain sluts,' said the princess, her voice soft, but cut with a prejudicial hiss. The hiss petered out as her lips tightened into a self-satisfied grin, polished little rows of chiselled dentin framed by big, wide, ruby-red lips. 'Gonna get yourselves killed, little darlings. Gonna get yourselves killed...' The cats, like the princess, were half-naked, though their lingerie, compared to hers, seemed both cheaper and less compromised by wear and tear, a few snicks and flirtatious rips supplying evidence that the ruination of their silk and lace was tailored rather than the result of misfortune. 'Popcats,' said the princess, dismissively. 'Tight-Lacing Society groupies.' The princess's lacing, I was about to observe, was just as tight as theirs; tight enough to displace her ribs, or to slice her liver in two. But I thought better than to interrupt her rant. I concentrated, instead, on the conversation piece of her own corset. It forced her breasts upwards so that they lay, shivery and wanton, immediately below her elfin chin, the extreme constriction of the stays having the effect of making her breathing thoracic, each inhalation and exhalation resembling the breathless pantings of hysteria, agitating the vanilla blancmange of her chest until I felt inclined to bite my lip, called once more to a feast at which I could not participate. 'Slaves, not just to men, but to fashion. To all the latest servile fads. Popcats!' One cat broke away from the wolf who had pinioned her against a wall. She slapped his face; struck a pose, putting a hand on her hip and bending her leg so that the slave tattoo on her left thigh – that image of an entwined rose and poppy that symbolised the union of sex and death – was suitably displayed, peeping above the garter of a tattered, white silk stocking. 'Foundation garments fitted with Invisible Scapula Contractors, no less. Huh! To develop the bust. Well, Duane, some floozies *need* developing. Yeah, they *really need all the development they can get.*' The insolent cat who had raised an unwise hand against her stalker was brought, savagely, once more into the wolfman's embrace, his gauntleted hand moving to her throat.

'Cats always seem to possess,' I pondered, retreating into myself, thinking that these confabulated alley cats – sex princesses of the streets – could have been sixteen, seventeen, even eighteen years old, though they had the plump-cheeked, doll-faced countenances of depraved little girls, '*neotenic* beauty.' My own sex princess's eyes flashed as she turned her head to look up at me, white tresses tumbling over a bare shoulder. But before she could offer a rebuke or continue her lecture on the failings of her feline sisters, the dragonman pre-empted her with a continuation of his thesis.

'A perfect example of the future in embryo,' he said, a thin smile gracing his armour-clad face, the green-blue scales – that made his face seem so like a wrinkled, gangrenous scrotum – bunching into knots of industrial-quality lamellae.

'What are you talking about?' I said. 'They're just a bunch of confabulated riff-raff on heat. The men hunting, the girls on the prowl. We'd better avoid them. They're high on the craziness of the night and they're likely to try to have some fun with *us*.'

'They prefigure what may be. The lost tribes of the perverse – when they were dispersed by the cataclysm that destroyed their cosmos – were but shadows, imprinted on this world by the blinding effects of The Abortion. But some tribes carried more of the original signatures of their homeland than others. The cats, for instance. And the wolves.'

'Oh, so you're a *cat* aficionado, are you?' said the princess.

'They best represent the manner in which Above and Below may be reconciled, *was* reconciled before our fall. They represent the new Cathay.'

'You really get off on being the social engineer, don't you?' said the princess, unable to hide her prissy disgust.

'He's a dragonman, Frenzy. That's what dragons *do*.'

'I know. But it all seems just a little too Atlantean.'

'There is nothing Atlantean about *me*. Atlanteans are neutered. Desexualised. I am like you, a creature without guilt or regret. My hopes for an alliance with the Sublimated Ones are in harmony with my aspirations to restore the multiverse of our home, the home we had before we were cast down by The Abortion.'

'Well, I guess everybody who's perverse wants that,' she conceded. 'But *cats*—' Her bile rising, she was unable to complete whatever parable of spitefulness, prurience and betrayal that – along with the flecks of sputum occasioned by her ire – had begun to bubble from her lips.

'Do you think our former home was as unsuccessful as this orphanage, this place of exile in which we now find ourselves; do you think it was as unsuccessful as the human bodies that we originally infected were to mirror our own true nature? No; our home had established a way in which perversity and civilisation might coexist! I know it, I know it in my dragon bones!' The dragonman's voice, unable to resist its rise to a crescendo, had alerted the lupine-feline foursome to our presence.

'Well, if it isn't La Gargouille come visiting,' said the cat who had been about to be throttled. 'How're things with you, Mr Anal Retentive?'

I pulled free the walking cane that I had earlier tucked into my cummerbund. Unsheathing the long, stiletto blade concealed in its ebon shaft, I contemplated that I had never knowingly killed a woman before. There had been the times I had turned myself into a suicide bomb; doubtless women, as well as children and even babes-in-arms, had died as a result. But I had never killed a woman with my own hands, by express intention. I had, however, at various times, eaten the brains of wolfmen. The shards of their shattered consciousnesses glittered, now, refracting the black light of buried desire. Introjected, voices rose from that glass-like sea, baying, wolfish voices; they confided their secrets; and suddenly, I saw through wolfish eyes.

'Atlantis dies, like Cathay died,' continued La Gargouille, his voice anonymous, eminently ignorable, just another in the multilingual buzz emanating from the busted beehive of my brain, 'because it has forgotten that the source of civilisation is the erotic impulse. It has chosen security over pleasure. To be reborn, we must turn once again towards gratification, towards joy. But joy which is ordered.' My attention was on the two catgirls, the breasts that heaved, struggling against whalebone, breasts that, if disparaged by my upper-crust rat, were opulent and worthy enough of regard to meet the criteria necessary to effect the radical excitation of surely any man – any man, that is, but myself. My gaze shifted, falling upon the umbilici that winked through the laced-up bodices; the taut bellies, the shrouded, useless organs of generation. My vision stuttered; breasts, genitalia, genitalia, breasts; and my attention, triangulated by primary and secondary sexual characteristics, created a feedback that induced a pulmonary overload; as I panted, struggling to get my breath, all seemed fluid, plastic, as if belonging more to the world of the dismembered mannequins spread-eagled across the street – refugees from the gaping windows of a department store – than to anything

organic, those erogenous zones superimposed, suddenly,
with imaginary crosshairs, points for desirable entry
wounds; ritual, sexual wounds; the kind of marks found
on the practice dummies wolves use to hone their skills.
And then I seemed to see right through flesh, cartilage
and bone, as if I had acquired X-ray eyes. Hyper-
ventilating, choking for lack of air, I focused on a symphy-
sis pubis, the bladder above, and the uterus stacked on top
awaiting to be skewered by my blade, the black handle of
which, greasy with sweat, seemed to urge my hand.

'This planet may well be racked again by another
War of the Liebestod: the orgiastic renunciation of this life
of the flesh. But this time it will not be a conflict between
continental powers; it will be a civil war. Out of these
flames will rise our liberation, a new order of domination
and submission, of rulers and ruled, masters and slaves;
an order whose salvation will lie in *desire*; an order of the
imagination.' The voices inside my head subsided; I let the
thin-bladed sword drop to my side and, grateful to be
released from my asphyxiating state of possession, filled
my lungs.

The cats, both caucasian, with a complexion the
city's depths had turned white, white almost as the
albino-like skin of my goblin princess, walked a few
yards towards us; stopped.

'We've heard about you, Miss Hoity-toity. La
Gargouille told us. La Gargouille so *likes* to talk.'

'Ah yes, the pseudo-cat. The rodent with A Name.'

'So high and mighty.'

'Posh, posh. Puts on the Milady.'

'She's a slut princess. Milady, malarkey.'

'You're right. Those undergarments. Expensive, but—'

'Uh-huh. So strategically torn.'

'Almost like a slavegirl.'

'Like a girl wanting a master.'

'Like a girl wanting to get raped. Meow!'

'You're right, my pussycat sister. *So* right.'

'And what about him. The big man. What do you say, big man? Does a poor kitty get her creamy-cream *cream*?' Her eyes scanned me, her gaze lingering at my crotch, pink tongue flicking across her lips, her appetite gone virtual, disconnected from reality, a fellatrix in fetters to an impossible dream – if she'd heard about 'Miss Hoity-toity', she hadn't, it seemed, heard about me.

'Forget it. He's a revenant. Don't you know anything about revenants?' She tittered, held up a hand and wiggled a little finger. 'Not even a *cat* could make a man of *that*.'

The princess seethed, two smudges of hectic flush enlivening her dead-white cheekbones. She stood akimbo, tail flailing – its displacement of air wild, yet angular, disciplined – as if she were performing an exercise with a *nunchaku*.

'Oh, the rat is upset with us.'

'She's jealous, I think. For a slave, jealousy can be more dangerous than disobedience. We should know, mmm, my cat-sister? But *are* you jealous, little ratgirl? Afraid we might have a little one-on-one–'

'Or even two-on-one–'

'With your big, bad, Brobdingnagian boyfriend?'

'Afraid we'll do something you can't, *pathetic* sister?'

The wolfmen folded their arms across their chests, like famished, mean-eyed nightclub bouncers. Distracted from *droit de seigneur* by our appearance, they seemed content to let their cats enjoy their playtime with the mouse before returning to the more serious divertissement of sex-murder.

'I'll take them out,' I whispered, 'crack their heads open like eggs, no problem. Fillet them, gut them, disabuse them of their right to exist—'

'And eat their brains.' The princess sighed. 'I know, I know. But listen, my beautiful zombie: this is a matter of honour. You have to let me avenge myself.'

'Hey, he likes to eat brains,' said a wolf.

'We should, I think ... *retreat*,' said the dragonman. 'We have, you recall, an appointment *elsewhere* ... an appointment of some *importance*.' It was with some satisfaction that I noticed that our guide had renounced his vapid philosophising. Transformed into a non-verbal creature, he sank beneath further notice, of me, or anyone else.

'You like our cats, revenant?' called the other. 'We'll let them eat *you*, if you like. Sometimes we show them a little mercy before we kill them. And then sometimes' – he made a gesture similar to that of the catgirl who had mocked me with her pinky, but with coarser emphasis – 'sometimes, we do not.' His shoulders quaked, animated by the dry laughter that rose out of his lean chest, his whole wiry frame seismic with irony. His hunting companion slapped him on the back; arched an eyebrow as he appraised the beauty and crimes of those he had been born to hunt.

'Yeah, they were trying to get back to the Heights. They want to be slaves again, the little sluts.'

'It can be very confusing, dead man. First they run away from us, then they run away from the humans, then they run away from us again. These girls can be hard to figure out.'

'Confusing. Yeah. But it's our fault in many ways, brother. We spoil them. We're just too soft.'

'It's the treachery they enjoy, the constant betrayal.'

'It's their way of getting attention. It's their way of getting off.'

'Yeah, even if in the end they just end up getting themselves killed.'

Both cats looked back at their genetic counterparts, flicking their fringes from their flashing green eyes with arrogant tosses of their heads; and then, with a synchronised twitch of the neck, returned to face me, the left eyebrow of each girl – in minxish mimicry of the wolfmen – arching with reflexive disdain, as if to accompany a tired disclaimer, a plea that they'd heard all this murderous rhetoric before, and were no longer impressed.

'You've insulted me,' said the princess, 'and you've insulted my man. I demand satisfaction.'

'Ha! She wants satisfaction!'

'Satisfaction'd kill the likes of you, *ratgirl*.'

'Look who's talking, *catgirl*.' The princess stepped up to the feline nearest her and, taking off one of her evening gloves – a long flute of white satin perforated at the knuckles to allow her talons access to her enemies – struck the offending pussy across her cheek, leaving a blush glistening with three lines of beading blood, and a challenge which could not be ignored. The wounded cat's hand went to her thigh, fingers fluttering about the switchblade that stuck from a garter. I offered the princess my sword; with her eyes unwaveringly on her opponent's weapon, now unsheathed and slashing at the air in an invitation to join battle, she took it, glowering with sullen pleasure.

'No,' said a wolf as the two girls took up fighting stances, the other cat drawing her own weapon from its frilly scabbard, eager to enter the fray. 'It is you who have been challenged, cats. It is you who have the right to choose the mode of combat.'

'And what's wrong with cold steel?' said a cat.

'You're up against an experienced swordswoman. Believe me, I can tell. Be prudent. Choose the cards.' The cat put out a hand, fingers splayed, palm outwards, seeking a momentary truce; held her knife aloft, to show she had no trickery in mind; drew herself up out of her crouch.

'It's true what my brother says,' said the cat. 'You challenged us. So *we* get to pick weapons. And I say, yeah, let the cards decide.'

'The cards?' said the princess.

'This way,' said a wolf, an outstretched arm indicating a recess – a cavity, that, perhaps, a round of artillery had opened up in the side of a building nearby. 'Everything you need awaits you.' He disappeared into the yawning darkness, a shadow rejoining its spawning ground.

The catgirls followed; we traipsed after them, the dragonman making little quasi-lingual noises of protest, but unable to renounce us, his charges. My calves were torn by the serrated edges of the steel-thorned undergrowth as we navigated our way through the scrap-metal wilderness to at last step through the hole in the exposed roots of the skyscraper's ancient, blasted façade. Inside, the illumination – candles jutting from a circumference of old wine bottles – revealed a grotto filled with girlish treasure: dresses and lingerie hanging from nails, piles of scavenged lipsticks, blusher, powder compacts, mascara, eye shadow and pots of rouge; there were glossy magazines, too, their pages open in imitation of fell birds, displaying illos of fashion models, slavegirls, the homes of the rich and famous, blow-ups of tumescent phalli. Broken glass exploded beneath my feet; and the catgirls each made a *moue* as palettes of make-up and ampoules of black-market semen were also lost to my shambling gait's destructive energies. I was standing, I realised, inside the first or second storey of an old department store – the one to which the dismembered mannequins outside owed their refugee status – a store that had served the wants, appetites and cravings of long-departed Metropolitans, their memory buried amongst the rubble of the streets even as the memory of their world's mechanics had been buried in the avalanche of the perverse. I retrieved my sword from the distracted heiress of Castle Duino; re-sheathed it; I was resigned to playing along with her game, no party pooper I, but a big brother worried, jittery, nonetheless.

'This is where we found them,' one of the wolves said to me, nodding towards the girls he had hunted down, but whom – whether for reasons of amusement, honour, curiosity, I really didn't know; cared not a jot – he had chosen to give a brief reprieve.

'Their little hideaway,' said his brother. 'Their little treasure chamber.' He laughed.

'A regular hole-in-the-wall gang, these kitties, eh?'

'Sure,' I said, biding my time, unsure whether to intervene sooner rather than later, this whole affair getting out of hand. The dragonman sidled up to me.

'This is all most unwise,' he said into my ear.

'What's that, dragon?' said a wolf. 'You been

polluting these good, perverse people's ears with your cant about building a new world?' He turned to me. 'La Gargouille here's pretty well-known in these dark, disastrous depths. He's a real travelling evangelist, aren't you, La Gargouille?' The dragonman stared at the floor.

'You can forget about recruiting us, dragon,' said the catgirl who was now acting as the other cat's second. 'Down here on the streets we don't want anything to do with your bullshit.' Rubbing his hands together, fly-like, as if in a fanciful detergent that might rid him of responsibility, the dragonman retreated to a point from which he might execute a swift exit if events took an evil turn.

'Sit over there, ladies,' said the wolf who had first suggested that the girls settle their quarrel by a more mysterious method of duelling than swordplay. 'The table's already been set up.' He looked me in the eye – mockery glinting in the corners of sclera as white as the bloodshot albumen of fertilised chickens' eggs – the reason for his involvement in the specifics of cat-rat conflict resolution becoming lucid as I met his stare and saw deep into his clouded soul. 'Our two little cat-sisters were going to play themselves, it seems. Just the two of them.'

'Until *you* came along, wolfy,' said the cat who had already sat down, 'and spoiled our game.' The field of honour resembled a card table. It stood in the middle of the seamy grot, its three legs straddling the relentlessly sweet, sticky remains of the candy bars, chocolate éclairs and sherbet dips that constituted the core of a catgirl's diet; a frying pan lay there, too, laden with congealed cooking fat where the severed penises of stray dogs had been prepared, a less sugary, if more coveted treat; posters of Atlantean music-hall celebrities looked down, censorious, their images bearing the cupid's-bow impressions of sustained kiss-attacks. A wax-smothered bottle, a smoking taper sticking out of its green neck, had been placed at the table's centre; beside it, a pack of playing cards and a crystal goblet filled with what looked like milk. 'We're always having rows, aren't we, Trash?'

'Sure are, Vicious. If those wolfmen had come along a few minutes later there'd have been one less kitty for them to kill, the poor boys.'

'Poor *frustrated* boys. We like it when they're in pain, don't we, sister?'

'*Mmm...*' The duellist called Trash looked up at her rightful Masters and ran her tongue about her lips in a display of lewd defiance.

'We rather like it when *you're* in pain,' said the wolf who stood by my side, smiling over the heads of the combatants to where his brother, who was drawing out a chair to accommodate the princess, returned a grin of approval. 'So let the duel commence. And our entertainment begin.' He pointed to the goblet.

'Yes, yes, I know what's to be done,' said the other wolf. Taking a sachet from his pocket he popped a pill from its cellophane; held it up between forefinger and thumb for my inspection. 'We confiscated these little *stimulants* from the prisoners,' he informed. Pink and round as a sugared comfit, it made a tiny *plop!* as he leaned over and dropped it into the crystal vessel, a concomitantly tiny splash of viscous, milky liquid leaving a spot of lactose on the tabletop.

The wolf who stood next to me took a handkerchief

from an inside pocket, a big square of paisley cotton; he held it aloft, readying to drop it and signal that the duel was to commence. 'The ladies cut the cards. Aces high. Lowest card drinks the philtre. It's simplicity itself.'

'Philtre?' I asked.

'This method of combat is really so tailor-made for cats. For rats too.'

'Philtre?' echoed the princess, in a delayed echo.

'The pill contains the neurotransmitter vasoactive intestinal peptide: the chemical that transmits word of sexual arousal to the female brain.'

'You mean it induces orgasm?' I said.

'Black orgasm,' said the wolf, the foolish son of the Canidae holding me by the arm, anticipating, perhaps, some physical manifestation of protest, though nothing at that moment could have restrained me if I should have decided to run amok through the dilapidated cavern and killed them all, both him, his friend and their doxies. But instead of breaking that incursive arm like a dry twig, I simply focused on the princess; shook my head. 'There's still a lot of dirty tek left up in the Heights. Chemical tek, genetic tek … More than they had in Cathay, at least. There are Atlantean pharmacists who, for a piece of gold or a piece of pussy, will supply you with just about anything.'

'It's hoarded, of course. Tek gets hoarded the world over,' said his friend.

'You got to appropriate it while you can. Soon, we'll be left with little more than two sticks to rub together. And flint-knapping's not my style. I'm a tek junkie. The confabulated got to make their *own* hoard. Anyway, I'm certainly glad our two little cats here showed the way and got their hands on this here *autoerotic medication*. I'm looking forward to the show.' I passed a hand over my skull, as if attempting to smooth away the furrows, the protruding rivets and bolts.

'This has gone far enough, Frenzy. Let me take care of things now.'

'No, Duane. I mean to go through with this. You just don't understand.' I understood enough to know that her gut aversion to things feline – her need to face down a cat – was inducing her to take a ridiculously lethal degree of risk. But she had always had a gambler's temperament. The chips were down; and she was hooked.

'Please, Frenzy. It's not worth it. I know cats have always bugged you because they say—'

'Because they say I'm frightened to *come*. No, Duane, I'm going to show that I'm not frightened. I may be half-human, but *I'm not frightened to be a rat.*'

'Half-human?' tittered her opponent. Stung by that teasing laughter the princess reached out and cut the deck, turning over her cards on the table. She had chosen the Three of Clubs.

'*Shit!*'

I shrugged the wolf's hand off my arm and was about to dash forward and smash the poisoned chalice to the floor, thereafter to smash the skulls of those who had waylaid us (in a fit of fancy, I conceived of tying them up, pouring cooking fat down their throats – perhaps treating them to a few of those dog penises, too – and using them as makeshift oil lamps, a glowing, crackling warning to all who came after to think thrice before pestering the walking dead); but as I put my foot forward, ready to lift an arm and bring an elbow into the wolfman's face, the catgirl who faced my little companion herself cut the deck, a smug, spoilt brat racing to the winning post unable to comprehend danger. She slapped her cards on the table, exposing the rank and suit of the card that was to decide her fate. It was the Two of Hearts. The catgirl's eyes darkened, streaks of jaundice engendered by the sallow light of the wavering candle infecting their pea-green shade. And if I had not known that they had darkened with fear I would have speculated that that narrowing of the eyes, that dilation of the pupils, had been innervated by lust.

The princess leaned back in her chair. 'Your health, Miss Cat,' she said, pushing the goblet forward with the four-inch-long, hooked, crimson-daubed keratin of a heh-heh, told you I'd have you, *bitch*, digit.

There are qualities of the superfeminine that all females of the perverse share, but which, in the personalities and flesh of catgirls, seem to find particularly intense expression. I am talking about a fire that is self-consuming, uroboric self-sufficiency. Girls who display such qualities of fanatical self-involvement to the *nth* almost invariably turn out to be cats. Egotistical, self-involved, all such girls care about are themselves. Intoxicated with their own beauty, idolatrously in love with the looking glass, they possess an autoerotic focus that is coupled with the inability to differentiate, to individualise those around them.

The doomed catgirl had withdrawn deep into her own image, so deep that the dividing line between depth and surface had disappeared. Her wide-open eyes and quivering lips were less indices of dread than stagy mimes – divorced of verisimilitude – that embodied the physical charm of apprehension without conceding to the ugliness of true fear. She was perfect, as lustrous and as brittle as a freshly-processed daguerreotype. With no dramatic motivation to trouble her – a mechanical toy whose gears and wheels were prompting a hand to stretch out and wrap fingers about a crystal vessel brimful with death – she prepared to tread the boards, win over the audience with her big scene.

The grotto became still as all attention settled on the one due to perish. Fastidiously, with a pouty disregard for any sentiment but sexual insolence, the catgirl lifted the goblet, then, after turning it to survey the lactescent contents, brought it to her lips.

'Kill her,' said the cat called Vicious. 'It's too cruel to stand by and let her die this way.'

'Too cruel, yes,' said the wolf who stood behind the princess, knuckles whitening as he gripped the back of her chair, bone about to pop through the drum-tight skin. 'It would, of course, have been better for her – for any cat – to have been bellied, breasted and sexed. As had been our intent. But the suggestion of a duel was just *irresistible.*'

And then the catgirl Trash put the goblet to her lips, upended it and threw back her head, the creamy elixir of death flowing from the corners of her mouth and down her chin. Drained dry, with the philtre already churning in her stomach – if her startled eyes were reliable indicators – she tossed the goblet aside, where, smashing with a tinkling that was like the screams of a thousand fairies, it joined the other shards of glassware that covered the floor. Staring into the princess's eyes – her own eyes expressionless but for the afterburn of her brazen staring down of terror – the cat seemed about to laugh, as if discovering that she had been the victim of a practical joke, the philtre a dud, no more than a peculiarly effervescent fizz-pop; but the laughter lines that had already half formed about her mouth suddenly creased into lines of an unassuagable cramp of pleasure. Trash, her hands clawing at her belly, nails snared and breaking in the laces of her stays, had doubled over, eyes clenched, a bead of blood dribbling from her nose, her mouth puckered into an O with an Indian file of little O's wiggling free of the parent in a long *Ooooo* ... The princess jumped to her feet; the wolfman stepped back; a chair fell over, was kicked away. The princess backed off, distancing herself from the girl whose writhings prefigured the theoretical conclusion to her own life; its denouement, she knew, could not be deferred forever, no matter how often she placated, with offerings of violence and blood – the nearest she dared come to the precipice of sexual abandonment – the deities of the perverse. She held up an arm, as if to ward off contamination, invisible rays of erotic angst radiating from the martyred face of the cat who was about to achieve release, almost flash-blinding her with its light of pure ecstasy, a light outside the visible spectrum, unknowable to poor capons such as myself. But I could see that she pitied her enemy, too.

'If only you would all unite,' said the dragonman, getting back into his stride. 'All this internecine bickering. It was the same in Cathay! We must concentrate the energies of the perverse if we are to build a new world.'

'Oh, shut up, La Gargouille,' said the princess. 'You're as bad as an Atlantean.' The table turned over as the cat fell to the floor, her hands clutching her abdomen, to squirm and slither amongst the glass. 'We just wanted to get to The Moon. Not to build a new world. We just wanted to get away from *this* world. This rotten, fucked-up Planet *Arschloch*. That's all. Leave us out of your grand plans. It's enough for Duane and me to be together someplace where we don't have to listen to people like *you*.'

'Yeah,' I said. 'And where people aren't always trying to dice-'n'-slice us.'

The princess knelt and cradled the convulsive, dying cat in her arms.

'My mirror,' said the cat. 'Please, take me to my mirror.'

'Can I help?' I queried.

'Take her over there, Duane.' The princess pointed to where a cracked pier glass had been propped against the remains of a service counter, a grimy neon strip proclaiming *Estée Lauder* hanging above by a single steel thread. I stooped; picked the girl up, her body slithering and wriggling deliciously in my arms; walked over to the freckled glass; placed her in front of it. The princess joined us, squatting down by the cat's side, holding up her feline sister's head so that she might come face to face with her reflection.

'Where do you come from, Trash?' said the princess. 'You're not originally from Metropolis, are you?'

'I'm Europan, like you, goblin girl. Sold myself into slavery when I was thirteen.' She moaned, her breaths coming in short gasps as she ascended the gradient that led to the pinnacle where she would soon leap, leap into the darkness, to fall on the rocks of joy. 'All cats want to be slaves, I guess. We just have a problem about choosing the right masters. Wolves, humans, humans, wolves. It all gets so confusing.'

'Pain slut,' said the princess, but without her former

venom, stroking the cat's long, golden hair. 'I knew you'd get yourself killed. Poor kitty, poor dumb, dumb kitty. Why is it you catgirls don't know the meaning of *restraint?*' The cat jerked her hips into the air, a hand fluttering above her vulva, not daring to make contact, as she fought to deny the chemical attack on her brain's pleasure centres.

'Restraint?' said the other cat, looking on, agog. 'We know what *we* are, rodent, do you know what *you* are? You can't run from destiny for the rest of your life.'

The dying one screamed, then seemed to snatch a moment of respite as the roller coaster trundled up the steepest, highest point of the ride, ready to send her over the top and into eternity.

'When I was a little g-girl,' she stuttered, sweat running down her face, a few yellow tresses plastered across her forehead, 'I had a big, oval mirror in my bedroom. I would look into that mirror all the time. It was in that way that I was first drawn into Lilith's web.' Her voice, though choked with desire, was also infused with a certain lisping innocence, as if someone else had possessed her body, the child, perhaps, who had first been taught this tale by other tribespeople many years ago. 'For that mirror had once hung in a den of demons, and a daughter of Lilith had made her home in the cold, glassy lake of its surface. Every mirror is a gateway to the Other World and leads directly to Lilith's cave. That is the cave Lilith went to when she abandoned Adam and the Garden of Eden for all time, the cave where she sported with her demon lovers. From these unions multitudes of demonesses were born, succubae who flocked from that cave and infiltrated the world. And when they want to return, they simply enter the nearest mirror. That is why it is said that Lilith makes her home in every mirror.

'Now the daughter of Lilith who made her home in that mirror watched every movement of the girl who posed before it. She bided her time and one day she slipped out of the mirror and took possession of the girl, entering through her eyes. In this way she took control of her, stirring her desire at will. So it happened that this young girl, driven by the evil wishes of Lilith's daughter, began to pursue the men who lived nearby. It was then that the villagers began to call her a catgirl.' The girl's eyes rolled back, the Big Dipper at the apogee of its ascent, bells ringing, sirens wailing, the ride set to terminate in the ultimate, heart-stopping thrill.

The girl screamed in a way that the wolfmen ~ connoisseurs of feminine cries ~ seemed to particularly appreciate; and their eyes ignited as, in an agony of desperation, she pawed at the filthy looking glass as if she would retreat into its cool, dark world; but the philtre would not let her escape its embrace. She arched her back, lifting her belly to the ceiling, her hand, no longer to be denied, slipping to clutch at the soft, wet triangle of her sex, tightening, squeezing, as if it were a sponge soaked with dark, red honey, her back arching further, more red, candied goo ~ it was too sweet-seeming to call 'blood' ~ streaming from her nose, her ears, the corners of her mouth and her navel. The princess wrapped the cat in her arms as the stricken one, her convulsions unremitting now, tossed her head from side to side, her shoulders inching towards her buttocks as her contorted torso folded in upon itself, an agonised, radical uroboric circle. Her tongue slipped between her lips, flicking towards the dagger-like heel of a sandal, as if she would pleasure it, as she herself was being pleasured, and take it with her in a suicide pack to The Moon, legendary land of the dead. With a violent squirm that burst the laces and stays of her corset she opened her mouth to emit a final, piercing cry; a scream above which I heard the sharp crack of her spine, and then the damp concussion that signalled that her neck had broken. Limp, her body collapsed onto the floor, as twisted and tangled as the wreckage littering the streets.

The princess stood, her legs astride the late cat, the virtuoso contortionist dead of her own histrionics. 'Let's get out of here, Duane. I've had enough.' She unholstered her pistol and, taking ball, wad and powder from her cleavage, began to reload. The wolfmen snarled.

'I can see we've gone too easy on you,' one of them said. The surviving catgirl seemed less concerned with castigating our presumption than satisfying avarice, creeping up to the beautiful corpse to forage its body for the jewellery a dead sister can neither appreciate nor need.

'Oh? Perhaps you'd like me to cut the cards again?' said the princess. 'You still have a prisoner left, after all.'

'It had occurred to us.'

'Tough patootie. *She* seems more interested in diamanté and fake gold, and *I'm* certainly not playing your games any more. So there. Not for any of you. And that goes for you too, dragonman.'

'But *Fräulein*, The Bridge—' The princess looked at me, her eyes adamantine with the manifold disillusion of the years, a rat used, abused but no longer confused, lifting her pistol in a two-handed grip and training it on the nearest wolf.

'Back off you big, bad gynocide.' The princess's prospective victim had already pulled out his knife, the thin blade glimmering in the candlelight; a gauntleted finger stroked the guard, as if trying to placate the itch that urged him to kill; gave up. And the word *Kill* seemed to shine, then, in big, flaming letters, from the notice board of his face. He crouched, inching forward, testing the princess's resolve.

'Let me oblige, Frenzy. That pistol won't—' It wouldn't, I was about to opine, have much effect on one whose constitution was designed to survive the tribulations of millennia. But, impulsive girl that she was, the princess fired anyway, loosing off a ball into the chest of the one who sought to call in her overdue debt to life. The wolf grunted, imagining, perhaps, the prospective laundry bill that rebuked him for carelessness – a red splash surrounded a tear in his cravat – and continued his tentative stalking of my nonplussed moll. 'Enough is enough,' I said, moving forward and sweeping the wolf off his feet, bringing his back down across my raised knee with such force that, not only was there a loud crack – like that of a bullwhip – reminiscent of the sound effect that had accompanied the breaking of the late duellist's spine, but a secondary, wetter and altogether more nauseous sound of meat pared, ripped from bone; coccygeal vertebrae erupted through his groin in a poetically apposite nemesis to the black orgasm suffered by his prisoner; the blood-slicked bone wiggled, an inverted tail, innards unravelling to either side of the exploded flesh, dribbling across the hips and down the thighs. I dropped the body to the floor. The wolf's upper torso writhed, its nerve endings still vigorous – it would take more than this to kill him – but he was unable to move his legs and thus effectively present us with further threat. I wiped my hands on the sides of my trousers, leaving a trail of crimson slime along the seams. The other wolfman backed slowly towards the hole in the wall that gave onto the street. The catgirl, who had completed her foraging and was draped in the baubles and trinkets of her dead, over-excitable sister, also beat a retreat, heeling the one she was genetically disposed to call master, her paradoxical nature so spontaneously perverse as to prove her, in a moment of crisis such as this, more loyal to the brothers, the murderous, lupine brothers who were sworn to relieve her of her treacherous existence, than to herself.

'You don't have to go,' said the princess to the pair of luminous green eyes that, disembodied, hung spectral in the ragged frame of the blasted masonry, before disappearing, winking out into the night. The hapless couple had disappeared, intent on whatever fell honeymoon their sexual proclivities would bring them. I looked across the grotto to where the dragonman hunkered, a hand shielding his eyes, sputum covering his chin, his whole body vibrating, each sinew and ligament like the string of a violently-strummed guitar. I walked over to him and pulled him to his feet. 'You don't have to—' The princess repeated. Her voice trailed off, disappointed, hurt almost, like a little girl's who had been snubbed by the class bully who is at the same time her only friend. 'You know, Duane,' she said, looking out into the darkness, 'I really think I might have gotten over my aversion to cats.'

'Is that good?'

'If I had a shrink, I think he'd say it was good, don't you?'

'We never did get to Vienna.'

'It's like I've gotten something out of my system. It's like—'

'Catharsis.'

'That's right, Duane. The malignity's been siphoned off.' I wondered if the ghost of her latest victim, supposing that departed spirit had been listening in, would have appreciated the princess's conversion. 'Cats is okay, I guess.'

'If you say so, goblin girl.' The princess screwed her eyes into tight little buttons, black with make-up, dark thoughts and inner vision.

'She showed me the way, Duane. She really did. All this time and I didn't know. But I know what to do *now*, Duane. I know what *we* have to do.'

I turned away from my neurotically inclined rat and, tightening my grip on the dragonman's lapels, lifted him off his feet, my face a fraction of an inch from his own so as to allow my cadaverous breath to threaten him with death by miasmic intoxication.

'You're supposed to be taking us to The Bridge,' I said.

'That's what I've been *trying* to do!'

'Don't get sassy,' said the princess, stepping over the corpse – something like her old self again – to inflict her own variety of badmouthing on our guide. 'You may take us to The Bridge, *control freak*, but I don't think we're so prepared to go along with your plans any more, are we, Duane? I think we've changed our minds.' Instinctively, I knew what she meant. A supercharged bolt of dark excitation shot through my bones.

'That's right. You think you're so different from those tribespeople we met in Times Square? You're not. And neither are we. We're configured to live on the dividing line between pain and pleasure, life and death. It's the

way we're made, dragon. A new Cathay isn't to be had
with bricks and mortar. It's to be had by realising ourselves, by journeying to become the creatures we already
are, the creatures we were *born* to be. That's our moon.
Nobody else's. *Ours.* We never learned to share with the
other children, did we, my sweet?'

'Right. Our playmates always ended up dead. Listen:
we're going through your matter transmitter. Both of us.
To hell with Duane doing a recce for you.'

'You'll be killed,' said the dragonman, surveying us
through his fingers. 'It only transmits patterns of energy.
You know that. If you go through in physical form your
atoms will be scattered all across sub-lunar space.'

'Yeah, well, maybe they would if I went through in
energy form. Truth is you don't really know *what* would
happen, do you?' I threw him against a wall and watched
him slide to the floor.

'We believe,' said the princess, positioning a leg so
that her one intact heel was poised to descend upon the
dragonman's Adam's apple, 'we believe in the spirit of
adventure. Don't we, Duane?'

'Adventure. Sure.'

'We take risks. Chances.'

'But you'll *die*,' interjected our guide.

The princess looked back at the dead catgirl and
then, batting her eyelashes with cat-like flirtatiousness,
looked up at the seven-foot hulk that towered over her.

'He's dead already. A reanimated, sewn-together
platter of cold cuts. A zombie. A filthy, walking carcass
with a little mechanical worm inside its head.' She pouted;
blew me a kiss. 'As for me, well—' I put a hand to her
cheek; stroked, dislodging a little soot that had become

impacted in her rouge. 'I'm reconciled with the perverse. I've made my peace. I'm not going to fight it any more. I'm a part of it. It flows through me. I'm its servant. Yeah, at long last I think I can see the end of the road.'

'I always knew all roads would lead here,' I said, with a fatalistic sigh, seeing the death-drawn ardour in my friend's lust-blurred vision.

'It's only the dead who inhabit The Moon, Duane. I think we always knew that, didn't we?' I kicked over some of the larger pieces of glass that were scattered across the floor, and then toe-punted them, sending them skittering out into the street.

'How do we use the transmitter, dragonman?' I said.

'You have to enter it at speed. That's why it's situated on a bridge. You have to take a run up to it, as it were, plunge into its vortex at about forty miles-per-hour.'

'On a horse?'

'We've been using carriages and teams of four. You need a carriage to carry the recording instruments.' I patted him on the head; looked at the princess; smiled.

'You still got that map?' She peered down into her cleavage, this pack rat swiftly stock-checking her miscellanea of ammunition, foodstuffs, the bric-a-brac of years spent fighting, running, hiding, to locate the crumpled piece of paper which contained instructions on how to reach our objective.

'Got it, Duane.' I knocked out the dragonman with a stomp of my foot.

'Then let's go.'

And so we left, the princess leading the way, her hips swaying with the passionate, sexual conviction of one of the early virgin martyrs, as, impudent and coy, she lifted her tail to treat me to the sight of her rump, the crease of her buttocks so well displayed and emphasised by the minimalist T of the *cache-sexe*.

Wounded, inveterate cunt-hound that I was, I followed, slavering, the scent of a just-out-of-reach potency stinging my nostrils, determined to track down the means by which we might both finally commit ourselves to each other and find a place amongst the stars.

We lay behind a knoll, the prospect before us cleared of junk, indicating that the road was regularly used for traffic; no coaches or wagons were apparent, though, as the dawn broke over the East River, showering the far bank of Brooklyn with needles of oblique light that threaded the tower-scudding clouds with jags of azure-tinted brilliance. The Bridge, its curveship, taut, strung with harp-like strings, thrumming silently like a spectral orchestra of the spheres, rose and fell from shore to shore, a beckoning gesture, a sign displaced from substantivity, its iron girders, its cables, as ghostly as that silent music, that thrum of weightlessness, chords of heavenly song that, for us, had spanned from Atlantis to Cathay, Cathay to Atlantis, connecting us one to the other, ourselves with ourselves, completing our journey and bringing us home. 'That patch of haze on the far side,' I said to the princess, stabbing an index finger towards where a cyan vortex of electrical discharge whorled into the air from the cratered macadam of The Bridge's surface. 'That must be the entry point. That's what we have to head for.'

'So how do we get past these guys?' she countered, nodding at the assembled police who crowded the intersection beneath us, their wagons forming a roadblock. Voices, carrying over the still morning air, had alerted us to the nature of the new imbroglio in which we found ourselves. From snatches of conversation we came to understand that Jules, who was, it seemed, alive and in an interrogation cell in the Heights, had subsequently, whether under duress or of his own free will, informed on us, telling the authorities not only who we were and what we intended, but of the entire plan involving the matter transmitter. 'Must be over a hundred of them,' she added, 'all armed to the teeth. But if we could steal one of their wagons—'

'Do you see who's down there?' I said, pointing to a wagon whose sides were barred, as if it were designed to hold wild animals for a travelling circus, though a face, like a shrivelled walnut, squeezed between the rusted iron verticals, advertised that here, rather than an exotic beast, was a freak-show act, a turn involving a miniature lady, old and dressed in rags, who, if half feral, was still vaguely human.

'I don't believe it, said the princess. 'Herzog, you filthy old woman, what are you doing here?'

'She doesn't,' I mused, 'seem in a position to offer assistance.'

'They're using her as a lure, Duane. To flush us out into the open.

'That wagon could be of use. Four good horses. We steal it, we could be across The Bridge in no time.' But the wagon looked heavy; I wondered if I could induce its team-of-four to gallop at the necessary speed? 'I'll go down there and—'

'That's what they want, fool. For us to go down there.'

'I'll go in astral form.'

'What's the use? Herzog won't be able to see or hear you.'

'There was something the necromancers trained me to do but which I've never once put into practice.'

'Oh yeah?'

'I think I might be able to enter her body.'

'What, step right into it?'

'Take it over, use it as a puppet. The only problem is, I believe, that the host body, in incorporating my own highly energised form, sometimes has a tendency to spontaneous combustion.' The princess frowned ... conscience-stricken, perhaps.

'I *suppose* my maid wouldn't mind. Not if she knew it was the only way of us getting out of here.' She pushed a talon through the packed roots of her hair, scratching, as if to investigate whether the irritative attack of conscience had subsided, or whether it might resurface, forcing her to perform a more radical act of bad faith. 'Spontaneous combustion – it's probably relatively painless. Isn't that so, Duane?'

'I expect that's right.' I stretched out, supine, behind the cover of the knoll, a knob of compacted rubbish and greasy, black grass that was an earthwork left over from a time when the ground we occupied had served as a battery, some kind of gun emplacement used by the perverse, or whatever had preceded the perverse, to signal proprietorship of The Bridge. Folding my arms across my chest, closing my eyes, I went into the mental procedure that precedes evacuation, summoning up the images and symbols that would trick my body into once again giving up its ghost. I floated skywards; rolled. The meat machine below stared up at me, its tenantless eyes those of a man in deep coma; I drifted away, slowly, allowing the umbilical cord – coruscating like a white-hot length of fluid steel

~ to snake out untaxed and give me the requisite amount of slack; and then, with a cursory salute to the princess, I rose, flew steadily across the intersection and along the road, bearing down on the ebon-lacquered, iron-barred wagon in which Mrs Herzog had been caged.

With a shudder, I passed through the flesh of the policemen, ranged ~ bored and stamping their feet to allay the chill morning air ~ across the mouth of The Bridge, their copper epaulettes and braid prickling my astral flesh with conduction and leaving, in my wake, a line of cops twitching with tiny, static shocks. I hovered above the wagon. Its driver napped, slouched in his seat, the horses ~ their keen senses picking up my presence ~ swivelling their eyes. The horses snorted, and vapour billowed from their flared nostrils; but, seeing that they were not about to bolt, I descended, feet first, through the coach roof. I checked my descent; reconnoitered. I was surounded by three walls, panelled with iron, the barred proscenium, against which the dwarf was pressed ~ declaring, to her bored audience, with rasping insistence, her demands for emancipation ~ directly opposite.

Reminding myself that communication was impossible, I drifted forward, attempting to rearrange the parameters of my energy form, to bunch myself up into a fist of invisible light. My body retained its familiar contours, but its essence now seemed concentrated in my solar plexus, like an indigestible ball of lightning. I willed myself into the tiny woman's form, my chest distending, as if it was swollen with a foetus that had decided to jump ship, preferring to board the crone, to use her as its surrogate. As my chest assumed a wedge-like shape, the rest of my body melted, in morphic sympathy, becoming a shaft

to the thoracic arrowhead. The tip of the arrow penetrated
Mrs Herzog's crooked spine, as if it had been fired from
a crossbow, the quarrel-like trajectory sucking the
remainder of my body inside, to leave me tunnelling up
the old woman's spinal column and into her brain.
Emerging out of the blackness of that tunnel to the sound
of a scream - her scream; no, I thought, my scream, *our*
scream - I discovered that I had my face, my leathery,
timeworn face, pressed between rusted bars, arms hyper-
kinetic, sawing maniacally, punching at air, legs jigging
incontinently against the floor, as I sought to bring the
kidnapped meat under control. A panicked voice rose up
from the cranial dungeon to which I had consigned it,
'*Master Revenant, is that you, is that–?*' Then I had it
gagged and chained; the screams were no longer shared; I
had control, the stolen body all mine.

My skin was prickly with heat, the energy source
which animated the diminutive muscles of my new flesh
threatening to short it out, melt it like a mechanical doll
whose innards have corroded, leaking acid. Suddenly
invested with incongruous power - I glimpsed a nearby
policeman stare straight at me, bug-eyed with disbelief - the
thin, bony arms prised open an egress, bending the cage's
bars to allow me to slip out of my confinement, no freak-
show act, now, but the strongman himself - haha, and in
what a disguise - come to wreak havoc amongst the
audience. I tumbled over as I hit the road; got up, cursing the
frailty of my novel, if temporary, shell; the rags that
swaddled my body had begun to smoke and I was giving off
an aroma of roast piglet. Cops were running towards me, one
taking up firing position, lifting a blunderbuss to his
shoulder. I swivelled on my heels; threw myself onto the

wagon's bodywork; scampered up the rungs that ran to the driver's seat. Halfway up I felt a tremendous blow to my thighs and buttocks, as if I had been chastised by a demonic schoolmaster, then heard ~ my ears refusing at first to acknowledge the truth ~ the roar of the blunderbuss. For a moment I went limp, hanging from the ladder by a single hand, babbling that I would return my homework assignment tomorrow, tomorrow first thing, *I promise, I promise*; then, as I forced myself to concentrate, sending more energy into my extremities, my head cleared; I rallied, my legs again finding purchase on the rungs and levering me towards my goal. As my eyes came level with the seat, the driver ~ alerted by the commotion ~ was ready for me with his whip; but as it unwound, swishing towards me, I reached out; snatched its tip from the air as if it were a fly; wound the braided leather about my wrist and then pulled, hard, to jerk the human off balance and tip him face forward so that, somersaulting across the road, he was left to negotiate a crash landing, leaving the imprint of his skull in the asphalt. I hoisted myself into the seat; took up the reins and, the smoke now rising thick and black from my combusting body, cried out, urging the team-of-four forward. There was the old, familiar *crack, crack, crack* of musketry, ball finding a home in the wagon's panels and Mrs Herzog's poor, shrivelled flesh. I turned the wagon about and got the horses into a trot, and then a canter. The police dived aside; but even so, some were still able to train their weapons, and I found myself speeding through a gauntlet of gunfire, hot lead finding accommodation in my gut, my thorax, my redundant dugs, as well as the careless body of the wagon, splinters of black lacquer flying around me, like confetti at a marriage for the dead. And then, as the front horses dispatched a cop who had tried to fire at close range, I sped out of death valley, the wagon's rear providing a shield for stray rounds as I bent over the reins and guided the horses along the road and towards the knoll, some hundred yards distant, where the princess, no longer concealed, stood waving and jumping in the air.

I braced myself against the footboard; struggled to rein in the crazy-eyed team, their necks bulging with veins hectic with terror; I tightened my grip, my old flesh's transfused vigour nearly wrenching the bits from the horses' mouths; the wagon slewed, sparks gushing from the iron-rimmed wheels as it shrieked to a halt.

The princess splayed her hands beneath her chin, her fingers linked, one knee bent in little-girl pose. 'Oh Duane, you look so *cute*.'

'I have to get out of this body,' I said, 'before—' My hair burst into flames. Unwilling to linger, I projected, the last sensation of my fugacious habitation: a searing agony, a terrible burning that was like an arsenic-laced catheter penetrating my arteries, my nerves, my brain. Not looking back – too unbearable, that sight, despite the facetiousness with which I was accustomed to view fear, agony and death – I arced through the air, diving behind the knoll to where my own body, second-hand, only five years old, if several previous owners and saddled with a lifetime's log of abuse, waited. I entered; my astral body, attuning itself to the demands of matter, became one with my autonomics and somatics; I opened my eyes; and, immediately conscious of the perilousness of our situation, heaved myself to my feet. I looked myself over; decay was running riot across my flesh, as if I were being eaten alive by microbots. Projection always left me weakened; but possessing another's body had accelerated my decrepitude ten, twenty, thirty-fold. I sniffed at the air; noted that I was transpiring, the putrid mush of my liquefying innards having seeped through my pores to poison the air. Microbots might well, these last few centuries, have become extinct; but the corruption encoded into my cells would strip the meat off my bones as efficiently as any weapon of the Liebestod. For three years I had been in debt to death, each day owing a little more, with the knowledge that my debt would some day be called in full; I determined to put what energies I had left to good use; today I would cheat the banker.

The princess was already atop the wagon. She had extinguished, as best she could, the flames that had been consuming her maid and now embraced her, the front of her corset blackened with the charred rags and flesh that was all that was left of Mrs Herzog.

'I need brains, Frenzy,' I said, stumbling towards the wagon, each step compounding the damage done by my recent out-of-body excursion.

'Brains can wait, Duane. Get this wagon turned around. The police are closing in.' I ascended, my enervation making the scaling of the wagon's ladder almost as arduous as when I had been incorporated with Mrs H. Looking back across The Bridge I saw that what the princess had said was true. A phalanx of cops was shuffling uncertainly towards us, muskets at their hips, as if they were set to charge. I swung myself onto the box seat, next to the princess, and took the reins from the petrified grip of her carbonised maid. The horses yielded to my urgings; describing a tight semicircle in the pitted road, we came about to face our persecutors; I checked the team's enthusiasm, fearing they would bolt; and we held our ground, the princess indulging herself in a brief display of pity, crushing the smouldering but still living remains of her oldest friend to her capacious breasts. As tears ran down her cheeks, and as the horses stamped and whinnied, I gritted my teeth, my gaze fastened upon the rising sun, the seagulls that dipped and pivoted over the dark, chained waters, their cries redolent of far-off Europa, Afric and dear, sweet Cathay, of the song of songs that was like a bridge of fire connecting them. I hollered, cowboy-ish, and we began our run, the horses protesting a little as they struggled against the inertia, and then settling into a rhythm, assuming a brisk pace.

'Yeah,' I said, my breath steamy as the exhalations of the funeral-black mares. 'If I'm to be the New Columbus, then let me conquer a new world for *myself*, not for the perverse, or those who would use our dreams to serve their own ends. A new Cathay, but for me and Princess Frenzetta!'

'Well said, Duane.' Mrs Herzog opened her eyes; looked from me to the princess, cornflower-blue pupils small, intense, as if scanning that other bridge, the blindingly white rainbow that led to eternity.

'Sorry, Mrs H,' I said.

'Yes, we're sorry, poor Herzog. It was the only way.'

'I understand, Master Revenant. And you, my little bonbon, what need have you ever had to say *you* were sorry? Anyway, it's best, like this. It's time for me to go. I can't look after you young things any longer. No, not where *you're* going.' And then her head slumped to one side and her throat rattled with the definitive overture of mortality. The princess let her slip from her arms; the maid fell between the horses. Before the princess could look down and indulge herself in a more debilitating emotion than pity, such as disgust, regret, or even guilt, I lashed the team onwards, and the tiny, burnt-out corpse disintegrated, like pulped charcoal, beneath their great hooves.

'What complete bastards we are, Duane.'

'True,' I said, bringing the reins down once more across the horses' backs, whipping them into a gallop. 'The confabulated, the normal. They've got nothing on us for sheer callousness.' The princess smiled, the dawn-streaked horizon accentuating her vicious dental work, one of her metal fillings radiant, refracting the glorious, cold-blooded light, a star burst celebrating an almost divine self-love.

'Just you and me, Duane.'

'Total egotism, Frenzy.'

'Utter selfishness.'

'Arrant solipsism.'

'Through-and-through narcissism.'

'The me-and-you mutual absorption club. Members only. No one else need apply.' I pulled her under my arm as I urged the horses to their breaking point, beyond which their hearts would surely burst; the thunderous concussion of their iron-shod hooves against the road surface threw up a shower of sparks; but as the team exceeded its physical limitations, becoming, briefly, an equine super-team, each horse seemed granted a stay of execution, their brave hearts racing to accommodate the strain. We achieved what I prayed was escape velocity as we tore through the first line of police. A fusillade punctured my legs and torso. Ichor ran down my trouser leg and pooled in the declivity between the footrest and the seat. 'Are you all right?' I said. The princess snuggled more deeply under the protective mantle of my arm. I looked behind. We had left the ranks of police scattered across the road, running for their lives, or else, limbs shattered, recumbent on the macadam, screaming imprecations against the gods and goddesses of the perverse.

'Just keep driving, Duane. We're nearly there.'

We smashed through the roadblock.

A ball hit me in the back of the head; and though the steel plate under my scalp saved me, the myriapod that shared my life wriggled in its burrow, like vermin shying from a relentless exterminator. I tried to calm it, murmuring *sotto voce* reassurances that our day was not yet done, scotching rumours drifting up from my cerebellum that held that we – dead man and parasite both – were committed to bidding farewell to this world, this existence; my lies tasted like ashes, and I had to spit them out.

'There's no going back now, Frenzy, are you sure that–'

'Keep *driving*, Duane. I think I can hear the sound of the sea breaking on The Moon's shores!'

'Is this really the only way?'

'The *only* way, Duane.'

'The Moon it is, then. Hang on!'

Ahead, the spinning cone of light, its fizzes and crackles audible, now, spiralling upwards into the rays of the rising sun – a sun splintered amongst the multitude of tuning forks that were the tensile cables strung on either side of us – sang out, the light cone trembling with sympathetic vibration; spun candy, it was like, blue-green candy floss glistening in the oblique rays that poured through the steel latticework; like children, we reached out, greedy-eyed, sticky-fingered, rumble-tummied; and then we were inside its whirligig of cyan brilliance, lifted up, it seemed, wagon, horses, us, all spiralling, hurtling skywards, banked into a road that was like a helix, conducting us to the stars.

I sat on a boulder, the sky naked, impeccably black, no light to compete with the earthshine that fell from above, burning like ice, the crescent of blue that dominated the horizon arresting my attention, hypnotising me as it had done for as long as I could recall, for all the centuries, the millennia, it seemed, that I had sat and waited, here, on this lonely beach. At last, I managed to subtract my gaze, turn my eyes, instead, upon the rocky grey expanse of the *Mare Serenitatis*, its basalt-like rocks carpeting the surface in a mile-thick layer of rubble. A little way off, in the gentle swell of a crater, was a seaside villa, its walls crumbling, its garden baked, frozen, destroyed, the promenade that ran past the front door overlooking but a sea of dust, the machines that had pumped water across the barren plains, kept out the killer vacuum and powered the artificial gravity well, no longer functional. Bathing in cosmic radiation – the great skydome ripped, perforated like a sieve – I tried to remember who I was and how I had come to be shipwrecked on this desolate shore.

An angel walked across the mare, his gown throwing up a skirt of dust as he shuffled, hands locked beneath his wide sleeves, head bowed – an eremite about whom the landscape coalesced – moving steadily, relentlessly towards me. As he closed, I looked down at the ground, studying the fine particles, reaching out, letting a handful sift through my fingers, enjoying the silky feel of dust against my skin; and it was only when his shadow spilled over me that I surfaced from my meditation, lifted my head and met his eye. He was a young man, white-haired, but, apart from that tonsorial signature of other-worldliness, having a look about him that would have served as effective camouflage amongst most of the human populations of the Earth.

'Hello, revenant.'

'Hello,' I said. 'I've seen you before, haven't I?'

'You mean in Afric? I was in another form then, as were my brothers and sisters.' Again, I directed my gaze between my feet, studying the enigmatic patterns of the dust.

'Am I dead?'

'To one such as myself you're as you've always been. Death is only the other, invisible side of life. Just as the perverse is the other side of normality. I live in both worlds, as you have done. Quotidian, perverse. The world of life, the world of death. But you should know all this, revenant, being one who has died and been reborn before.'

'I'm dead, then. Not even my astral body survived.'

'Yet you are here.'

'You mean I'm *really* here, on The Moon? I'm not just hallucinating?'

'As soon as you entered the matter transmitter your body was smashed, converted into energy, and then sent out to … everywhere. Your atoms are scattered across space. Didn't you know that the transmitter wasn't working?'

'I knew. We knew. It seemed the only way. But you haven't answered my question.'

'In Cathay, you were dead. They remade you. Is it so hard to believe, though your corporeal shell is destroyed, that you have risen again?' *It isn't enough*, said an inner voice, *to settle for the modification of the flesh; all of reality has to be rejigged if something truly perverse is to be created.* And it occurred to me then that if I was alive, I had perhaps always been alive; and that, perhaps, I had never gone to the Nam; never fought, been killed and resurrected as a zombie; that, perhaps, my earthly existence had always been a dream.

'Is it then they who're dead?' I said, pointing up at the blue crescent I had left forever. 'Were they ghosts all along? Insubstantial? Unreal? Was I the only living man amongst them?' And as I said those words I felt myself surfacing from the dream of death, knowing that death's fears and horrors could no longer torment me.

'I see both living and dead. The distinctions between the two states of being are more nebulous, perhaps, than you would suppose.'

'I – I can't remember my name.'

'Is that so bad?'

'No,' I said. No; it didn't really seem so bad at all. It was good, so good, not to have a name. Not to have memories, a past. But better, far better, than simply not being an agglomerate of desires, fears, needs, loves and hatreds, was a state I seemed to stand on the edge of, the vertiginous, joyful precipice of never-having-been.

'She's waiting for you,' said the angel.

'Who?'

'You know who.' Yes, I did know. All had been ghosts, except one. He stretched out an arm, gesturing towards distant mountains. 'Go to her, revenant. You don't have much time left.' And then he turned on his heel and began walking back across the plain.

'Wait,' I called. 'I need to know more. I need to know what I've become, where I'm going.'

But the angel continued to walk away. And soon he had disappeared over the truncated horizon, swallowed by the blackness of infinite space.

I walked for days, it seemed. I walked through seas of dust, along rills, across craters; I walked through abandoned prison camps, and then the villages and towns of freemen and the settlements of those escaped slaves who, so many centuries ago, had turned to The Moon for sanctuary; and at last I came to the mountains.

'Duane?' I heard. 'Duane, is that you?'

'Frenzy?' A figure appeared from behind a cluster of rocks. We stood on a peak, the cratered desolation of our new home far below. 'The angel said I would find you.'

'Are we dead, Duane?'

'I don't know. Does it matter? The angel didn't seem to think so. He said that the distinction between life and death is artificial. Life and death are the same thing.'

'The matter transmitter killed us, didn't it?'

I shrugged. 'I suppose so.'

'Well, we knew it would. We knew that this was really the only way we'd ever get to The Moon.'

'As dead people?'

'As dead people, Duane. It's true what they say: the souls of departed tribespeople really do migrate here.' She walked up to me; I opened my arms, and she pressed her cold body against my own, her forehead snug against my chest. 'At least we didn't end our days in a cheap hotel.'

'Alone and sick.'

'And old. How strange to think of being old.'

'They would have found me murdered, in a dirty, un-made bed surrounded by cheap liquor bottles, hypodermics, old newspapers, the soiled, smudged pages of my one remaining book...'

'Cheap hotel rooms are for the living.'

'To hell with the living, *I* say. Dead's cool. Let's build our own heaven.'

'And what would that be like?'

'It'd be like Duino, I think. Close your eyes, Frenzy. Can't you hear it? The waves of the Bay of Sistiana beating against the cliffs. And we two on the battlements of the castle, looking out over the sea, or over The Karst. And there are angels all about us. Angels everywhere!'

'Oh yes, Duane, yes, yes!'

I looked out over the dusty plain. There were angels in the sky, winging above the barren seas; and there were angels inside me, too, singing in my heart.

'I'm like you now, Frenzy,' I said. 'I can see them. They really do exist!' I felt the princess's tail snake about my thigh, its venomous tip investigating my perineum.

'Let's do it, Duane. That's why we came here, after all. Let's do it. We can't die twice.'

'I already did,' I said.

'Wiseguy. So make it thrice.'

'You got it, goblin girl.' Tonight – for us, a night eternal – she was at her loveliest, crude-tongued, *déclassé*, a blue-blooded rodent who had become a real *Rattus norvegicus*, as common, vulgar and as sluttish as you could wish. I pushed her roughly up against the rock face; tore off her *cache-sexe*; and was shocked to discover a twinge of sensation in my genitals. I cried out, encouraging passion to riot, to overthrow the tyranny of my life's impotence. Roughly, I jerked her thighs apart; unzipped my trousers, scared of letting this moment of grace disappear.

'Oh, it's going to be wolfman-style is it, dead man?' I relaxed my grip, telling myself that I was manhandling an aristocrat, one whose pretensions – qualified, albeit, by her serving-wench lustiness – I was unwilling to puncture, much as I was willing, of course, to puncture her.

'Sorry, Princess Frenzetta.'

Her illusions intact, I attacked her intacta, pricking and perforating her hymen with the monstrous lead-filled hose pipe that sallied forth from the folds of my coat.

The princess threw her head back, her teeth bared as she screamed her rat war cry of Ee-ee! Ee-ee! Ee-ee! Behind her eyes, visions of rat cities deep beneath Trieste, beneath Prague, Vienna, Zurich. Duino was burning, flames licking the sky, goblin soldiers gambolling about its ruins rejoicing in a funeral pyre dedicated to Man. Perverse, she lifted her hips to meet me, her mouth a great O as she gloried in the destruction of everything she had called home. *Wriggle, squirm, wiggle, slither–* Oh, for more verbs of such insistence! She squealed; I choked; she gagged; I poked, thrusting myself into her, savage, self-obliterative, burying my life, my death, inside the folds of her sweet, virginal flesh. The moment of death, said the angels circling above, is the moment of orgasm, fulfilment; just as fulfilment is secreted within the thousand-petalled rose-poppy of death. Pedants! This is the other, invisible side of life. This is the other, secret life which is mine to enjoy, today and forever. I tore at her corset, freeing her magnificent breasts; palpated them, as if they were wineskins; I was drunk, but I intended to get drunker. *'Ein Glückliches fällt–'* cried the princess, abandoning herself to her own intoxication. A white incandescence, like a flare, lit up the dark, cobwebby palace of my skull. The doors that led to the lands of going and return were thrown open; the inferno roared. From East to West, from West to East. All that was left now was memory; all that is ever left, at the end of the road connecting death and birth; so strange for a man like me, a creature without memory. And not so strange, for what was left – see, look, there below – was the faces, a whole gallery of faces, friends, enemies, victims, faces of hatred and benediction. On the grey plain, figures had begun to materialise. Men and women who were the ghosts of those who had populated the prison camps in which the children of the perverse had been incarcerated so long ago, thereafter to live in exile, generation after generation, surviving as best they could. And there, there – the ghosts of the escaped slaves, the persecuted; and there, too, the ghosts of those tribespeople who had died on Earth, those who had only ever dreamed of The Moon; and all of them, no longer lost but found; to be lost, I knew now, was to be found; for the princess and me – we were ghosts and we were more than ghosts; we were of the angels, terrible, enraptured, and all was transformed by the peace we were becoming part of, all the unknown past, all the nameless faces as nothing but a host of figures dancing, dancing, dancing themselves to eternal life, the surface of The Moon a New World – Nirvana City, the New Cathay! – and all names becoming the one name of Love, the beautiful kingdom of the lost. Ah—

    Am not. Was not. Never been, never to be.

    'Oh, Duane, *du, du, du, du, du Schweinhund*!'

    Yeah. Nirvana, baby.